Dark Luminous Wings

Edited
by
Kelly A. Harmon and
Vonnie Winslow Crist

Pole to Pole Publishing
Baltimore

Dark Luminous Wings

ISBN-10: 1-941559-20-4
ISBN-13: 978-1-941559-20-8

Dark
Luminous
Wings

Under the awful wings

Which brood over land and sea,

And whose shadows nor lift nor flee—

This is the order of things,

And hath been from of old:

    First production,

    And last destruction;

So the pendulum swings,

While cradles are rocked and bells are tolled.

~ Mors et Vita, Richard Henry Stoddard, stanza two

Table of Contents

Enchantment Lost
Brian Trent

I need you to find my childhood. I know where it is. I'm hiring you to recover it, and return it to me."

Jack Saylor waited for the ancient woman to continue. Standing across from where he sat, Sylph Tørnquist of Tørnquist Corporation didn't look ancient. She appeared to be a precious twenty, if he didn't stare directly into her eyes. Platinum hair piled atop her head, her slender neck like that of a Cycladic statue connecting her oval face to a limber body clad in a velvet coat dress with a pinched, scalloped waistline. She appeared young, radiant, and unblemished…

…if he didn't stare into her golden eyes.

"You *are* a recovery specialist?" she asked.

Jack gave her a boyish grin that managed to be smoothly defiant. "You know perfectly well I am."

"My childhood is in…a rather inaccessible location."

"Just tell me where."

The young-looking woman stared absently at the fireplace mantle. The books there were actual paper set in actual leather; Jack could practically smell the aged parchment from where he sat. But the crystal collection was the real focus there. Each was of some kind of winged creature—birds, angels, pegasi, dragons, butterflies. Lovely, perhaps as ancient as their owner, yet in the candlelit gloom each pair of wings also appeared to be icy fangs, jabbing menacingly towards the ceiling. They glowed in the candlelight like volcanic stalagmites.

"You would have to break some rather heavy laws, Mister Saylor. Is that a problem?"

"The only problem," he said, "is you not getting to the point. You can afford eternity, Miss Tørnquist, but my time has value. Let's dispense with the foreplay, shall we?"

Sylph Tørnquist's gaze flared like stadium lights. In that moment, Jack seemed to feel the gravity of her two-hundred-and-forty years, despite—or because of—her chemically preserved youthfulness. Her ominous glower changed her face from delicate heiress to vindictive banshee, and Jack figured it was a handy tool for controlling Tørnquist Corporation's board meetings.

"Very well," she said, apparently seeing that he wasn't about to wilt. "I'm sending you the location now." She blinked, and Jack's optics bloomed with a crisp business card. In delicate oxblood lettering, the coordinates of her childhood appeared like petroglyphs in a glacial wall.

"Will that be a problem?" she snapped.

"Yes," Jack said, minimizing the card with a blink and doing his best to keep his smile hoisted. His sun-blushed cheeks betrayed little of his shock. "But problems are what I handle, Miss Tørnquist. That's why I command my non-negotiable fee: I deliver the goods, always."

"The goods." She seemed to find the expression amusing. "I don't know if my childhood was good."

"I have questions," Jack said.

"For the job, or your curiosity?"

"To do my job, I rely on curiosity."

She absently touched a crystalline angel. The room's candles glinted in a starry spray across the trinket's outstretched, feathery wings.

"You want to know why I hid my memories there," she whispered.

"Seems like an awful lot of trouble and expense."

"The trouble was for others to deal with. The expense is irrelevant." She sighed. "Do you know what Snapshot is?"

Jack leaned forward, steepling his fingers beneath his chin. "It's a program for freeing up memory storage in your head. 'Reduces the clutter,' as the commercials put it. Your memories are compressed into a kind of highlight reel. Instead of every phone number and random face from a lengthy life, you get a 'best-of' overview, right? Keep some memories, extract the rest into holocubes." His gaze strayed to the crystalline, winged menagerie.

"I used Snapshot to have my childhood extracted," she explained. "I no longer remember why I did it."

"And then you sent it way out on—"

She fixed him with a stare that was simultaneously hard and desperate. "Yes."

Jack stood. "One last question. How the hell did you get it there?"

"Tørnquist Corporation made its fortune through strip-mining. My father sent a team two centuries ago. I secretly paid one of the employees to smuggle the holocube there, and bury it."

Jack was already accessing the web, running a search on Tørnquist Corporation field teams from two hundred years ago.

The ancient woman seemed to notice the flicker in his eyes. "You won't find a record of it, Mr. Saylor. The mission was a failure. We never learned why. We received confirmation of their landing, but nothing else."

"And you never sent anyone to investigate?"

She looked surprised, as if he'd queried the color of the sun. "It was an illegal mission even back then. And the window for landing only comes around every hundred years, so…"

Jack nodded, thinking: So your company decided to cut their losses and pretend it never happened. *Extracted* the story from the history books. Paid off employee families and presto! Some human lives vanish in a puff of edit.

He moved towards the door.

Tørnquist called after him. "What now?"

"Now," he said, glancing back to her, "wire your payment to my orbital bank. I'm flying off to obtain what you want. No problem."

§

The problem was 600 miles per hour.

It was his vessel, the *Harpy VIII*, flying about like a hawk in a hailstorm as it bore down on his destination. It was the musical pinging of debris striking the ship's steel-resin hull, rattling and showering and strafing her. It was the panicked, multi-hued configuration of his display warning that the *Harpy* was in trouble: a nightmare swarm of crimson speed warnings and yellow altitude advisories and blue ladar fields. It was his stomach lurching into his throat as—a gigantic chunk of ice slammed into one of the *Harpy's* wings like a hammer, and suddenly she was spinning like a wounded bird shot out of the black sky.

I'm flying off to obtain what you want. No problem.

A snowfield and knobs of icy hills rushed at him as his ship plummeted. He had launched three orbital mappers on approach, trying to scan for a proper landing zone; two of these probes now visibly impacted into the terrain below, sending out glassy ejecta plumes.

Jack's fear morphed into outright terror. There was a shriek of metal, a hiss of ruptured coolant, the crumpling of the chassis like an imploding womb around him.

Jack screamed in agony. His bio-readout instantly displayed a diagram of the human body, with angry medical crosses flickering over its damaged portions. His screams fogged an oxygen mask as it settled like a jellyfish over his mouth, hissing air into his throat.

Jack's head lolled, the medical crosses blinking more rapidly now, like scarlet flies eager to feast. He smelled the stink of roasting meat.

Before unconsciousness took him, he realized *what* was roasting.

§

"Don't waste soup on a dead man!"

"He isn't dead."

"He has to be! Just look at him!"

Jack's eyes opened and peered into a metal bowl filled with liquid and stringy green tendrils. The odor was pungent and vaguely offensive, like something rotting in a heap of freshly mowed grass, and he thought: *biofuel. Someone is feeding me engine fuel.*

Still, his lips moved instinctively, slurping in the slimy muck. The algae clusters popped like blisters in his mouth. It took him back: six years earlier, when his poor deceased *Harpy III* had been shot out of the sky over the Gobi desert, he'd been forced to cut its fuel lines and suck the green stuff for two cold, bitter days until rescue.

Hungrily gulping the soup, Jack finally looked up into a circus nightmare of giant tribal masks, and what appeared to be the interior of an igloo.

"See?" cried a masked figure. "The winged man is alive!"

"I'm alive," Jack confirmed. His captors bobbed nervously around him, brandishing silver-tipped harpoons. Goggle-eyed countenances painted green, white, blue, and black, contrasting sharply against the ice-blue curvature of the igloo.

How the hell did I get into an igloo? he wondered.

One of the motley figures took the bowl away. Then, to his astonishment, the figure bent almost directly into Jack's crotch and sniffed at his stomach. "No leakage," the masked thing noted. Its goggles were rimmed bright white, like a photonegative raccoon. "It sounds impossible, but he may yet live."

"It *is* impossible," retorted a woman in a scowling blue mask.

"My name is Tartok," the raccoon-mask told him. "I am captain of these people. I thank you. We all thank you."

"Um, thank *you*," Jack replied uncertainly. Deciding he was safe for the moment, he conjured his bio-readout. Jack's heart fell when he considered the report.

Broken ribs. Burns over sixty percent of his body. He recalled his screams in the cockpit, and the smell of roasting flesh.

Well, Jack thought. Could be worse. Upon impact, his internal seedclusters had released their specialized nanomachines, pinching off nerves that were trying to send reports of scorching agony to his brain. Other machines were industriously repairing his cells and even his flight-suit's integrity. It would take weeks before he no longer looked like a melted candle, and he'd slough off the ruined skin like an especially nasty reptile, but he'd survive.

The woman in the blue mask pushed him. "How many more winged men will come? How many more people will you snatch away?"

"Hold on. My name is Jack Saylor, captain of the *Harpy VIII*."

The woman turned to Tartok. "He's a spy for Shostak! The bastard called into the Great Sky and summoned this winged man!" She pointed to Jack's sleeves, where the *Harpy's* logo was displayed: feathery wings and splayed-out claws in reflective decals. "Others will follow!"

Jack frowned. "I'm not here to spy for anyone. Who are you people?"

Her eyes were wrathful behind the goggles. "I am Miko-of-the-Hurrier. How can you do this to a child?"

"You have me at a serious disadvantage." And then, before Jack could say more, he suddenly realized what he was looking at. "Your masks... those are biovisors! You painted them in weird designs, but—"

Miko seized him by the lumpish, melted collar of his biosuit with one hand and wrenched him towards her. "It's true then? There are others out in the Great Sky? *How many* others?" The panic in her voice was terrible; Jack felt it transmit to him like an electric current.

Tartok touched her shoulder. "Miko! Release him!"

She complied, but her hands were trembling and she began a tight pacing through the igloo, like a frustrated bee trying to communicate an unprecedented encounter with its hive.

Jack shifted his ruined body into a more upright posture, and his blistered lips said, "Where's my ship?"

Captain Tartok bowed. "We thank you, whatever your intentions. Nothing of it shall go to waste."

Jack blinked for several seconds, and then the awful realization twisted in his stomach. "You salvaged my ship." Over Tartok's shoulder and against the igloo's curving far wall, the picked-over remains of the *Harpy* were strewn about like a dissected specimen. Steel plating, heaps of wires, the only remaining wing...these people had fallen upon the metal carcass like vultures.

Doing his best to stave off the surge of hopelessness in his chest,

Jack's attention fixed on the sight of his ship's instrument panel amid the wreckage. He took a shambling, injured step towards it.

Several harpoons came up around him; Miko nearly jabbed her silver-tipped weapon through his eye. Jack seized her weapon, jerked it towards the igloo's swamp-green algae-lanterns. Along the weapon's stock, block lettering read: EMERGENCY TETHER PITON – WARNING – CONTENTS UNDER PRESSURE.

"This is from a landing gear," Jack said in amazement. He regarded the igloo, noticing the rattling, corroded O2 processors embedded in the ice. "And those are a ship's enviro-units!"

Miko tried to pull her weapon free. Jack frowned, surprised at the difficulty she was having. He released his grasp and she tumbled backwards into the snow. He bent to help her up, and narrowly avoided receiving her harpoon in his throat.

"Do not harm our guest, Miko!" Tartok commanded.

She glared through her blue goggles. And in that moment, Jack noticed a detail of her silver uniform he hadn't before. It was like a baggy clown suit around her fragile body, but there was faded stenciling on the sleeve:

Tørnquist Corporation.

§

Tartok removed his white-lined mask, and his breath came in vaporous swirls as he sat beside Jack. He was a sandy-haired, gaunt-faced creature, but without the mask his voice was warm and comforting.

"My daughter," he said at last, displaying his suited forearm. An old job-status wristband glowed to life. Pixels crawled into place along a cracked, faded display. Jack found himself looking at the digital photo of a young child wearing a small, green mask.

"We painted it together," Tartok explained, his forehead creasing with angst. "Dark plankton green—her favorite color, the color of life and hope and food. She was so excited when I explained that summer was coming, that its light would replenish the batteries and pools."

The image dissolved, reformed into a second picture. This time, the girl was without her mask, and was grinning happily alongside her father. A mop of dirty blonde hair fell around a pale, emaciated face…a countenance resulting from living in a low-g hell like this. Tartok had his arm around the little girl, and her joyous smile made Jack's heart pang in anguish. He wondered if he had ever made anyone smile that like.

"Where is she?" Jack asked softly.

"You truly don't know?"

"I'm not from around here."

"He is going to sacrifice my little girl to the summer sun."

"The summer sun?"

"He knows all this!" Miko-of-the-Hurrier protested, and she snatched the instrument panel from the wreckage and held it out, wires dangling from its undercarriage. "See?"

Jack stared. There was enough battery power remaining for the panel to display a digital rendering of the outside terrain. Before crashing, his orbital probes must have fed it enough data to construct the map. On that vector-drawn topography, a single bright dot flashed mirthlessly.

The holocube!

Two miles west of his current position.

"Tartok," Miko cried. "Please listen to me! The winged man is not our ally! Look at the dot on the map! It proves he knows where Shostak's encampment is."

Jack lurched to his feet. "You said your little girl is going to be sacrificed to the summer sun. *When* is the sun coming up?"

"An hour," Tartok said helplessly.

"*An hour?!*"

Jack felt himself go dead inside. He located his helmet on the floor, snapped it onto his suit's neck ring, pressurized it, and trudged to the igloo's steel pressure door.

Then he went through, stepping onto the exterior of the comet.

§

Outside, the valley's dirty white terrain was cluttered by igloos, hemmed in by bony, freakishly-shaped cliffs. In the black sky, there was a scintillating haze of gold flecks that were probably particles of ice, weakly hovering on the edge of the comet's gravity and reflecting the pending, once-a-century summer.

Jack watched the gold flecks and thought of Sylph Tørnquist's eyes.

How many miners had been a part of her company's illegal strip-mining expedition two centuries earlier? Enough workers, apparently, to maintain a breeding population when their expedition failed and marooned them here.

Jack trudged along the village path, passing igloos until he attained the foothills and began a difficult, terribly weakened climb. The lower gravity helped, but after only a few meters of ascent he had to stop, gasping in his helmet from the effort.

An hour until sunrise...

He glanced back to the village. The ancient miners must have repurposed their failed ship to construct these modular habitats. Their descendants now trickled out in a nervous, uncertain herd, following at a distance.

What had it been like for their dimly remembered progenitors? Sent here in secret to strip-mine in defiance of the law. Their ship crashing while attempting a landing, much as he had: landing on comets was no easy feat. Attempting to contact the larger universe... and failing. Forced to adapt, the ship raided and salvaged. Pools dug for the biofuel to propagate, to provide them food. A once-a-century summer that made the pools green and the batteries come to life.

Then, as the generations passed, a reversion to this species of tribalism...

Jack sighed, feeling small before this hidden, terrible episode of history. And suddenly, without warning, he was looking down on himself from the sky.

It was like a third eye had opened in his brain. He saw his hunched, blackened, melted biosuit from a vantage point somewhere high above.

Jack upturned his face. Nothing but black sky and the shoal-like glitter of ice particles that he could see, but a grin broke across his ruined face as he realized what was happening. The orbital mapper! He remembered seeing two of them crash, but the third one…it must still be up there! Since the *Harpy's* death, it was sending out electronic queries to find him. Like a dark angel, gliding above the cometary terrain on mechanical wings.

Jack closed his eyes and peered through the probe's optics. He watched as two of the igloo dwellers hurried to catch up to him.

"We have less than an hour until sunrise," Tartok said, wheezing in his mask and rebreather. "Do you need us to… carry you?"

"No. But you could tell me about Shostak. Who is he?"

"He was my most trusted scout once, seeking places for new algae pools to be dug. With summer coming, we wanted as many as possible, you understand, to grow green before winter sets in again. Shostak was the best. He was my friend." The man hesitated, eyes twitching in sorrow behind his goggles. "I don't understand what madness possessed him. Some say he spent too long out on the ice. Whatever the truth, he never returned to the village. He set up his own camp and convinced others to join him. Preached that when summer arrived, it might bring us a better world, if we were willing to…"

"Sacrifice," Miko said softly, and she touched Tartok's shoulder. "For many months, our two camps stayed away from each other without incident. Then last night, Shostak led a hunting party into the village and kidnapped the captain's daughter. We believe she is to be the sacrifice. When you arrived, we thought you were here to capture others." Miko squinted at him. "Why *are* you here?"

He sighed.

What can I tell them? he wondered. That an immortal woman on Earth whose family sent your ancestors here was feeling nostalgic for a childhood she can't remember? That this nostalgia must have been stoked by knowledge that the forbidden comet was coming around again, making its hundred-year flyby of the sun?

Jack looked kindly upon Tartok and Miko, seeing himself reflected in their goggled gaze. "I'm here to stop the sacrifice. I'm here to get your little girl."

§

He spotted Shostak's village through the orbital mapper before he saw it with his own eyes. The rival camp had carved caves directly in a mountain of dirty ice, making it appear like a nightmarish termite mound. At the mountain's feet lay a snowfield, crowded with more than a dozen people: the apostates, presumably, who had siphoned off to this opposing ideology. They ringed an icy altar, upon which a diminutive shape squirmed beneath restraining hands.

Sunrise was eight minutes off; a dawning light already revealing the intricate patterns of the snowfield. Intersecting layers and crisscrossing filigrees radiated beneath their feet. A billion-year history of solar voyages, encoded in cosmic ice like pages of a book.

Jack hesitated at a single icy boulder and regarded his two companions.

"Stay here," he told them.

Miko scoffed. "You can't face a dozen people by yourself!"

"I'm the winged man from the Great Sky. That gives me certain advantages, Miko."

She twirled her harpoon. "I don't come from the Great Sky, you condescending bastard, but I can still impale a target from twenty meters off."

"I believe you. Doesn't change anything."

"The hell it doesn't!"

Jack had to choke back his laughter. Two hundred years of isolation, and certain idioms were as immortal as the Tørnquists themselves. Jack was a lifelong admirer of spite and defiance, and it was clear that Miko had both in spades. He was really starting to like her.

"Listen," he said. "Tactically speaking, it would be better if I met them alone."

"But—"

"They know *you*. They won't know me, Miko. I'm counting on that making an impression."

Miko looked ready to argue, or threaten, or maybe just skip right to the part where she jabbed him in the throat with her harpoon. But she finally relented when Tartok gave a silent, reluctant nod.

With that, Jack strode out across the snowfield. Once he'd covered half the distance, he cranked the volume on his shoulder-speakers: "Lord Shostak!"

The rival camp turned towards him in surprise. Even at a distance, Jack could see that they all wore bright yellow masks.

In seconds, several of Shostak's people were airborne. They leapt off the hilltop, flinging themselves up in the low-g, and fired their harpoons. Pitons cracked into the ice around him. They retracted their bodies along the cables in a stunning display of speed and accuracy. A moment later, Jack found himself surrounded as if by a grinning bunch of space spiders.

He held his hands out in a non-threatening posture. The efficient dragnet unnerved him. And then the ugly thought:

Maybe it was these people, and not Tartok's gentler group, who were fated to rule the comet one day. Maybe it was their flavor of aggressive superstition, obedience, and blood-lust that gave them an awful advantage on this crucible of the void.

Jack regarded the bobbing yellow masks. "Your leader," he said. "Take me to him."

He let himself be carried—it was a welcome reprieve for his legs. He watched himself from above, seeing Miko and Tartok hiding anxiously by the boulder.

Seeing Tartok's daughter was forcibly stretched across an icy plinth.

Five minutes until sunrise.

When his captors set him down, Jack was facing a tall figure donning a bright yellow mask rimmed with red.

"Shostak," Jack guessed. He looked the man up and down, noting the old mining uniform, the Tørnquist Corporation logo. He noted something else, too. Hanging by a necklace of yellow wires was…

The holocube!

Maybe it had never been buried by the ancient miners. Or maybe it *had* been interred, only to be rediscovered by this master scout and adopted as… what? A fetish artifact? A symbol of priesthood?

"Who are you?" Shostak demanded.

Jack displayed his sleeves. "I'm the winged man. From the Great Sky."

The girl on the altar turned her little mask towards him.

Shostak was silent for a long while. "It was *you* we saw arrive," he muttered. "In your craft, appearing out of the darkness. You…why are you burned?"

"When you have wings, you can't help but fly near the sun."

"He comes from the others!" someone from the crowd shouted, but Shostak remotely muted the man's suit speakers from his wristguard controls.

"I'm here because *you* wanted me here," Jack insisted and, inspired by Shostak's little demonstration of power, decided to respond in kind. Using his link to the orbital mapper, he ordered the probe to rotate its geodesic hull, until he began to glow from reflected sunlight, the wings on his sleeves like angry red stigmata.

The effect on the crowd was immediate. They threw their harpoons into the snow and bowed.

"Sunrise is upon us," Jack boomed, "And… um…you wanted something, right?"

What *did* the man want?

Shostak held out his arms, dropped to his knees, his harlequin face glinting in the dawning luminosity. He touched the holocube around his neck. "The Enchantment! I know I must sacrifice for it! I've brought the captain's daughter for that purpose! Surely you see!"

"Absolutely," Jack muttered, stalling for time. He noticed the curling knife in Shostak's hand; a nanosteel boring knife, re-appropriated for this nasty business. The girl's young throat would open like tissue paper around its diamond-hard blade.

Two minutes until sunrise.

"I've seen the visions!" Shostak insisted. "I *will* sacrifice!"

Jack bent and scooped the girl into his arms. "I accept your offering, Shostak. I'll fly her away into the Great Sky, and then you'll get your—"

In the distance, a geyser erupted from a crevice, expelling rock and ice as Sol's touch heated and stirred the gases beneath the comet surface. The clifftops were suddenly weeping great torrents of snow into the endless black—the cave-riddled mountain resembled a chunk of dry ice—and Jack felt a thrill of panic as his shadow stretched grotesquely across the steaming, sizzling snowfield.

"Where's the Enchantment?" Shostak demanded, leaping back to his feet. He brandished the knife as the world cracked around him. "*I deserve to ride it!*"

Jack instinctively recoiled from the man's vehemence; Tartok's daughter was stiff in his arms, her mask hard against his shoulder.

Shostak's eyes grew wide behind the goggles. "You're here to trick me! *She* is my sacrifice! I *must sacrifice* to earn the Enchantment!"

Another geyser erupted; the shock blew Jack off his feet and he dropped the girl. The crowd began to shrink away, disturbed by the violence of the sun. When he got to his feet, he saw an image he knew would haunt him all his days: Shostak's grinning sun-mask as the man dashed towards Tartok's child while she stood, bewildered, on a field of steaming, popping ice. Shostak's blade was like plasma in his grip.

"The sacrifice!" Shostak screamed.

Jack clenched his eyes shut. Mentally he redirected the orbital mapper yet again. Sunlight burned directly into the man's goggles.

Shostak threw back his head and howled. He fell upon his knees, sliding through gray slush mere inches from the girl. Jack wove around erupting geysers, grasped the holocube from Shostak's necklace, and snapped it free. Then, as the man continued his terrible howl—of pain, blindness, and betrayal—Jack scooped the girl once more into his arms and jumped into the sky.

He glided dreamily, came bounding down, and made another kangaroo hop, covering breathtaking tracts as the landscape sizzled and exploded. Miko and Tartok rushed out to intercept him.

The ground directly beneath Jack split like a cracked mirror.

In the fraction of time afforded him, Jack threw the young girl downward towards her father. She sailed into the man's arms; he and Miko caught her together, and then the trio scurried out of the deadly valley, rushing back to the safety of their valley.

Then the geyser erupted beneath Jack's feet and blasted him from the comet's surface. He careened into space.

Flying alone in the great and endless sky.

§

"This is Jack Saylor of the *Harpy VIII*," he broadcast into the void. "Emergency S.O.S. Anyone copy, over?"

For a long while, silence was his only response as he drifted in empty space. Then an answering signal found him:

"This is Listening Post Franklin. I copy you, but the pingback suggests you're transmitting from the comet. That's a clear violation of IPC Conservation Code 4423-B77."

Jack sighed in deep relief. "Come pick me up and we'll chat about that. Meanwhile, I need you to prepare an emergency rescue for about seventy people, maybe more."

"*Seventy* people? What the hell are you talking about?"

"I'll explain later. Just pick me up, goddam it."

Jack chanced to swivel open his protective visor. The comet's tail flared ahead of him, the piercing rays of Sol causing his visor to darken until it was like squinting at a lighthouse through a very deep smog.

Jack drifted in the void. His meal of algae slid unpleasantly in his stomach. He regarded the holocube in his clenched fist curiously.

I'm flying off to obtain what you want, he had told his employer.

Jack snapped the holocube into his suit's chestplate holoreader. A display appeared in his eyes:

CONTENTS LOADED

"Access," he said.

§

The amusement park was like a magical, storybook kingdom come to life.

Little Sylph ran ahead of her father, eager to reach the steam-train. Other kids were already climbing aboard. It was a wonderful train! Blue as the sky, with massive eagle wings painted along its flanks, and the train's name—the Enchantment Express—in large, elegant letters. Children giggled as they settled into their seats, eager for the train to begin its journey around the sprawling length of the amusement park. Sylph had seen the train advertised in commercials. Now, after months of nagging her father, he had finally brought her here! She would ride the Enchantment!

She hurried towards an empty seat.

"Sylph!" Her father's hand caught her arm.

"Hurry, Daddy!"

Mr. Tørnquist knelt in front of her. "Do you like this train?"

"The Enchantment is wonderful!"

"Yes. It is beautiful."

Sylph let out a chirp of delight and tried climbing into the spare seat again. To her confusion, the elder Tørnquist pulled her back to the station platform.

The train whistle blew.

"It's leaving!" Sylph cried. "Come, Daddy! We need to board it!"

"You're not going on the Enchantment, Sylph."

"But you took me here to—"

"The Enchantment makes you happy?" he asked, a cold tightness coming into his voice. "Well, happiness is not free. Nothing is given to you in life for free. Sacrifice, Sylph. You must be willing to sacrifice if you want happiness. It's time you learned this lesson."

Little Sylph sobbed in his grip as the magical train pulled away, drawing off its cheering children, the sunlight glinting off its painted wings.

"Sacrifice," he repeated, and then he steered her towards the helipad where the company copter awaited, while the sun perched like a cruel eye on the horizon.

The Devil You Know

Nemma Wollenfang

It was semi-dark when Sister Ava lit the taper candles around the church. Their limited light barely defined the extensive aisles and looming windows and left the dark corners untouched, but it did not matter, only a little was needed to commune with God.

She was just finishing up, straightening prayer mats ready for the morn's service, when there came a peculiar scratching noise. Had rats gotten into the vestry again? It wouldn't be the first time. Yet as she looked about, the pews were as quiet as the graveyard beyond.

Scraaaaatch. There, again, at the main doors—a scraping like claws on wood.

An animal, Sister Ava decided, *likely searching for food.*

Brushing her hands to relieve them of dust, she made for the back dormitories, thinking of warm broth and her modest yet cosy bed-pallet. Two steps and she stilled.

"Help..." a voice whispered. Or had it? The sound was so faint it could have been a curl of wind. "Help," it went on, undeniably real. "Help me, please..."

No one else was about at this late hour, and Sister Ava wondered what she should do.

What if it were some ruffian, seeking to rob the collection? That had happened before. But she pushed aside her unease. *This is God's House. I am obligated to help any who seek it.*

Taking up a flickering taper, she shuffled back to the main doors and reached for the bolt. It was heavy in her frail hands and slid free with a painful whine—old and rusty, just like her bones. Holding the candle aloft, she peeked out into the eventide gloom.

Nothing stirred. The mud-laden street was empty—save for a lone horse tethered at the nearby Inn and a stray dog prowling about the butcher's shop.

"Please..." that same voice grated—at her feet.

Sister Ava gasped. There, on the marble steps up to the abbey, knelt the most wretched creature she had beheld in an age. Ropes of matted hair hung to her knees, riddled with twigs and leaves, mud smeared her translucent skin, her lips were chapped and flaking, and the smell... Oh, the smell! Rotten and ripe. Like soiled smallclothes. She held a hand to her mouth.

"Please..." The creature held up a trembling hand. The candlelight caught the glint of tears. "Help me..."

At the end of the street came the orange glow of flames.

"She went this way!" a gruff voice hollered. "Where are ya, witch?!"

The creature's eyes widened—stark white in the dark—and she grabbed at Sister Ava's habit. "Help me," she begged, with volume now, "I claim sanctuary. Please let me in. They mean to lynch me!"

She's little more than child, Sister Ava realised with a start. It was difficult to tell beneath all that grime but she was surely no more than fifteen.

Sister Ava shook away her disgust.

"Come, child." She ushered the girl inside.

"Thank ye," she muttered, as she crawled around her feet. "Thank ye, thank ye."

Sister Ava barely had time to nod, for the mob had rounded the corner. They were at least twenty strong. All angry, all hostile, all clutching torches and hoes and scythes and other sharp things. Lopsided tricorns and ruffled lace-caps sat atop their heads, and some substance splattered their cloaks and shoes; dark and slick. It was hard to tell what in the murk.

Some even came ready with planks and kindling. Not just a hanging, then.

Mr. Scott, the inn-keep, led the band; a broad man with a red face and a bristly beard. He had fiery hair and a temper to match—his wife and daughters could attest to that. And right now he was striding closer, a noose already in hand as he scaled the steps to *her* abbey.

"What is this?" Sister Ava barked, with as much authority as she could muster. The man was so tall, so prone to anger. "What do you mean by terrorising this small girl?"

He paused, seeming surprised by her outburst. Few dared to question him.

"That ain't no girl, Sister," Mr. Scott said defensively. "That there is a witch!"

"Witch!" the crowd behind him agreed. "Witch! Witch!"

The girl's hands curled tight around Sister Ava's habit, pulling the robe taut.

"How do you know this?" she asked.

"She plagued our grain with hundreds of field mice!" one man claimed with an angry snarl.

"She cursed Goodman Higgins with the bloody flux!" another announced.

"Aye, and she tried to turn my husband into a hog!" a woman proclaimed, gesturing to the robust man on her right—who's waistcoat bulged at the seams. "It didn't take, mind…"

"Please, marm," the girl at her feet whined, "I don't know what they mean. I ain't done no harm to these folk."

"It spews poison and lies," Mr. Scott blustered, reddening. "The witch needs to be burned. You know what the good Lord's book says: 'thou shalt not suffer a witch to live.'"

"Aye, that's right," someone in the crowd agreed, though Sister Ava doubted that many present had even learnt their letters. Let alone consulted the Bible. "Burn her! *Burn her!*"

Ridiculous, Sister Ava thought, *such primal simple-mindedness.*

"She is a child of the Lord," she called out, "same as you or I. How else could she pass the threshold of His own House?"

That gave them pause.

Several dropped their heads, shuffling their feet like chastised children.

"Now away with you. Leave this girl in peace." When the assemblage only shifted uneasily and exchanged wary glances, she added sharply, "Be gone!"

They dispersed then; a few at the back to begin with and then more. There were still the rebellious few who lingered. Mr. Scott and his brothers, Fin and Angus. But Sister Ava did not wait for them to leave, stepping inside she pulled the door shut with an echoic boom.

§

Across the fire, Sister Ava watched the girl as she huddled in a fur pelt and nursed a steaming bowl between her hands—her own eve's rations. She was certain she had not seen the girl at mass before… and yet, that was strange, for she had watched most the townsfolk grow from babes. Nor did she bear familiar coloring; neither the coppery red hair nor the flaxen corn mane that was most common in the region. Where had this starveling waif come from?

"Are you feeling better?" she asked after a time.

"Yes, marm, thank ye." She blew on her bowl and sipped. The chills had abated somewhat with the warm broth but the odd one still shook her slight frame.

She must have been so very frightened. "What is your name, child?"

"Me mam called me Lily."

"Lily," Sister Ava repeated with a kindly smile. "That is a lovely name."

"Ye," the girl said, taking a large gulp.

She did not resemble a lily, Sister Ava thought. Lilies were pure and delicate, all soft petals and pearly white. This girl was hardness and dark edges; of swarthy native stock, *old* blood, not good god-fearing folk. But then, her origins were not subject to judgement.

Seeing another shake, Sister Ava retrieved another, thicker pelt and placed it about her shoulders. The abbey was a cold place, with its stone floors and draughty halls.

The girl wrapped it closer. "Yer a kind one, marm."

"Call me Sister."

"Sister…" The word twisted about her tongue as if it felt odd. How very strange. Where had she come from that she would not know it? Convents covered the length of the land. Curiosity would have to wait though, for there were more prudent matters to address.

"Why did they call you such?" she asked. "Do you know why they called you 'witch'?"

At that the child grew worried, wide eyes darted with a rabbit's skitter.

"They say…" she paused, breaths quickening.

Sister Ava reached out to pat her knee. "Do not be afraid, child. Speak."

"I's so afeared that if ye know, ye will send me away, back to *them*."

Poor girl, Sister Ava lamented. Suddenly she did not appear as wretched, more akin to a frightened soul in need of reassurance. "Have no fear. I shall neither judge nor shun."

After a moment, Lily seemed to accept this, and took a deep breath.

"They say that me mam were a bad woman, with evil an' lecherous ways. She had no husband, see. She an' I, we lived on the outskirts o' town, out in the Fens."

"Where is your mother now?" The girl spoke as if she were no longer living.

Lily dropped her head, lips tight. "Gone. Them folks outside stoned her an' burnt our hut. I barely got away with m' life…"

That dark stickiness that speckled their cloaks and boots. It had likely been blood.

Oh, poor child. "What of your father?"

"Got none," she shrugged, "as far as I know."

"What of other family? Grandsires, aunt, uncles?" Was she really so alone? Was there no one who could be fetched?

"I got many uncles," the girl nodded hastily. "They visited the house a great deal when I were little, when mam lit the red light in her winder... though I never saw them long. They came to see mam in her bedchamber an' I never learnt their names."

Ah, so that was the way of it.

"They say that because I got no da I must be the Devil's own spawn, his little witch. That's what that big one was shoutin', with all that red hair."

"Mr. Scott." He began this? As a pillar of the community, he'd be hard to go against.

Misunderstanding her unease, the girl grew defensive. "It ain't true, ye know! I don't hold with those ways, an' me mam always told me that I had a da once. He were a sailor, a tar on some slave ship, but he loved her well enough. They meant to marry, they did, only... when last he went to sea he never came back..." Her ardour ebbed then and she eyed the dregs of her bowl, becoming morose. "I were still a babe in me mam's belly then."

Too common a fate for a woman these days. Sister Ava patted the girl's cheek and her fingers came away sticky. Ah, the mud. She needed to wash.

"None shall harm you within these walls, child. The abbey is well-protected."

As Sister Ava prepared a water basin, the girl sat by the hearth in silence. It took some scrubbing, and several buckets of water, but finally they uncovered the flesh beneath all that dirt. Her clothes were beyond saving, it would be the fire for them, but now she looked more like a young woman than some heinous marsh-creature, and a rather comely one at that.

"Are they still out there?" she eventually whispered.

"Yes." From the window, Sister Ava could see Mr. Scott and his brothers hunched in a doorway across the street, standing sentinel.

Glints of silver caught the moonlight—hidden weapons? One still clutched some kind of cudgel in his meaty palm.

"All I want is to be left alone," the girl mumbled. "I never hurt no one." Beneath those tats it was hard to tell, but Sister Ava was sure she saw the shine of tears again.

They wanted the girl and planned to get her, but not tonight, not on Sister Ava's watch.

She meant to protect this vulnerable child with whatever power she possessed. No matter how high Mr. Scott might be, some places were still beyond his reach.

After the girl was washed and dressed in a clean garb of undyed wool, Sister Ava set her in her own straw cot. "Dawn is still long off," she said. "You should get some sleep."

With a vague nod, the child curled up, exhaustion taking her.

§

Days passed and still the brothers stood watch. Cloistered inside, Lily was safe from them, but for how long? Sister Ava thought they would give up after three nights of wintry chill but they were a determined lot. And with each day the girl grew more restless.

"Do not fret, child," Sister Ava tried to assure her. "The Lord will deal with them."

The girl looked unconvinced. "Will He?" She knew better than to believe platitudes.

When another three days passed, and the brothers were joined by two field-hands and the smith's boy, Sister Ava began to lose heart. Why did they persist? Why not find some other occupation? There was enough work needed doing. Why target this young girl?

They even began taking alternate shifts watching the abbey, so others could get rest.

Her prospects of survival diminished every hour. In sheer desperation, Sister Ava made a suggestion one day. "Perhaps you could take up the cloth, join our sistren in the church."

Perhaps if she was an official bride of Christ they would leave her be. With shorn hair, wimple and veil, the wildness in her might even tame. Those men would not hound a mouse.

The girl thought on it a while—perhaps the option was appealing to her—but when she spoke her tone was slow and measured, as if she wished to cause no offense.

"Me mam followed Cernunnos and them Old Gods, as did her mam before her. It would be disrespectful to their spirits if I were to change me followin' now."

Sister Ava could understand that, even if she did not condone pagan heresy.

§

It took another week before Sister Ava could muster the courage to leave the abbey and approach the men, and by that time there were eight of them. One of the field-hands pointed as she descended the steps and Mr. Scott looked up. *They were stripling boys not long ago,* she reminded herself. *I used to scold Fin when he chased geese, and give a pitcher of milk to young William to take home for his sickly mother.* But they were men now, and much more intimidating for it. As she neared them, she clutched her rosary for strength.

"Why are you here every day, Mr. Scott?" she asked. "Why do you shadow this place?"

"You know why," he said. "You nuns harbour a daemon within."

"She may follow some pagan god but she is far from evil. The girl is no daemon."

"Aye, she is. She's the Devil's own kin. She beguiles folk with her innocent face."

A few of the surrounding men nodded with solemn looks and muttered agreements.

"She *is* an innocent," Sister Ava persisted. "The crimes you accuse her of are absurd." *Commanding rodents, spreading disease, transforming folk!* It was madness.

"That's what you say now, Sister," Mr. Scott sighed, "but give it time... give it time."

There was an odd, knowing glint in his beady eyes.

"What do you mean?"

"You'll see," was all he said.

Brimming with righteous indignation, Sister Ava returned inside with a huff and a shuffle. The men were fervent in their belief and ignorant in their fear. Eventually they would see the error of their judgement, she was sure.

"Check her back!" Angus called behind her. "Look for slits. The dark ones are known for their wings! An' they hide 'um beneath their skin. They're a sure sign that she's *His* child! I wager you'll find 'um if ya just—" She shut the abbey's door before he could finish.

That was before things started to happen. Bad things.

They started out small: a statue of Saint Peter fell in the undercroft and cracked, some coins from the collection plate vanished. Small things, dismissible things... Sister Patience developed a rattling cough that would not shift, and several of the altar boys fell ill with the sweating sickness. Such ailments were commonplace, always had been. But then, one morn, Sister Ava awoke to find her nails bleeding, scarlet around the rims, and later in the week a tooth broke free.

At other times, she may have attributed this to old age and a wearying life... had it not been for the suspicions Mr. Scott had planted in her mind, suspicions that had grown each day. For whenever a tomb was chipped or a glass plane broke without explanation, Lily was always there. Perhaps not close, no, usually distant, but she was within sight—peeking around doorways or sat in distant pews, just watching with those dark, dark eyes.

"It's nonsense," Sister Ava told herself, appalled by her growing worries. They were unfounded and ridiculous and dangerous. "You're allowing Mr. Scott's fears to infect you."

But the incidents escalated. A swarm of mosquitoes took residence in the confessional, the roof of the dormitory developed leaks that could not be patched, and when the kitchen-sisters cut into the freshly picked marrows the whole crop was riddled with maggots. And, perhaps the most disturbing, was the incident with the candelabra. During choir practice one morn, the iron-wrought frame fell and shattered, barely missing the conducting abbot.

A flock of nuns bustled forward to help him to his feet.

"Do not fret, sisters," he assured them. "I am well."

No one was seriously hurt—thank the Lord—many sustained only superficial cuts and the abbot bore his dislocated wrist with good cheer. But he did not see the way Lily looked.

None of them did.

In a daze, Sister Ava stared at the girl. She stood stoic, still, bizarrely calm...though with the slightest up-tilt to her pale pink lips, as if she found the whole thing *humorous*.

Her earlier words echoed back. *I must be the Devil's own spawn.*

"You saw it fall," Sister Ava said, suddenly certain. "Why did you say nothing?"

"Sister Ava," the abbot said, placating, "I am sure that if Lily had seen she would have—"

"Why did you not cry out?" Sister Ava persisted. "Or call a warning?"

Something sparked in the depths of the young girl's eyes. Anger, shame, regret? It could have been all three. But it was with nostrils flaring that Lily grated, "I saw naught."

Her eyes appeared so strange—a beguiling mixture of dark and innocence.

"You did," Sister Ava mumbled, feeling numb.

§

As time passed, her suspicions solidified into chilling fear. Her blood crystallized in her veins whenever the girl drew near and more often than not she held her breath without meaning to, until her face turned blue. She kept clear of her room at night, where Lily still slept, choosing to rest instead on the hard pews. A pained back was her reward. So she sought to share a cell with Sister Marie, who'd taken a vow of silence and could not ask why.

Lily. It was awfully close to Lilith—the supposed name of the Devil's own bride.

And Sister Ava never had managed to examine her back as Angus suggested. Always she kept it concealed. Even while washing she kept her back to the wall. On purpose, perchance?

The others did not see it; the nuns who passed Lily by with kindly smiles and nods of greeting saw nothing of her darkness. Sometimes Sister Ava wondered how they could be so blind. But as the days wore on, and more things went amiss, they too grew uneasy. And Sister Ava found herself... not hoping exactly, but nurturing the possibility of Mr. Scott's view.

What if he was right? What if she was a witch?

To shelter one such as her was tantamount to blasphemy. The papacy was very clear about what should be done with such creatures. If she were to ignore one of Satan's ilk and allow it to spread its evil, then she was a sinner herself. But what to do about it?

The answer came one Wednesday eve when, by chance, Sister Ava had to step out of the abbey and take a basket of vittles across the street to the ailing Mrs. Bates. As she passed by the watchful men on her way to the house, she paused by Mr. Scott, chewing her lip.

"Bad things have been happening," she said.

They stared at each other for an indefinite moment, knowledge passing between them in their looks alone.

Slowly, he nodded. "Leave the abbey doors open on the morrow. It'll be sorted."

§

That night, as Sister Ava lit the tapers about the abbey's church, she left the doors unbolted. Nothing more. *Let God judge what happens next.* Fate lay in His hands.

Nightmares plagued Sister Ava's sleep. The girl screamed, calling for her 'mam,' while flames devoured flesh, blistering skin from bone. There was fire, fire everywhere!

She awoke in a shaking sweat. Then remembered—the main doors were unbolted.

"No," she said, "no…" and holding a hand to her brow, she rose and dressed swiftly.

What had she been thinking? Lily did not deserve whatever fate lay in Mr. Scott's hands. Fear had overruled her compassion, made her cave to the horrors whispered in her ear. Even if Lily was what folk claimed, what Mr. Scott and his compatriots believed, that did not make her inherently evil. No, no one was born that way; they all chose their own paths. Even then that choice was not set in stone. Had not the Lord's own son absolved those sinners who died beside him on the cross? Proving that anyone could be saved should they repent their misdeeds?

Lily deserved another chance—a guiding hand that Sister Ava could, *would* provide. If there was any such badness to overcome, she would help her to do it.

The stone flags were ice-cold underfoot. Sister Ava swiftly slipped her feet into her leather shoes. She would bolt the doors. That's what she would do. She would walk into the church and bolt the doors and forget she had spoken with Mr. Scott. Later she must ask for forgiveness, do penance, wear a hairshirt if she must. It would be harsh on the skin, chafing, but she deserved such torment. Never had she done such a wicked, shameful—

A scream shattered the silence. A harrowing scream and the sounds of men grunting, struggling.

Lily.

Hurrying as fast as her frail legs could carry her, Sister Ava shuffled out of the dormitories and down the halls. She reached the pews in time to see Lily vanishing through the great wooden doors that fronted the abbey—dragged by two brutish men.

"No, wait," she called.

Neither listened.

When she reached the outdoor steps, she breathed hard and clutched at her chest. The beat of her heart was rapid and painful. There was a gathering outside. No, not a gathering, a mob—all with flaming torches of red and gold and snarls upon their faces, just like that first night. They looked much worse in the daylight; features distorted with their malice.

"How should it be done, brother?" Sister Ava turned to see Mr. Scott and Fin to her left. "Best it be at the end of a rope?" Fin went on, "Launch her into eternity?"

Mr. Scott shook his head. "Death by fire is the purer way, the only way to cleanse her corrupted soul."

Sister Ava could only gape. They had a pyre all ready at the centre of the town-square—stocked high with wooden planks and broken branches and splintered furniture. Many must have helped to compile it and many stood to watch.

Lily growled like an animal as the two men dragged her down the last of the steps, gripping an arm each. She did not give them an easy time of it, she fought them tooth and nail. The girl twisted and kicked and bucked and snapped her teeth—as feral as any beast.

The crowd parted like the Red Sea, clearing the way even as they shouted obscenities. Sister Ava stumbled forward, but when the girl's eyes found hers she fell to her knees.

"Ye promised me protection," she cried, her girlish voice breaking her heart. "Ye promised! None shall harm ye, ye said! I would've offered to leave if that's what ye wanted!"

The fierce accusation stung, lancing deep, and Sister Ava felt the depth of her betrayal.

"I'm sorry," was all she could say, "I am so very sorry."

She'd failed her utterly!

There was no forgiveness in the child's eyes. "Curse ye!" she spat.

It was with some wrestling that the two men carried her atop the wood-pile and tied her to the post, but they managed. And even as they descended people threw more sticks and branches from all sides and brought forth the flaming torches—so eager to see the girl burn.

The kindling ignited swiftly, with wicked fingers of orange flame creeping to the top.

"Daemon spawn!" the crowd jeered, "Devil's daughter! Satan's doxy!"

What have I done? Hands on her head, Sister Ava cried, "For mercy's sake stop!"

Strength found her then; she rose and dived for the crowd. Even as she fought her way through, she both knew and dreaded that the cloying mass would hold her back. They were strong and she was frail, they were young and determined and she was old.

Age and infirmity went against her.

Still at the rear, she forsook the fight. It was hopeless.

Fire licked its way up to Lily's post, surrounding her, trapping her, *engulfing* her. Sister Ava knew when flame met skin – the screech she unleashed was an unearthly howl.

Had she possessed the strength to reach the girl it would not have mattered, there was nothing she could do. Only prayers could help her now—clasping her hands, she squeezed her eyes shut and prayed, prayed for divine intervention! For someone's, *anyone's*, assistance. What was her deity's name? Cernunnos? Perhaps if she concentrated hard enough she could block out the cries, the agonised babbling. Perhaps she could banish the wildness of the crowd and the nonsensical words rolling off Lily's tongue.

Laughter silenced the jeers; laughter rich with mirth and mocking.

There were no more screams.

Opening her eyes, Sister Ava slowly looked up. The crowd had fallen quiet, a thrum of something intangible rippled through them. All eyes trained ahead.

The laughter continued, overlaid by a strange kind of chitter, as Sister Ava followed their gazes. Amidst the red and gold the girl stood free, her arms upraised and a smile upon her childlike face, as if she enjoyed the heat that consumed her bindings and licked at her skin and withered her clothing to ash. What chars her skin bore healed, into fresh pink flesh.

Sister Ava's mind was a static blank, even as she stared.

"Not possible," she muttered. "It's not possible."

Before them, the fire rippled and burst in a wave of heat and noxious black smoke. People cried out then, falling backwards, some began to scream and run. Within the flames the girl surveyed all, her black hair whipping and sparking with embers. They fled before Lily, the now-terrified gathering, like sheep from a wolf's teeth.

What Sister Ava was seeing could not be so. Behind Lily something moved, something vast and horrifying, with obsidian horns that branched from its skull and piercing black eyes that sliced like a blade. Two vast, leather wings unfurled from its back—dark and terrible. Shadows and oblivion. Cut sharp as cleavers. Within their lengths, flecks sparkled like mica in the black. Hands tipped with black spines wound around the soft skin of Lily's ash-smudged belly, in what might have been an embrace. They drew three rivulets of blood. Now she understood—that had been no agonised babbling she'd heard, it had been an invocation.

A summoning.

Devil or God? Good or Evil? Sister Ava's instincts screamed the latter.

"I withheld before," Lily called, in a voice booming with power. "I understood yer fear and restrained m' fury. Even after ye butchered m' mam, even after ye burnt our home. We willingly harmed none and meant only to live in solitude. But ye sought us out, drove me away, and here *again* ye mean to ruin me as ye did her, to cast m' remains to the wind!" Her eyes glinted, black as polished flints. Her lips curled menacingly. "You, who in yer ignorant rage understand naught! No longer. Now, ye will know what true wrath feels like!"

Two vast, leathery wings unfurled from her back—a match for the creature's own.

With that, she held her hands out, palms forward. "Ye reap what ye sow."

Another ripple and the fire travelled out, towards the fleeing in a sea of orange death, scorching, rendering all to black dust. As the firestorm blew her way Sister Ava fell, covering her wimple with her hands as heat seared the clothes on her back.

All around was screaming, and the stampede of panicked feet.

And laughing, always the laughing.

Curled in a ball, Sister Ava found that she could not move, all she could do was pray. Had she not prayed for divine intervention? That creature behind Lily was anything but. Whatever it was brought Hell-fire and chaos and death!

Oh, Lord.

When, eventually, she found the will to look up again, the world was silent. She was whole and well, yet others had not been so lucky. No people shuffled about the streets, no dogs barked, no horses snuffled. There were none left to make any noise. Only piles of smoking ash and charred bone. Where Mr. Scott and his brother had stood now lay a pair of skulls. All around was devastation; black and crumbling—the once-proud town in ruins.

The pyre was gone, as was Lily.

Whimpering, Sister Ava rose to her feet and turned.

No glowing embers, no blackened bricks. The fire had left the abbey untouched.

The *Wyvern*

Jason J. McCuiston

Captain Noah Oggs chewed the end of his pipe and tried to ignore the agony in his legs as he stared out the forward windscreen at the clear blue sky. They had run out of pain killers last night, but they were still a full day from Salt Lake City and home. If not for Old Nate's herbal tea, Noah knew the pain would be completely unbearable. He rubbed his thighs so hard his fingers turned white, hoping Smith had set the bones well enough that he wouldn't be crippled for life. "Report, Mr. Hargreaves."

Benjamin Hargreaves did not turn to face him; just kept a steady hand on the big brass-trimmed oak wheel and watched the endless horizon. Doubtless, the first mate was tiring of the frequent and identical reports, but Noah needed to feel like he was still doing something.

"Cruising at 8,000 feet at a speed of just under 50 miles per hour, Captain. Still on course for home; no problems in sight." Hargreaves's smooth, articulate tone did not betray exasperation, but Noah imagined he could see the younger man rolling his eyes.

"Engineering?" Noah half-turned his head and snapped the order around the stem of his unlit pipe.

"Same as five minutes ago, Captain." Carla Gomez made no attempt to hide her consternation at the constant demand for reports. "Same as five minutes before that. We're in perfect flying trim; good on batteries, good on helium, good on everything except our captain. Why don't you go get some rest?"

"You just worry about keeping the *Cibola* in the air, Carla, and let Smith worry about my well-being." Jasper Smith, former medic in the Royal Air Fleet, had been noticeably absent since informing Noah of the lack of pain killers in the medical supply closet late last night. Noah rubbed his thighs and wondered if he would soon be looking for a new medic for his crew. Smith's problem with pills had been the reason for his dismissal from His Majesty's service.

"What are you going to do with Reese, Captain?" Hargreaves still did not turn. "You realize it was an accident, right?"

Noah frowned and almost bit through the stem of his pipe. Bill Reese was currently locked up in the airship's tiny brig. The aging deckhand's negligence while exploring the ruins of one of the Lost Angels islands had been the reason Noah was now confined to his command chair in misery. Due to the unexpected injury, they had been forced to cut the salvage mission short and were now returning home without enough plunder to cover the cost of the expedition. "I don't know yet. Probably pay him and cut him loose."

"He's a good man with loads of experience, Captain. He'll be hard to replace." Hargreaves did turn this time, to give Noah a pleading half-smile. The good-looking first mate was always trying to make his wishes Noah's commands. Noah frowned, knowing better than Hargreaves how good a crewman Reese was, but that Reese's actions on this trip had been inexcusable. Since Noah was the one actually suffering the painful consequences, he was not about to waffle this time.

Noah saw the black shadow erupt across the windscreen before he could continue the argument. "Full stop!" An immense storm cloud had somehow jumped into existence not two miles ahead of the airship. The writhing, roiling, bank bristled with multi-hued lightning and growled with low thunder. It stretched across the sky like the black wings of the Angel of Death.

The temperature on the bridge dropped noticeably.

"What the hell…." Hargreaves turned the wheel to starboard to guide the ship away from the oncoming storm while Gomez worked leavers at the engineering panel to shut off steam to the engines. "Wherever that thing came from, it's still coming on, Captain. Our best bet is to try and run around it, and fast."

Noah rubbed his thighs and gnawed on the pipe. Even at top speed he knew there was no way to get around that massive front. "Climb," he said. They were already nearly at the ship's maximum altitude, but if they could push the limits, they might be able to get above the freakish thing.

"You're kidding, right?"

"Dammit, Carla, I said climb."

The engines roared back to full power and Noah felt the deck shudder through his chair; Hargreaves turned the wheel to port and pulled it back. The *Cibola's* nose rose and the black cloud seemed to grow taller; trying to catch the small airship.

"All hands on deck," Noah shouted into the command tube beside his chair. "Somebody let Reese out of his cage! Smith get your ass up here!"

"Madre Dios. We are not going to make it," Rosa whispered from behind him. A fork of green lightning lashed out. The ship rocked, tossing Noah from his chair. A peal of thunder crashed around them like the end of the world, punctuating the pain sawing through his legs. Everything was white and on fire, then suddenly black….

§

Noah opened his eyes and saw that the sky was perfectly blue; not a shred of cloud remained. He smelled a hint of smoke and noticed that the engines were not running. He also noticed his legs hurt like hell. "What happened?" he asked the ring of faces standing over him; Carla, Hargreaves, Smith, Old Nate, Reese, and the two youngsters: Jaquan, and Karan Tanaka.

"Lightning strike," Carla said. "Port engine's gone. Could've been worse."

"Where's the storm? How long was I out?"

"Must have been a wildstorm," Hargreaves said. "Though I've never heard of one this far from the frontier. You were out less than ten minutes; the storm's been gone over five."

"Like I said, could've been worse."

"You've had quite a spill, Captain." Smith, the pale, skinny medic pushed his thick glasses up his long nose. "You should let me give you a sedative, and spend the rest of the trip in your quarters."

Noah waved him off. He could see there was something else on the faces of the crew, something that looked like fear. "What is it?"

Hargreaves stepped back and waved toward the windscreen. "There's that." Noah pushed himself painfully up in his command chair and followed the first mate's gesture. "We've tried to hail her, but there's no answer."

Filling the forward view was a monstrous grey dirigible, its long gondola pocked with gun-ports, studded with winged bomb racks, and its dorsal edge surmounted by a row of machine gun turrets; a war blimp like nothing he'd seen before. It looked ancient in design, but brand new by its royal markings and the sleekness of its airbag. It just hung there in the open sky like it had always been there and would remain in that spot for eternity. Noah's stomach knotted up; he guessed from the bone-grinding pain in his legs.

"It's the *Wyvern*," Reese whispered from the corner of the crowded bridge. The old deckhand was paler than the junkie medic and looked in more physical distress than Noah. "It's the *Wyvern*, come back from hunting the Hodag!" Reese crossed himself and started mumbling a prayer in the depths of his brushy beard.

"What's the *Wyvern*?" Karan asked. She was new to the ways of airmen; they'd caught her as a stowaway coming back from Fresno four months ago, and she'd been indentured ever since.

"It's a myth; a ghost story to scare newbs like you." Noah knew the tales about the *Wyvern*, every airman in the Pacific City States did.

He almost stopped Old Nate from telling the tale, but decided it would give him time to come up with a plan.

"Sometime about three hundred years ago," the cook and quartermaster began, "after unifying the city states under his family's rule and establishing the Rowland Dynasty, Prince Walter declared that he would take the Royal Air Fleet's flagship into the uncharted Wyld to hunt down the Hodag, the Leviathan that had destroyed the Old World three centuries before.

"For months his carrier pigeons returned to the royal fortress in Saint George with reports of the ship's incredible adventures. The reports told of glowing rivers of magic flowing through indescribable landscapes and the towering ruins of ancient cities haunted by mystically-crazed savages and unliving monsters; of fantastical beasts and impossibly beautiful vistas; of unimaginable terrors experienced in the face of the unpredictable wildstorms which hurled untamed magic into the atmosphere, reshaping matter and energy in defiance of all mortal understanding."

Old Nate's voice dropped to a sinister timbre as he concluded, "The last pigeon brought a scrawled suicide note following the crew's disastrous sighting of the Leviathan. The royal family and the fleet promptly destroyed the note in hopes of sparing Walter's legacy. Of course, rumors got out and that only caused the legend to grow ever more evil in the ensuing generations."

"And that's the *Wyvern*?" Jaquan asked, his dark eyes wide as he pointed at the mysterious war blimp.

Noah looked at the faces of his crew and could see the effects the tale and Reese's behavior were having, and not just on the youngsters. Jaquan, the brawny kid Noah thought of like a son was scared but tried not to show it; not in front of Karen, the flirty young woman beside him, who was mustering her own bravado as best she could.

"That's not the *Wyvern*," Noah said. "What that is, is a prime piece of unclaimed salvage; royal or not. If there's no living crew aboard, then she's for the taking. There may be parts that can repair our engines, and they might have painkillers in their sickbay. Anything else onboard is fair game, too."

"You mean to board her?" Reese was horrified.

"Mr. Hargreaves, please put Reese back in his cage as it appears he will be of no further use to us this voyage. The rest of you prepare to go aboard; side-arms, tools, and carriers. I'll remain on the bridge and coordinate with the coms and my binoculars.

"Mr. Hargreaves, you take Smith and Tanaka and search the medical bay and the weapons locker. Carla, you take Old Nate and Jaquan and find engineering and the galley. Once you're back with necessities, we'll make another trip for the goodies."

"Captain," Hargreaves said, "if I may. We don't need to board her. We could launch a grapple line and tow her to Vegas. Even with one engine, we could make it by nightfall. We'd make enough selling her there to pay for repairs, medicine, supplies, and fuel; and you could rest in a real hospital."

"I like that idea," Karan said. Noah was not surprised; he knew about his first-mate's fling with his young servant, just like he knew about her plan to use Hargreaves to eventually supplant him as captain. In fact, if he hadn't been so preoccupied with keeping abreast of their little intrigue, he might have noticed Smith's relapse and Reese's drinking problem.

"Guess what, kids: my ship, my rules. You might have contacts in Vegas, Mr. Hargreaves, but I don't. And I know that if we did haul that thing in, we'd be lucky to get 30% of her value from those cowboys. And that's *if* we didn't wind up in prison for looting royal property. We go aboard and take what we need, what's worth scrounging, then we leave her in the middle of the desert sky with no one the wiser. Now, get moving."

As the crew began to file out, Noah caught Jaquan's arm and held him back. When they were alone, he said, "Boy, don't make me regret taking you on instead of turning you over to the magistrate when I caught you stealing." He never had in the past three years. "You keep your eyes and ears sharp, and you look after Old Nate and Carla. They both got families, big ones, and Old Nate's about to be a granddaddy."

Jaquan smiled and patted Noah on the shoulder. "And I thought you split me and Karan up so we wouldn't get 'lost' over there for a couple hours."

Noah laughed though he wanted to tell the boy not to trust that girl. "Couple hours, my ass. More like a couple minutes, then you'd be useless for a couple days. You just keep your head on a swivel and do what Carla tells you to. Now, hand me my binoculars."

Ten minutes later Noah sat alone on the bridge. His pipe had broken in his fall, so he caught himself chewing on the neck strap of the heavy binoculars. With the engines down, the *Cibola* was strangely silent; he could hear the wind rustling over the canvas airbag above and whistling through the outer decks of the gondola. The ship creaked and groaned in a familiar way as he heard his crew tramp down to the boarding deck; heard the loud thump of the grapple cannon fire.

He raised the binoculars and saw the line disappear into deep shadow beneath the war blimp's long, sleek body; it was midday, so the sun glistened on the top of the dirigible while casting its belly into complete darkness. In short order, Mr. Hargreaves had the relay lines secured and the heavily-dressed crew began to hook safety harnesses to the pulley systems, allowing them to glide across the fifty-foot gulf 8,000 feet above the Mojave.

Just as he dropped the binoculars to his lap, he thought he saw movement on the other ship. He jerked the optics back to his face but saw nothing. He lifted the handset from the chair arm. "Coms check."

There was a second's delay before he heard Hargreaves' voice crackle through the wired device. "Number One is good." Quickly, each of the other crew members rattled off their call signs through the handsets they carried on their belts. Each set was connected to a wire, which was then bundled with all the other wires and jacked into a spool of cable hooked directly into the bridge coms. Jaquan would carry the spool over to the other ship, then mount it at a central location so the individual lines would feed slack as needed as they moved through the ship.

Noah raised the binoculars again and rubbed his aching legs. He swept the darkened gondola of the other ship but saw nothing. Hargreaves led his crew, one by one, across the lines and onto the derelict. Soon, the call came back: "All aboard, Captain. We're splitting up now; my team is heading fore, team two is heading aft."

"Be safe," Noah said before setting the handset down. He felt a knot in his gut and a cold chill on his skin. He rubbed his face and frowned. "I'm just letting all Reese's superstitious horseshit get to me."

A bloodcurdling scream ripped through the com.

Noah snatched the handset out of the air before it fell to the floor. "Report! Report! Report!"

"Number One reporting; nothing yet, Captain." Hargreaves sounded surprised; confused.

"Carla reporting; same here. Why you so jumpy, Captain?"

"Anybody hear feedback on their coms?"

"Negative." No one had.

"Carry on." Noah dropped the handset in his lap and raised the binoculars again. He fingered the dial to maximum magnification and painstakingly began to pore over every inch of the mammoth dirigible. She was a great blimp, not an actual rigid airship like the *Cibola*, though she did have an armored exoskeleton of winged, interlocking mesh surrounding her long airbag, and a steel walkway, spaced with machine gun turrets, across her dorsal line connecting nose to tail. Her darkened gondola was at least ten times the size of the *Cibola's*, and probably loaded with heavy cannon and all manner of artillery shells. The absolute embodiment of Death From Above.

A ray of sunlight slid around the tail's shadow and fell across a sigil painted on the rear of the gondola. It was a great black dragon-thing, blade-like wings menacingly splayed. Noah felt cold sweat break out over his entire body and that knot in his gut dissolved into ice water. "It can't be...."

Noah picked up the coms handset again. He flicked the thumb switch. Nothing happened. He flicked it over and over.

Nothing.

He dropped the useless device and raised the binoculars. He caught sight of Hargreaves, Tanaka, and Smith moving past a row of portholes on the uppermost deck. He gave a tight sigh of relief. Noah swung the optics toward the stern in hopes of catching sight of Carla's team. He stopped amidships.

He saw people; maybe a dozen of them. At least he thought they were people. They were moving in the shadows, but remained dark even when they passed a porthole bathed in reflected light.

Noah closed his eyes tight, then tried to strain them into the binoculars for a clearer view. The shadows continued to move, but that's all they were. Shadows. But cast by what? Or by whom?

"We've reached engineering, Captain." Carla's voice was cool and confident as ever. "No sign of life so far, but everything looks in working order. In fact, though the tech on this thing is ancient, it looks like it rolled out of the factory this morning."

Noah snatched up the handset and flicked the thumb switch. "Carla! Keep on the lookout; I don't think you're alone over there!"

"Captain," Hargreaves' voice cut in. "We're in the medical bay. We've found no evidence of crew, but this place is immaculate. Even the glass alcohol and peroxide containers are full, intact, and unstained."

"Mr. Hargreaves, can you hear me?"

There was no reply. Noah dropped the handset and raised the binoculars. This time, there was no mistake. He saw figures moving past the portholes, closing on the forward deck where he knew his first mate's team to be.

"Oh my God." Noah focused the binoculars on the moving figures. He saw them disappear into an interior chamber.

Karan Tanaka's scream cut through the sky separating the two aircraft. Noah heard it clearly though it did not come through the coms.

The coms crackled. "Captain! The crew! No—!" Hargreaves' panicked voice was cut short by gunfire. Five quick pops, then silence. The shadow figures emerged back into the corridor and turned to head aft.

"No, no, no, no…." Noah felt tears welling up in his eyes. He swatted them away and tried to think. He was trapped in his chair on the bridge with no coms. Someone or something was hunting down his crew over there; on the ship he'd ordered them to board. He'd already lost three people, and now he was about to lose three more; the three who meant the most to him.

He tried to stand but the pain that shot through his legs took his breath away and dropped him into the chair like a haymaker. He gasped for air and clung to the binoculars and the useless handset like they were talismans against evil.

"Reese!" Noah flopped out of the chair and began to drag himself across the stamped-metal floor. If he could get to the brig, he could send Reese over to the *Wyvern* to bring Jaquan, Carla, and Nate back. The shadow people had four long decks to traverse; he only had two short ones.

Crawling through the hatch from the bridge into the outer corridor, he smacked one thigh so hard he was sure that he knocked the knitting bones loose. He screamed, bit his tongue and tasted blood, but dragged himself on through. He was shaking and weak by the time he reached the stairs leading down to the main deck.

Gritting his teeth, Noah pushed himself over the edge and bumped his way painfully down to the lower deck. He was bleeding from his brow and mouth, and had added a dozen new bruises to his broken legs, but he pushed all that out. The only thing that mattered now was saving his crew; his family.

"Reese," he said; he had meant it to be a shout. He tried again, louder this time, as he pushed himself further down the corridor. "Reese!"

"Captain?" The old deckhand's bearded face appeared behind the narrow door's barred window.

"Coms are down. You've got to get over there and get Carla and her team back right now. Hargreaves, Tanaka, and Smith are already dead. You've got to go now." The words tumbled out of him as he dragged himself against the wall, fumbled his keys out of his pocket, and wrestled with the secured hatch.

He flung the door open to find Reese curled against the back of the tiny cell. "I ain't goin' over there, Captain! That's the cursed ship; the ship of the damned!"

Noah's fear and pain exploded into rage. "I'll show you the damned, Reese!" He pulled his revolver and leveled it at the shaking man. "Get your ass up and moving, and get over there and save your crew's lives. I'd be able to do it myself if it wasn't for you, you son of a bitch."

"I can't, Captain! I won't!"

"You will!"

"No…."

The thunderous report startled him. Noah had pulled the trigger without thinking—without even meaning to. He blinked, and Reese's brains and beard were scattered all over the tiny, smoke filled cell.

Noah dropped the gun and backed away from the hatch, shaking and his ears ringing. He couldn't believe he had done it. He was truly alone now, and it was up to him; broken legs or not. He took a deep breath and tried to force the murder from his mind. He crawled toward the bow, where the relay lines were secured and the safety harnesses were stored. Legs would be useless dangling from the ropes, at any rate. Maybe he could get close enough to the ship to shout a warning.

It seemed like it took him forever to reach the front of the ship and climb out onto the frigid deck. Noah fought horrific images of his crew being torn limb from limb by the shadow people every aching inch of the way. When he finally reached the bow, however, he saw a happy sight.

Carla, Jaquan, and Old Nate were slowly pulling themselves back across the relay lines from the *Wyvern*.

Shivering against the cold, Noah pushed himself up against the bulkhead and relaxed. He wiped blood and tears from his face and wished he had his pipe for a smoke. Once his crew were back aboard, they'd cut the lines, fire up the one good engine and limp back to Salt Lake City and try to put this nightmare behind them.

He saw the shadows on the ropes.

"Carla! Jaquan! Nate!" He screamed but his ragged voice was torn away by the high winds. He could only watch as the unnatural dark things scurried along the lines behind his unknowing crew. They moved in quick, jerky motions, not like human beings at all; Noah thought of the coiling winged serpent on the ghost ship's gondola.

The first shadow reached Old Nate. In an instant, Noah remembered meeting the brawny cook when he was a boy, apprenticing to his father. They had practically grown up together like brothers. Nate's scream carried, higher and louder than Noah would have expected. The big man convulsed, shaking the tethers and relays, then went limp. He hung like a piece of laundry on a line as the shadows crawled over his body.

Old Nate's scream had warned Jaquan and Carla, however, and they frantically increased their speed; both shouting in panic. The shadows still moved faster.

Noah was weeping, unable to speak as the tears froze on his cheeks. He tried to look away but could not as the shadows caught Jaquan. The boy fought against the things, screaming and cursing, but his fists had no effect, while ribbons of blood erupted on his dark skin and his clothing was torn to shreds. Suddenly, Noah's adopted runaway burst in an explosion of blood; a red cloud in a blue sky.

Noah threw himself onto the deck, a rock in his throat and his cut and torn hands stretched out toward the dead boy. Stinging tears blinded him, so he did not see Carla's death. He heard it, however; a long, high, wailing scream of rage, terror, and sorrow. It was the scream of a widowed mother knowing she had just orphaned her three young children.

Sobbing and shaking, Noah dragged himself back to the supply chest where the safety harnesses were stored. He wiped crunchy tears and snot from his face and saw the shadows closing on the deck. He fumbled inside the chest with ice-cold hands and snatched a parachute.

Noah only had time to get his arms in and the chest strap buckled before the first shadow crawled over the guardrail. Noah looked up into the thing's face and saw the memory of a man. A nightmare memory to be sure, but the revenant that towered over him had once lived and breathed, had loved and hated, had been a friend and a companion. Yet all that had ever been human had been torn away and replaced with evil by the wild magic which had reshaped the world. All this Noah saw in the burning green orbs of hellfire that stared out of its empty eye sockets.

Noah rolled off of the deck and into the firmament.

He wrestled with the leg straps of the pack as he tumbled in freefall. The great tan orb of the earth rushed up at him one moment, the cigar-shaped aircraft outlined against the blue sky fell away the next. His fingers were numb and unresponsive. He knew he only had a matter of seconds to secure the parachute and deploy it before he was past the point of no return.

Noah buckled the strap on his left leg and decided that was enough. He snatched at the ripcord and screamed as he was suddenly jerked skyward by the deploying chute. The single strap cut into his groin and both of his broken legs felt like they were snapped in two again.

The pain subsided to a steady throb and Noah became aware of the wider world. He looked up, past the white edge of the parachute and saw the two airships hovering high above. He blinked as the sun slid past them and in that instant, the *Cibola* burst into flames. It was already breaking apart into pieces of smoke-trailing debris by the time the thunderous report reached him; tendrils of black and white smoke and fire hanging in the sky.

The *Wyvern* remained where she was, unharmed by the explosion as if she were just an image projected onto this world and not a horrifying thing of reality.

Noah watched as a huge black cloud suddenly appeared in the clear blue sky and enveloped the great warship like protective wings.

In a moment, the cloud and the *Wyvern* were gone, leaving only the falling wreckage of his ship as evidence that it had ever been.

He looked down and saw the unforgiving Mojave climbing up to claim him, and he knew that the story would soon die with him, and that Reese's murder would be avenged. All of them would be.

After all, Noah had been the one who had sent them to their deaths on that cursed ship.

Knight of the Broken Table
D.H. Aire

*A*nswering His Royal Highness's summons, I hastened to the
castle, hoping against hope this wasn't like last time when
he needed me to clean the jakes. I know that's not the kind of thing
which is normally the role of a knight. Then again, my Order has fallen
on hard times as had the Kingdom of Lasdrah, itself.

"Ah, Sir Harold," said the balding and rather rotund King, rising
from his well-worn throne. The torch light cast shadows across the
dingy tapestries gracing the walls, depicting the legendary tales of my
Order that so few credited these day, believing the creatures the Order
fought mere fancy.

"At your service, Your Majesty," I replied, bowing.

"Sir Harold," he said, starting to pace with his hands behind
his back, "it's come to my attention that a dragon is threatening our
demesne."

"A dragon?" I muttered. "But Your Majesty, there's been no report
of a dragon across the entire continent in centuries."

"True," he replied, frowning. "That's why I'm sending you to deal
with this."

"Uh, where is the reported sighting, Majesty?"

"Elmer's Croft," he replied, sighing.

"You mean castle."

"With Elmer, it's more of a croft."

"I, uh, shall leave at once, Your Majesty," I answered, thinking, *Elmer? Ye Olde Gods, a dragon sighted at the Prince-in-Exile's duchy.* Well, it was more of an old keep, now just a broken structure abutting the tower. I also knew the King was actually asking me to spy on his only son and heir.

How I wished I was not the last knight of the realm that, according to legend, drew the last straw when it came to establishing a kingdom. *Dragon?*

§

It was a day's ride to Elmer's Croft down the King's Road. Farmer children didn't even venture close to glimpse me on my faithful stead. Once they might have. Centuries ago, Lasdrah had been considered a no-man's land, bordering the Old Woods and the Forbidden Lands— which meant at the very edge of the known world.

My Order met the challenges Lasdrah faced, but at a terrible cost. There were fewer and fewer members as we confronted what came out of the Forbidden Lands, driving the evils and ills back at the cost of life and limb, prevailing against dangers far more terrible than the oldest tapestries dared boast.

Even worse than the steady loss of knights, was that Lasdrah, which had never been a prosperous land, became less so. Its pasturage and farmland producing less and less. Once there were mining concerns, but what copper and other precious metals had been here were long gone, and long stretches of the land left desolate in their wake to this very day.

So, when I came over the hill and glimpsed the croft, I reined back and stared. There was billowing black smoke and, indeed, a dragon, of sorts, outside the croft's palisade wall. It fanned its ebony wings, which soon beat like a bellows. Then, with a loud creaking, the black scaled dragon turned about on rutted wheels before lurching ponderously forward across the field. The creature's maw opened wide and spat fire.

I swallowed hard, spurring my mount forward, approaching warily, trying to make sense of what I was seeing, as my nose wrinkled at the acrid smell in the air.

"Stoke more to the fires!" Prince Elmer shouted, waving his arms as the dragon-headed, armored— Well, giant teapot best described the wagon with dark metal wings. The mechanical creature rolled forward, without horses or oxen drawing it.

The black smoke it spewed thickened around me as the wind changed direction. My mount suddenly refused to take another step. I coughed, urging my stead to the right and out of the smoke.

Once clear, leaning back in my saddle, I shouted, "Milord Prince!"

Prince Elmer hurried from his hilltop vantage, waving, "Harry! Come to see my triumph at last."

I encouraged my mount toward him, keeping clear of the dragon, to my mount's vast relief.

"Soon I shall besiege the castle," the Prince exulted, "and force Father to recant my exile."

"Oh, Uncle Harry, thank the gods!" shouted the fifteen-year-old Princess Alexandra, running from the croft.

It had been awhile since I had last seen the princess. The young lady was devoted to her mad father, particularly since her mother's untimely death when she was a little girl. The loss of his wife had tipped the Prince's sanity. She died at the hands of the King's half blind old cook, who accidentally put rat poison on the spice rack and, you can guess the rest. Alexandra's mother did not exactly enjoy her tea that day.

The other thing about our future queen is that she has not grown up to be particularly ladylike. His Majesty had lined up tutors and ladies-in-waiting to take her in hand, but she found ways to escape them, which often meant I was tasked to find her. She would only return when I trained her in staff, dagger, and later sword… and told her legends of the knights of the realm.

"Father, Uncle Harry's here, so you won't need to assault the castle after all."

The Prince shook his head, "But I want to besiege the castle."

I dismounted. "Your Highness, you know your father's castle stinks. Threatening it with fire may drive out the remaining…" I was about to say rats, but that was a sore subject, "…mice. And your father so loves to race them in the dungeon. He won't thank you by ending your exile for that."

"He'll have no choice, Harry. He'll have to acknowledge me as Court Wizard and stop calling me the Court Jester."

"Father, uh, shouldn't we invite our guest inside for cake?" the Princess asked, gesturing to the ancient tower covered in green gray moss, which looked rather crooked, leaning slightly to the left.

"Cake? Of course. Come on, Harry. You remember how wonderful Epiny's cakes are."

I winced, hearing that name. "I would love to… and learn more about, uh, that."

A sweating, rather burly blacksmith slid open the armored metal scaled door in the mechanical dragon's side, with a ringing clang. The man hastily ducked his head before he bumped it beneath the outstretched wing. He shouted inside, "You forgot to retract them again!"

"Sorry!" echoed a reply from within the creature.

The man glared, then looked at me and blinked, seeming almost relieved as I accompanied the royal family-in-exile back to the partially standing stone gate. It all seemed fitting, somehow—a broken castle for a broken man.

§

"Harry, this will work," Elmer said with glee during our dinner in reverse. Alexandra had Epiny—who served as cook, seamstress, and her lady-in-waiting—bring out an assortment of cakes. She set one before the prince, who muttered, "My favorite." Next came the entrée, and finally, the soup.

I drank liberally of the wine until I felt fortified enough, electing to sample my dessert in honor of the prince's etiquette before enjoying the rest of my repast. "My Prince, are you planning to make this your version of the legendary Trojanian Horse?"

The Prince grew quiet, "What? No, uh, of course not... Um, it is a masterpiece, is it not? The steam engine is better than the Imperial design I, uh, borrowed. It only truly needs the crew to stoke it with coal." He smiled. "I designed the mechanics and mechanisms. Had quite the time training the blacksmith and his sons to make them."

"You sound like you were, uh, inspired," I said with a sinking feeling.

"Yes, a gift from the old gods."

I noticed the Princess's worried look. We both knew there were those of The Faith, who felt the belief in the spirits and their sorcery were as much heresy as the mechanical creations reportedly cropping up across the continent. I glanced around, wondering if the legend that this had once been a stronghold of Believers might have further bent the Prince's mind.

"The dragon can practically run itself. Well, the crew drives it, but I can set the gears to work proper patterns and set all its movements," he said, with a smile that seemed to belay the truth of that.

"You have been working on it all this time?"

"Well, I had to build the foundry first—and order all the metal, of course, from the Empire... Ended up smelting down what they thought useless junk to keep expenses down. Building the dragon, though, that was the true challenge."

"Father has spent all our coin and more on this venture," Alexandra said with a wary look.

"Because this will work! Once my dragon appears to run out of coal Father will certainly bring the metal beast inside... Won't he?"

"No, my Prince," I sighed. "He won't. That dragon looks like a giant toy and when he doesn't see you, uh, casting your spells; he's going to know the truth."

"Oh," the Prince said, then smiled, "how is this, then? I shall be seen casting incantations before he takes it inside the walls. I will set the gears, and at a time of my choosing it will come alive and threaten the castle. I'll warn Father that only by my casting protective spells on it can I keep it sedate. He will doubt me, but when the dragon awakens spewing fire, threatening his castle… That's when I will prove myself the greatest wizard of the realm." Then the Prince's eyes rolled upward and he slumped forward, his head hitting the wooden table with a thump.

Alexandra sat back. "Sorry about that. It is taking longer and longer for the drug in the cake to put him to sleep."

"Princess…"

"It's all right, Uncle Harry."

"This isn't fair to you, child," I said.

"A choice between my mad father or the grandfather who would force me to dress in those ridiculous fashions and play court to… never mind, I'm sticking with Poppa, who—believe it or not—is the closest thing there is to a wizard. I only have to worry about getting blown up."

I shook my head, thinking it best not to comment.

Epiny went over to the door and gestured to the blacksmith outside. In his permanently soot-stained work clothes, the broad-shouldered man entered and gave a slight bow to the Princess, who nodded. He crossed the room, hefted his liege, and carried him off to his bedroom for the night.

"Will there be anything else, Your Highness?" the blonde-haired Epiny asked from the doorway, her blue eyes twinkling as she winked at me.

"No, that will be all, thank you."

"Ahem." I rose, feeling my cheeks grow warm trying not to think about that wink. This was going to be a long night. "I'd best be getting to bed."

The Princess nodded and smiled. "Of course… Good night, Sir Harold."

§

The bed was the room's sole accomplishment. I stripped out of my jerkin and pulled off my boots, careful to keep my weapons close at hand. I no sooner blew out the flickering candle than I heard a scraping sound and heard feet padding close.

I drew my knife from beneath the pillow, when I heard her chuckle, "Harry, I do hope that's your dagger you're holding."

"Epiny, what are you doing here?" I rasped, sitting up, seeing her silhouette from the wan moonlight streaming through the window.

"Before dinner Her Ladyship reminded me how cold your old bones are likely to get in this drafty place," she said, climbing into bed beside me.

"Epiny," I mumbled as she slipped next to me under the covers, leaned close and kissed me.

"Oh, you are pleased to see me..."

"Um, Epiny, this is, uh, unseemly."

"Yes, it was so much better when you used to sneak into my room in the palace."

"That was long ago... I thought... I thought when you decided to accompany Alexandra and, well, the Prince..."

"Is that why you stayed away? Because of my time with Prince Elmer?"

"He needed you. Loves you."

"No, he only needed me. I was a passing fancy." Epiny turned her head. "He's his toys to keep him entertained. It's Alexandra I watch over."

"He's worse, isn't he?"

She sighed, "Well, perhaps better to say more inspired."

"That's what worries me. How inspiring is it around here?"

"Well, the Princess says she feels we're being watched at inconvenient times—and, believe me, it's not any of the servants."

"Is it possible he's found a relic?" I asked almost in a whisper.

I felt her tense, hesitate. "He has these small glass marbles."

"Marbles," I muttered. "How many?"

"No more than two dozen. You know he's always had a few, but since we came here he's added to his collection."

"What color?" I asked, bolting upright.

"Why, they're black."

An old god itself? I feared, knowing that should be impossible.

"What, Harold? Don't tell me you were afraid that the Prince has lost all his marbles?"

Shaking my head as I cradled Epiny close, I told myself I had to be leaping to conclusions. Perhaps, the Prince had only stumbled upon an elemental spirit or merely trapped a ghost to help him with his dragon. "So serious, Harold," Epiny murmured, tickling me, making me forget such worries as we laid back down.

"Stop," I whispered as we rolled beneath the blankets.

"Harold, you really should have visited," she muttered. "You silly fool."

She kissed me again and I hope she did not notice my errant tears of joy as I thought, *One dragon down, one to go...*

§

I woke as she rose at dawn. "Epiny?"

"Shh, I've got work to do."

"So do I... It's just that, well, I've missed you so."

She chuckled, "Then, come fight dragons more often." That said, she slipped back out through the secret panel.

I blinked, wondering how I could have missed seeing that there. Then again, I apparently had missed a lot of things.

§

Prince Elmer was eating eggs and pancakes, while quietly drafting I knew not what on a large piece of velum. "Yes," he shouted, waving his quill, "All I will need to do is lay track between here and the palace walls and my dragon will be there in no time at all!"

Princess Alexandra looked up from her meal. "Uh, Father, track? Metal track?"

"Yes, the dragon moves too slowly on its rutted wheels. So, I'll just order track to be laid like the Western Empire is doing crisscrossing their territory. Hmm, come to think of it, I'll need to modify the wheels like they do, too."

"Father, with what money?" Alexandra rasped.

"Money? Money! I'll sell the rest of our properties."

"You've already sold them all, except this one, while also taken loans that are coming due, Father."

"Hmm, well, I've your dowry..."

"You've already spent that, too."

"Well, we shall have the treasury when your grandfather dies. Surely, we can get loans against that."

I winced, knowing the palace was in deplorable condition as was the Kingdom, which was not because the king was miserly by choice, but trying to explain that fact to the Prince would be rather pointless.

"No one will loan you more money, Father--not after they realize you've spent it all building the dragon."

"Tsk, tsk," he said, waving his hand, "it won't be a problem, my dear."

"Father, we already owe more than we can ever repay..."

I stood there, thinking wistfully of tapestries back in the throne room and suddenly laughed.

The Prince turned to glare at me as Alexandra looked imploringly.

"Your Highness, if I may be so bold as to suggest a solution?"

§

Once there was a broken table around which the Knights of the Realm sat with our King. The members of the Order swore vows to right wrongs and protect the people of Lasdrah from the horrors of the world, injustice and, of course, serve the royal line to the death, if need be.

I could practically see my liege sitting around that long ruined table cursing from one end of the realm to the other once he received the news. *Oh, to the hells,* I told myself, *I am the last Knight of the Broken Table—people will be coming from leagues away, even crossing the border, to see me fight the dragon.*

§

"Get your tickets!" the barkers cried at the croft's impromptu fairground's gate. Fluttering with the breeze were faded pennants and the royal banner of Lasdrah, displaying one of the fabled giant grey-haired mice. Wicked sharp teeth barred, the mouse wore chain mail and wielded a short straw in place of a sword.

No, I've never been sure what the founders of Lasdrah were thinking when they came up with it. But at that moment, as someone who's drawn the short straw himself a time or two, I will tell you—I understood the sentiment perfectly.

"If you get barbequed, I will serve you to that horde out there," Epiny cried, then hugged me, chain mail and all. "You are mad, you know that?"

§

His Royal Highness sat in the makeshift Royal Box beneath its striped canvas, likely left over from one of the Prince's attempts at building one of the Western Empire's famed hot air balloons. The King gaped as Elmer's dragon came out of the barn that had long served as his workshop. It plodded forward, metallic wings pulled back against its sides on its rutted wheels, foul black smoke pouring from its chimney. As I dismounted my horse, who clearly seemed to think he was getting too old for this, refusing to take one step closer, my liege yelled, "Sir Harold, you are crazy!"

"Thank you, Your Majesty," I replied, hefting my shield as I marched toward the dragon, neck swiveling so its head could track me.

Its red glass eyes seemed to glare. Its maw opened and fire shot toward me. Ducking, I muttered, "Shit."

My horse bolted, racing from the field. *Coward,* I thought, while knowing he was showing more wit than I was—since Prince Elmer had apparently tweaked his creation yet again, increasing its range by a good three yards.

I don't know if you have any idea how heavy chain mail, long sword, and my shield, emblazoned with a broken table, are. Let us just say, running is not for the faint-hearted.

"At him, Sir Harold!" the King shouted in delight as I backed away, waving my sword at it, trying to get back into position and safely out of range.

The crowd roared.

The dragon creaked, wings fanning out, making it oddly seem all the more menacing. Its wheels strained and it lurched forward one foot, two—which definitely was not according to the script. Oh, I will say this about it, those lurid glass eyes were a nice touch. It really looked pissed, then its mouth opened again.

I dropped hard to the ground as flame burst above me. There were cries from the collected crowds in the stands. I rolled just in case my cloak had caught fire. Based on the shrieks stopping, I had put it out.

Well, perhaps, this was not the best idea, after all—I had rolled closer to the dragon. I got up off the ground and ran zigzag as I would to confuse an archer. The dragon backed up and its neck swung around, while the blacksmith and his sons continued to stoke the steam engine.

Then the whole of it swiveled around, the wheels on one side going forward, while those on the other side reversed, changing its position.

I charged forward, holding my shield high, hacking at its metal side, which rang like a bell. Those within shouted, then the neck and head swung around, striking my shield. I toppled, muttering, "Hey, that's not part of the plan…" *Elmer, what have you done?*

The dragon backed up, its glass eyes reflecting the light all round us and for the briefest instant I thought it winked at me.

Swallowing hard, telling myself it had to be my imagination, but fearing it wasn't, I ducked under its neck, preventing the latest spew of fire from reaching me.

Flames shooting past, the crowds cheered. I glimpsed the fallen walls of Elmer's Croft and felt a moment of kinship with its tipsy tower, knowing I was an idiot for doing this.

The Prince strode forth in what at best could be termed second-hand robes with white stars embroidered across them. The dragon, thankfully, took its scheduled break, allowing the smith and his apprentices to stoke the fires, readying the bellows for the next act.

Prince Elmer shouted, "Harken, Oh, Dragon! The wizard that brought you from the depths of hell shall aid our Knight Errant this day!"

The crowds cheered louder than ever. I coughed as the breeze brought the fumes my way. Sweating from both exertion and the awful heat the dragon's body gave off, I glanced at my frowning King. That made me glance back at the Prince, who was waving his hands and marching closer to the dragon—far closer than agreed, as I saw the dragon's head swing away from me.

"Hey!" I called out. "Guys, Elmer's out of position!"

The neck stopped, facing the Prince. I banged on the dragon's side with my shield, "Guys! The Prince is too close!"

I heard coughing and a muffled shout through one of the vents as moving gears whined, faintly hearing, "Stoke, boys! We need to make this look good!"

"Shit," I muttered, throwing my shield to the ground, and glanced about, doing the only thing I could think of: I rammed my sword horizontally between the dragon's metal plates.

"Look out!" I heard someone shout distantly from inside. I used the sword hilt as a step and climbed the dragon's back.

The yelling of the crowd was deafening—and the dragon's wing wrenched forward, threatening to knock me from my perch.

The Prince laughed, throwing powdered dust that exploded into sparks, shouting, "HAVE AT THEE, DRAGON!"

I clutched the metal beast around the neck before I could fall off the damn thing, then drew my dagger and glanced back at the smoking chimney behind me as the wings creaked up and down, rocking me to and fro. Grimacing, I thought, *that chimney makes for one ugly looking arse, I mean, tail.*

The blacksmith within was shouting that they needed to get the bellows working harder. They had missed the Prince's cue.

Aw, hell, I thought, inching forward, ramming my dagger into one of the thing's glass eyes. Red fragments and a bit of the mirror behind it shattered as I yelled into the gaping hole, "HE'S TOO CLOSE!"

The blacksmith screamed, "What?!"

"TOO CLOSE!" I screamed.

"Sim sim salabiminy. Beast... Begone!" Prince Elmer screamed.

"Shift that gear! Back it up. Back it up!" the blacksmith cried, which is when I fell off the ruddy thing and hit my head.

In my haze, I could have sworn the dragon glared down at me as its neck lowered. Its lurid, remaining eye filling with darkness as I passed out, thinking I heard someone yell, INTERFERING HUMAN!

§

"Harry!"

"Um," I murmured, my hand going to the small pouch I wore on a chain around my neck as the Princess ran into the tent.

"Harry, you bloody idiot," Alexandra said.

"Ow," I rasped as she hugged me close and kissed my cheek. "Princess?"

"You marvelous knight! Grandfather asked Poppa to bring the show to the palace parade grounds. Our exile is over!"

"The show?" I muttered.

"You are the star," Epiny said and laughed.

"The what?" I rasped.

The Princess grinned, "Poppa's the wizard he's always wanted to be and all because of you, Sir Knight."

"Um, that's wonderful," remembering the wicked gleam in the dragon's glass eyes, now single eye, and knew it was vindictive beast.

That's crazy, I told myself, wincing, knowing it wasn't. Prince Elmer had at least some of his marbles inside that metal dragon. *Apparently, Prince Elmer had become a wizard in fact, whether he realized it or not.*

Smiling, the Princess looked from Epiny to me, then back again, "Uh, I think I shall go talk to father now..."

Epiny nodded, grinning at me, with a welcome, inviting gleam in her eyes as the Princess hastily left. "No ribs broken?"

"Uh, no, I don't think so," I muttered, lying.

Epiny leaned close, "My hero."

Princess Alexandra paused at the entrance, "Oh, Harry, I almost forgot. You will get to slay the dragon six days a week!"

"Six... days..." I winced, glimpsing past her the dragon through the tent's opening as children peered around the edges, staring wide-eyed at me.

A crowd ran along the dragon being pulled by a team of horses back toward the barn. Its head bowed forward. Its single eye seemed to suddenly meet my gaze and look into my very soul.

The moment passed as the dragon continued by, straining cords of rope slung under the dark wings nestled against its iron sides as wisps of dark smoke trailed behind it.

"Uncle Harry, we have sold out for the next four shows! We're going to be rich!"

"Wonderful," I muttered as Epiny squeezed my fractured ribs, holding me close.

"You blooming idiot," she whispered in my right ear as the King's guards ushered the awestruck children away and the Princess practically danced from the tent.

I winced. "My dear, that's essential to being a Knight of the Broken Table... Now, please let go..." I gasped. "I can't breathe."

Fluttering
Evan J. Osborne

*T*he sun dipped behind the horizon giving up its relentless* assault upon the impenetrable emerald canopy of the deep Brazilian rain forest. The sun's eternal war against the trees went unnoticed by the small expeditionary camp that had been living within the eternal gloom of the deep jungle for months now. The native guides in their curious mix of western clothing and traditional tribal gear nervously rushed about the tiny camp setting up the fine meshed nets that Dr. Charles W. Borganis had brought with him all the way from Harvard's entomology department.

Charles walked out of his stuffy travel stained tent and into the warm thick air of the jungle camp to oversee the placement of those many nets. He bustled around the camp pointing out t in the trees to the locals where he wanted the nets to hang ensuring that the widest area possible was covered. He had come a terribly long way in search of new and rare species to discover.

So far he had found several interesting variations on already discovered species, but nothing new, nothing that would cement his name in the annals of entomological history. He was about to conclude his expedition, which had already run a month overdue, when he heard tales of rare and bizarre insects that dwelled deep within the forest—deeper than any expedition had gone before. One creature in particular had ignited his curiosity more than any other. In a tale he'd heard told by the shamans and elders of the local tribe, they spoke of a massive black winged moth bigger than any on record. The moth was feared by the tribe who said it brought death and ruin to all in its wake.

Charles didn't subscribe to the locals' foolish superstitions about the death and ruin, but the descriptions of that moth sounded like it could be a new species of *Lepidoptera Saturniidae*, one that might rival the Atlas moth in size and the White Witch in wingspan. Such a specimen would be his chance to have his name go down in history. All he needed to do was to capture it, and with the multitude of nets he had brought it was almost a forgone conclusion.

Charles smiled to himself as he went over the different variations of his last or first name attached to the end of the scientific label of the mysterious giant moth. He was still lost in thought when the nets were finally hung and the native guides picked up their scant belongings. They left the camp in a hurry, all the while muttering quietly amongst themselves as their eyes darted about the darkening tress. Charles noticed their curious behavior and made his way over to his translator, Hugo Oliviera.

"Where the hell are they all going?" Charles asked.

"They won't stay the night in this part of the jungle," Hugo said.

"Why ever not?"

"I don't know. They keep going on about evil spirits. I told you to let me hire some men from my village. Natives spook too easy," Hugo said.

"At least they had the decency to string up my nets before they left. I do hope they will be returning."

"They should. This tribe are good people, just superstitious."

Charles reached into a small cooler and pulled out a pair of bottles of Brazilian beer and gestured around him at the hanging nets, "here's to a bountiful catch, eh?"

Hugo took one of the bottles and popped the cap off with the flat of the machete he always seemed to carry with him, "I'd rather be using these fancy nets to catch fish, but you're the one paying."

The two men shared a laugh along with the tepid drinks and watched the camp settle down for the coming night. Finally, the setting sun's dying light could no longer provide illumination to the world underneath the boughs of the great rubber trees and walking palms, plunging the perpetually dim world into complete blackness. Then, the forest, which was always a cacophony of sounds, erupted into a symphony of insect song produced by a million different performers. Charles smiled at the sound, knowing that tonight would be the night he discovered something truly momentous. He could feel it in his bones. After giving his nets one last cursory inspection, he returned to his tent to sleep the noisome jungle night away.

Inside the tent, Charles sprawled on an uncomfortable folding cot and wiped the sweat from his grimy face. He loved his work more than anything, but he didn't relish the time spent in the jungle away from showers and beds. He tossed and turned on his tiny cot, excitement and heat keeping him from slumber.

He couldn't do anything about the excitement, but he could do something about the heat. He reached into his bag and rummaged around for the small portable fan he had brought, hoping the increased air flow would help him relax. Instead of the smooth plastic of the fan, his hand closed around a small clay jar. It had been a gift from one of the shaman of the local tribe, and contained an herbal paste said to ward away the black winged moth.

Charles pulled the stone plug from the jar and was nearly overcome by the acrid stench that escaped from within. Inside the jar, the tarry contents looked no better than it smelled, and he shuddered as he recalled the old shaman had told him to apply the salve liberally to his head and neck. Charles shoved the stone plug back into the jar and placed it deep in his pack. He would have to get rid of the jar before he left the country, as he doubted any sane customs agent would allow such a thing to enter the United States. The Brazillians might not even let him leave the country with it.

Near the bottom of his pack, he found the small fan that he had been searching for earlier and clipped it to a piece of fabric that hung down from the top of his tent. He flipped it on, and a small artificial breeze blew across his face bringing him some relief from the oppressing equatorial heat. Thus, Charles eventually fall asleep.

The small buzzing fan proved to be just loud enough to mask the sound of large dusty wings fluttering around the camp in the blackness of the jungle night. Nevertheless, all night long, broken images of wriggling worms, gnashing teeth, and dark flapping wings danced through Charles's dreams. When morning finally came, he awoke unrested to the dim green light of the jungle morning with a head that felt ready to split open.

Charles clutched his head with his hands as he stumbled out of his tent and rubbed his temples in an effort to dispel the pain. He stopped suddenly and looked around. His aching head was soon forgotten. because all around him his nets hung heavy with twitching specimens in a wild array of colors, shapes, and sizes. However. it was in the net in the center of the camp that drew his eyes. It hung low, and he saw something so large he thought they had caught a night flying bird of some sort. He walked over to inspect the creature and let out a wild whoop of jubilation when he saw that it was no bird but the giant moth for which he had been hunting.

The rest of the camp was awakened by his highpitched cry. Men came stumbling out of their tents clutching machetes and old rifles thinking some trouble was a foot. Charles turned to the men who had started to file into the center of the camp, and saw that they had all smeared themselves with the same herbal paste the old shaman had given to him. Even his trusted guide, Hugo, had applied the acrid ointment liberally across his head and neck.

"I suppose the natives aren't the only ones easily spooked," Charles said, pointing at the paste smeared across Hugo's head.

"Better safe than sorry, boss. It's what my father always preached," he said with a shrug.

Charles rolled his eyes and ordered the men to collect the insects from their mesh prisons. He attended to the recovery of the massive black moth himself, all the while marveling at the size of the now dead creature. His recent comparison of this moth to the Atlas moth was woefully inadequate. His moth was far bigger than the Atlas, even bigger than the Australian Hercules Moth.

Charles reached out gently and removed the creature from the net with surprising ease. Unlike the rest of the specimens who were tangled hopelessly in the fine strands of the net, the great dark moth was perched gently on a fold in the net as if it had landed there. As he held the massive moth, a small chill ran up his spine. The shaman's words about death and ruin echoed in his mind,. but he chided himself for his foolish thoughts.

Charles carried the large obsidian insect over to the collection table and placed it in a display box. He was awestruck as he measured the wing span and wrote down a detailed description of the specimen. Charles puzzled over the apparent lack of any anus on the abdomen, but after recalling how the Atlas moth had no mouth, decided perhaps the adult phase of this moth was incapable of eating, too. Another mystery, was the structure of the moth's head. Instead of a small mouthless head adorned by large pheromone seeking antennae, the creature had a massive head equipped with a sharp piercing mouth piece. Charles brought out a field microscope to get a closer look at the bizarre proboscis.

The moth's mouth part was sharp and made of tough chitin perfect for piercing. Charles couldn't fathom why a creature with no digestive tract would need such mouth parts. He longed to dissect the moth's iridescent body to learn the secrets it held, but out in the field was not the place to perform such delicate work. Taking his time, Charles carefully packed up the moth to ensure it would survive the return trip to Boston. Satisfied the crown jewel of his collection was packed safely, he went to surpervise the workers packing up the rest of the specimens.

The morning passed quickly as they sorted the insects caught in the last night's nets. Their task was not even half way completed, when the natives who had run away the previous night returned to help them break camp. The added hands sped the work, and by nightfall they were on their way back to the Amazon river and toward civilization. Charles was so excited by his discovery, he forgot about this morning's pounding headache or how it had faded so quickly.

Ten hours in the air and half as long waiting in lines at various airports, finally saw Charles back in Boston. The bulk of the collected insects were transported to the University for the under grads and interns to scrabble over. The massive black moth, however, he kept for himself. He was adamant about being the one to perform the initial dissection. He knew it was a selfish decision, but it was his to make—besides the long trip home had caused his headache to return and he was in no mood to deal with jealous colleagues.

With the plastic box containing the giant moth under one arm, he stepped through the doorway of his quaint cottage. His legs quivered like half cooled jello and he steadied himself against the nearby wall. With his free hand, he wiped his forehead and realized he was running a fever. Charles hoped that he hadn't contracted malaria or some other tropical infection that his multitude of inoculations had failed to protect him against. Though he had been diligent about taking his anti-malarial drugs, one never knew what they might pick up mucking about in the rain forest.

Charles stumbled over to his study where his desk and well worn chair sat beneath a still ceiling fan—its trio of lights dark and lifeless as the eyes of the moth in the case. On the way to his desk, he hit the switch, and the fan spun to life. Beneath the fan's now bright lights, Charles collapsed into the thick cushions of his office chair and placed the specimen box on to his desk. He leaned back, letting the waves of weakness and chills wash over his body along with the cool air blown about by the spinning fan. Charles took several deep breaths and massaged his aching temples. Satisfied the moment of weakness had passed, he opened his eyes, eyes that were bright with fever and excitement. It was time for the serious work of dissection. And throughout the rest of the day and into the early night, Charles examined the body of the enormous moth.

Hidden inside the insect's abdomen, past the tough black chitin, he found none of the familiar organs shared by other moths. Instead of a digestive tract, all that was contained within the abdomen was an empty sac that presumably had once held eggs and other reproductive organs. When he dissected the rest of the body, Charles found the adult moth was nothing more than a biological vector to spread eggs.

The large head with its curious piercing mouth piece was the last part of the moth to go under his knife, To his amazement, contained within the head of the insect were two large glands filled with a clear liquid that could be excreted from the tip of the piercing mouth piece.

While removing the glands to be studied later in the lab, Charles managed to get a drop of the liquid on his hand and discovered it had powerful numbing powers. Though only a single drop of venom had landed on his skin, his entire hand quickly went numb.

Why would a moth with no digestive tract or reason to feed need such a powerful venom? he wondered. *Why would it need mouth parts that pierce through flesh and bone?*

Charles thought about species of insects that laid their eggs in the still living bodies of animals to use them as hosts. It was an action most commonly seen in the Tarantula Hawk or Spider Wasp which laid their eggs on living spiders so that their young would have a food source once they hatched. He laughed nervously as he scratched the back of his head, which had begun to itch, as he thought of dozens of writhing larvae eating their way out of still living hosts with sharp black fangs.

Charles wiped the sweat from his brow and looked up at the closed window beside his desk. He slid open the window and allowed the night breeze to wash over his face, sending shivers down his spine. He turned back to his desk and packed everything away, content that with the dissection finished, his legacy was preserved. He stood, intending to make his way upstairs to his bed, but was soon overcome by a wave of exhaustion and dizziness. Charles stumbled over to the low couch that he kept in his study for those occasions when he couldn't be bothered to make the short trip to his room. He collapsed onto the couch as the room spun around him. All the while, the pain of the headache he had developed in the Amazon forests throbbed on. He passed out of consciousness and into a world of dark and twisted dreams unlike any he'd ever experienced before.

In the horrid dreamscape, he ran through echoing halls chased by snapping jaws that hid in the shadows. Pain dripped down around him onto slime covered beings that wriggled and wrapped themselves around his body, causing him to fall. He landed in a stone lined pit filled with blood and floating bits of meat. Fat wriggling things scraped feverishly against the pit's walls with sharp chitinous jaws searching for the light that lay just beyond.

Charles became aware long enough to know that something was terribly wrong. He tried to get to his feet, tried to reach the phone that sat on his desk. but his limbs wouldn't obey his brain's commands. All he managed to do was roll off the couch and fall to the floor where he lay in a painful sweaty heap. He moaned incoherently as he hit the floor all the while a terrible noise like the scraping in his dreams, echoed around him. He rolled on to his back and stared up at the ceiling fan watching its blades go round and round. The fan's arms cut through the air making a small fluttering noise.

Again Charles slipped into the nightmare world.. Filled with dread, he took several stumbling steps in the dark unsure of what to do, until a noise made the choice for him, and that choice was run. Breaking through the silence, a dry fluttering sound began to grow like hundreds of big dusty wings beating. Charles continued to run until he reached a ruined city. His bare feet slapped against the cold hard stone that lined the empty streets that stretched out before him for miles. Looming above him like waiting gallows, tall broken buildings stood sentry along the road.

He had no time to marvel at his surroundings, for no matter how fast he ran the fluttering sound grew louder as if it was born on the backs of dusty wings that drew ever closer. He looked into the shattered windows of the buildings hoping to find some aid, but saw nothing but dust and bones. In his haste to be away from the dreadful noise, he turned down a blind alley and collided with a wall made of stacked bodies. He stared in horror at the pile of corpses, all of which had gaping holes in their hollowed out heads.

When Charles scampered away from the corpses with their ruined heads, he tripped over his own feet and fell to the ground as the terrible fluttering intensified. He clapped his hands over his ears to shut the noise out, but it made no difference, because the noise wasn't coming from outside. The darkness surrounded him for the last time as a cloud of shadows swarmed about him beating him into submission with their dry black wings.

Outside of the dream, his eyelids snapped open revealing a pair of blind, bloodshot eyes. His mouth hung slack, tongue gone dry. His hands still pressed against his ears in a futile attempt to shut out the noise from the dream. Charles's prone body twitched and jerked until some dark impulse caused him to lurch to his feet and take several unsteady steps towards the open window.

If his eyes could still see, he would have viewed Boston at night. It was a sight Charles once took great pleasure in, but now it went unnoticed. His hands rose up shakily to his head and held it. Instead of trying to alleviate the pain of his headache with a gentle massage, Charles's hands pushed into his head breaking past a dry layer of skin and a skull made eggshell thin by the ceaseless scraping jaws of the larvae that had been placed there by the great black moth. A small moan of relief escaped his mouth as his hands pulled outwards tearing open his own head like a rotten pumpkin. He fell to his knees, welcoming death, as darkness spilled forth from his ruined mind born on black wings.

Dozens of little black moths, much smaller than the great moth that had deposited them in Charles head, flew about the room in a curious orbit around the now dead doctor of entomology. They danced, as if in thanks, about the ruined head of his corpse that served as food and home before they turned as one and flew out into the cool summer's night.

The baby moths flew in a tight group into the sky until they were well above the city lights. They waited in a circling flock until the sun crept up from the horizon and turned the black sky an unhealthy shade of pink before splitting up. Then, each mothling went its own way in search of food and a nice warm place to lay eggs of their own.

To Touch the Sky

Claire Davon

*T*here were so many feathers it looked like a congress of ravens had molted in the yard.

Emory picked his way to a small indentation in the bare dirt. It was as if someone had slammed a hand into the earth and left these feathers behind. He plucked one of them at random. He twirled it around, admiring the way the vane and the downy barbs spread out. One side was wider than the other, indicative of its use in flight.

He picked up another that appeared to be a contour feather, only it couldn't have lent its color and shape to any known bird. Both items made his hand sink, as if they were made up of more than vane and barbules and rachis.

His young sister Stella banged open the screen door to the outside and stopped. Her mouth worked as she surveyed the scene.

"What did you do?" she asked.

He reached for another flight feather. He didn't see any down or semiplume quills, but perhaps they were under the bigger ones. He would check after he dealt with Stella, who would be trying to figure out a way to get him in trouble.

"Not me, Stel," he said, wading out of the pile to meet his sister on the concrete slab. "I came out for some air and found this here. What a mess."

"More likely you did it."

It was a cliché to live in the basement—technically the bottom apartment of their three-story house, but how many teenagers could say they had their own space?

"Yeah, like I'd be able to get a couple of thousand feathers and dump them in the yard. Fat chance."

Stella tossed her hair, her lip curling in disdain. "Sure."

Emory gestured to the rusty wheelbarrow lying on the slab. "I'll clean up," he said. Stella's eyes widened.

"Seriously? Mom has to beg you to do the dishes. What gives?"

He turned the too-heavy feather over in his hand again. The downy barbs brushed against his palm, making his skin tingle.

§

He piled the feathers in the middle of the basement, black barbed quills dominating the space. Spreading them out over the floor, he started sorting them. There were the usual kinds of flight feathers: primaries, secondaries and tertials were all there, along with tactrices, emargination and alula. All feathers that aided in lifting a bird in the air, if he remembered correctly. There had been a time when he'd been crazy for all things avian, and his lessons flooded back.

Once they were sorted, he began to place them in their correct position. It didn't take him long to assemble a magnificent set of shimmering black wings, almost two and a half times as wide as he was tall. With this many feathers forming a wing, it would be big enough to keep a person aloft. These wings would be a dozen feet across and black as night. People would look and point at their bearer in the air. At *Emory* in the air. He snorted. No matter the size of the wings, human bones were too heavy to allow man to fly.

He had been reading too much fantasy. Emory picked up a feather and studied it. It was a tertial feather, not considered a true flight feather, designed to act as a protective cover for the primaries and secondaries.

The place where he had plucked the feather from looked empty and he set it back, breathing a sigh of relief when it was back in its correct spot.

The shrill voice of his mother calling him for dinner broke the spell. With one final look at the array, he headed to the kitchen.

§

"What the heck?"

Stella stood on the stairs, eyeing the spread. Her expression was unreadable.

Emory's shoulders rose at her unexpected intrusion. He turned to face her. The wings seemed more substantial, as if tendons had joined the feathers and fused them together.

"I thought I locked that door."

"You forgot."

"I remember now. Get lost."

"Not until you tell me what that is." Stella pointed at the display that dominated the available space in his living room. "Are those from the backyard?"

"That's my business."

"I want to know," she said in a wheedling tone. "Tell me."

One glance into her set face told him he wasn't going to get rid of her any time soon.

"Yeah, sis, they're from the yard. Don't tell Mom. She'd freak about the mess."

She took one more step closer to his precious wings. The way her gaze kept going to them told Emory he was going to have to make sure he locked the door from now on. He'd double bolt it to be sure.

"I won't tell," she said, dragging out the last word. "If I can touch them." Her gaze didn't move from the feathers.

"Sure. Next time." He fought to keep his voice from quivering with the lie.

"Promise?"

"Yeah."

With a final look at his living room, Stella went upstairs. Emory breathed a sigh of relief and ran to make sure the door was secure. Then, he strode to the wing and bent down to snatch up a feather. He expected nothing but one downy plume and he staggered back, losing his grip when the thing came up in one piece. It landed with a thwack that seemed to reprove him for releasing it. His hands shook, matching the trembling in his body.

He picked the appendage up with both hands, grunting as he levered the wing so it was parallel to the ground. He hadn't done anything but put the feathers in the proper order, like fitting together a jigsaw puzzle, but now they were whole. One wing was over six feet long and as dark as crow feathers, with a shimmer only apparent up close. Together, they were larger than condor wings, bigger than the wandering albatross. The heavy bulk strained his seldom used back muscles. He laid both down on the floor, lining them up as if they were in flight.

All his younger self's notions of wanting to fly asserted themselves. All the times he'd spent reading about birds, surfing the 'net for birds, wishing he were Icarus so he could touch the sky. The wings had come to him for a reason. It was madness, of course. There was no chance that they would work on a human.

§

"Knock, knock."

Forgetting the wings were strapped to his body, Emory turned toward the basement door. The feathered appendages swung around, crashing into the TV stand, almost knocking the flat screen over. The extra weight sent him tumbling to the floor, arms, legs and wings splayed. "God damn it."

"Knock, knock," came Stella's voice again, followed by a loud rapping. "Knock, knock, knock, knock, knock. Let me in."

He'd stalled her for a week. His time was up.

"Gimme a minute, Stella." He cursed under his breath, struggling to get the harness free. Stella knocked again, and then began a light, rhythmic tapping. The noise flowed through his brain like water dripping on his head, making him want to scream.

"Stop it, Stella," he cried, his tone strangled. "Or I'll never come up."

"Yes you wi-i-ill," she said. "Or I'll tell."

He managed to extricate himself from the straps and went to let Stella in.

Her eyes widened when she came down the stairs and sighted the wings. They were a dark cloud that dominated the room, drawing the eye from any angle.

She went down on one knee. "They're amazing," she said with wonder in her eyes. Her fingers caressed the feathers in an absent motion. Emory felt a phantom shiver in his back, as if she were touching him.

"They are," he agreed.

"Can I try them on?" She gestured to the straps. "Looks like you've set them up."

Stella would sneak in when he wasn't home to try the wings on. He could see it in her eyes, the avarice, the need to touch them, the desire to feel them on her back. He would have to act before she could get back down here.

He would wait until the early hours when everyone was sleeping. Then, he would go to the cliffs by the beach. The worst that could happen, was he would fall into the ocean, which was survivable.

Satisfied with that decision, Emory smiled at his sister and let her stroke one of the wings. It was only for a little while.

§

He was securing the straps when a fierce pain dug into his shoulders and back. He cried out and fell, writhing, on the area rug.

After a time, the agony calmed enough for him to stagger to his feet. His clothes were damp with sweat. To his surprise, the wings were still attached.

Then, as he watched in disbelief, the harness slid to the ground but the wings stayed on his back. He took a tentative step forward. The unfamiliar weight took him down again. The agony in his shoulders flared as if someone had driven hot needles through him. He got his knees and hands under him, and once again rose to his feet. He tottered again, but managed to find his center of gravity and he remained upright.

The full-length mirror beckoned. His reflection showed feather and tendons behind him like dark shining clouds. Using muscles he didn't know he had, he tried to move a wing, and was rewarded with a small shift that he felt throughout his body. Emory turned until he could see his back in the mirror's reflective surface.

There were livid marks around the junctures where the wings had sank into his body, Wing met flesh and tendons pierced his skin like they were part of him. It was his fantasy come to life.

Above him were footsteps and the muted sound of conversation. He cried out as white hot agony suffused his body, blurring his vision. With a rending sound the array dropped off him. The sounds stopped at the basement door as if the people were debating knocking. He held his breath, struggling not to whimper, tears filling his eyes. After a moment, the people moved on without knocking.

Emory stared at the red holes on his shoulders and back. When he moved his arms the wounds flared with agony. It didn't matter. The wings were the thing. They would hold his weight; these were meant for human flight. But not anyone. Only the person who had recreated them.

It was time to act. He would go to the cliffs tonight.

§

Nothing moved in the early morning stillness. Their suburban residential area was quiet in the time between the bars closing and the dawn walkers. It was the perfect time.

He opened the basement door, trying not to make any sound. The door creaked and he cursed. Heart pounding, he waited, but heard no movement from upstairs. After a few long moments that seemed to stretch out into eternity he eased the door all the way open. Cool air hit him like a slap in the face. It would be colder at the beach, and foggy. Grabbing his Pierce College sweatshirt from the top of the pile, Emory put it on.

He had to angle the wings sideways through the trunk of the family SUV and across the passenger seat to get them in. Hopefully the same miracle that had happened in his basement would happen tonight.

Feathers brushed against his right arm as he worked the gear shift, trying to slide down the driveway without much noise. He didn't breathe until he was around the corner from their place.

Sure enough, there was fog when he got closer to open water. It was going to make his flight more difficult. On the plus side, there wouldn't be people out and about to see him. He would be able to try out his wings under the cloak of darkness.

The drive to the beach took little time in this quiet hour. Spotting a cop, he slowed, but the man ignored him. He already had the story rehearsed if he were stopped. This was Los Angeles. Angelenos saw much stranger things than wings.

§

The cliff was north of Malibu, a sheer drop both awe inspiring and a bit scary. The ground was flat, with little scrubby plants and rocks. The roar of the ocean seemed distant. He had meant to look online to see how far down it was. He had chosen this spot thinking he could survive a fall, but now doubts came rushing at him.

Emory picked up the wings and slid them into the harness, and then, he put the entire apparatus on. He was beginning to adjust the straps when stabbing pain shot through his shoulders and back. Tears trickled down his face, the agony threatening to overwhelm him. After a time, the pain lessened. He tore the harness off and flung it away; a smile lighting his face when the wings stayed behind.

Trying to remember the layout of the beach, he plodded through the dense fog. There was one spot on this cliff where people dove off and lived to tell the tale.

He tried to draw one pinion in, and it furled in as neatly as if he'd had wings all his life. He unfurled the wing again, and it soared behind him, a dark beauty that disappeared into the fog. He flapped his wings and a whooshing sound filled his ears. Though it was like hiking with an eighty pound pack, his smile grew wider.

He wanted to get a running start, soar out to catch the wind, and then flap into the sky. Or go into the water.

Emory backed up almost to the SUV. He still held the key fob in his hands. He pressed the lock button, and then stashed the key under the left front wheel. Best case scenario, he would come back for it and drive home. He didn't know how he'd drive the car with wings, but he'd figure that out in the morning. Worst case, he'd have a long walk back up to the road.

The ocean air chilled his lungs. He clenched and unclenched his fists. The wings did the same in response. With a whoop, he dashed toward the cliff edge. He counted off his steps. Thirty feet, twenty, ten…he jumped as hard as he could off the edge.

He was falling, plummeting toward the ocean below. He had been wrong, this wasn't going to work.

Then, he caught the air and soared upwards. Emory flexed his muscles and was rewarded with a flap. His shoulders strained against the unfamiliar weight. A whoop of triumph tore from him. He tried to bank, and to his delight, turned to the south.

With a series of strokes, he went higher until he couldn't hear the ocean. He kept hoping he would get clear of the fog, but it seemed to go on forever. His hands and feet grew numb with cold. He couldn't feel his face and his nose was running. It was all part and parcel of being in the air. Next time, he would be better prepared. He shouted into the fog, his cries snatched away by its dense thickness. He had done something no other person had ever done, except Icarus. He was flying.

Emory flapped again, feeling the burn in his shoulders. He wouldn't be able to fly much longer. Cursing his tendency to laze on the sofa instead of working out, he pivoted on one wing to turn back to the cliff. He wasn't sure where he was, the fog was so dense. He had lost track of his surroundings.

He flew back the way he thought he had come. He shouldn't be too far from his starting point. He had been in the air at most ten minutes, but was already too cold and tired. He couldn't afford to get so exhausted that he plunged into the sea.

There had to be some markers or guideposts over the ocean. Worst case, he could head to Santa Monica and use the Ferris wheel as a guide for landing. That would be a long way back, though. Better to figure out where he was.

He listened for the ocean. His pulse was racing; he felt lightheaded from it. Now, he realized how foolish he had been to do this without preparation. He had been so anxious to get the wings on that he hadn't thought the plan through.

He couldn't hear the surf. His arms and shoulders ached with the unfamiliar strain of flapping. His thighs were also shaking from holding his legs up to serve as a tail. Being a bird was supposed to be easy like in superhero movies. He'd need to practice. He would go out to the desert and jump off the rocks. Nobody would pay him any attention there.

For a moment the fog cleared. The cliff face was below him, so close he could almost touch it. With a sigh of relief Emory lowered his feet and prepared to land.

But the wings pulled him away, moving under their own power. He cried out, but his shout was snatched away in the wind. Fog closed around him, so thick he couldn't see. Heart pounding, he twisted around, pulling with his tired legs as well. Still the wings kept flying with powerful strokes that took him somewhere unknown. He thought he saw lights down below, but couldn't be sure. He could be over ocean or land, or nowhere at all.

"Stop, stop!" Emory tugged at his shoulders but couldn't get a grip. He started crying, tears slipping down his cheeks. Of course they had a mind of their own. What had he expected?

He was too tired to do more than struggle weakly. He saw glimpses of lights and thought he had crossed the Santa Monica Mountains. He hung down, not trying to stay upright, letting his body dangle while the wings carried him.

As if waved away, the fog vanished. It took his eyes a moment to focus. The familiar markers of Van Nuys airport, its surrounding runways, and nearby houses caught his eye. Emory would have laughed if he hadn't been so tired. The 405 was behind him, even at this hour there were the red taillights and shining headlights of traffic. It appeared the wings were taking him home.

His street came into view. He banked right in a diagonal path across the neighborhood. He was so high, that the telephone wires that bisected the backyards in this area were far below him. To his horror, the fog closed in again. He could see nothing as the cool mist brushed against his nostrils and his hair, filling his mind and lungs with the acrid wet scent of morning haze.

He screamed when he was yanked up, his hands fisted in futile anger. He stopped, hovering like a hummingbird, his body dangling. Then, the wings folded and he began plummeting toward the ground. He was whimpering as he gained speed, the wings still furled. He could see little in the fog, just vague shapes in the whiteout.

There was a whooshing noise in the distance and his ears buzzed. His trembling shoulders smarted. Looking down he saw that his body was shrinking. The wings tore free and followed him down, black shapes growing larger as he shrank.

He was the size of an infant now, diminishing so fast his perspective kept changing. Then, he was no bigger than a house cat. Below him was his yard.

Emory was the size of a baseball when he struck the earth, making an impact crater, still shrinking as he died. The wings landed a moment later, shattering upon impact into a heap of feathers scattered over the ground.

Then, they waited.

§

Stella pushed into the kitchen as streaks of sunshine dappled the room through the curtains. Mom and dad weren't up yet, and the house was still. She didn't hear any movement from the basement, but that was no surprise. He was probably sleeping between those wings. Her hands tingled with the remembered feel of them against her skin.

Something in the yard drew Stella's gaze. Spilling juice down her t-shirt, Stella gasped, her attention focused on the yard. Glittering in the early morning sun like black diamonds, lay feathers. They were everywhere, scattered from a central point of bare dirt.

"Em? Emory?" She went to the basement door and knocked. Stella paused and rapped again before turning away.

She slid out the back door, creeping on tiptoe toward the sight.

In the middle of the feathers was a small impact area in the dirt. There was a tiny beige rock there which Stella considered pocketing before deciding against it.

She picked up a feather, stroking it. It flowed through her hand like silk, her fingers sliding over the individual strands. Stella touched her nose with it and giggled. It felt warm, as if heated by the sun. Something primal rose up in her, a need to keep these marvels safe.

Stella went to get the wheelbarrow. If she hurried, she might be able to gather all the feathers before Mom and Dad got up. She searched the ground for that strange pebble she'd spotted earlier, but she could no longer see it. Then, she put the pebble out of her mind. She had to hurry.

They were her feathers now. Her wings.

Hers.

Treasure
Rebecca Gomez Farrell

*W*ind thundered past the slats of the storage cabin. Hidden* within a barrel of fish guts, the stowaway braced herself for lurching. But when the ship pitched sharply sternside, Enkid knew it was no ordinary squall. A storm this bad would force the captain out of his quarters despite his usual drunken stupor, creating an opportunity to filch the beveled, green-glass vial he wore around his neck. It held hemlock tincture, a rare poison that would come in handy for someone in Enkid's line of work. Someday, she might not find a boat on to which she could escape from the Creftish guards and their immense gangmares, as she had three days ago.

Enkid scrambled up the rope ladder to the deck, determined to make her way to the captain's quarters near the gunwale before the storm burned itself out and the sailors noticed an extra head in their midst. Crewmen yelled at each other in the dimness of a crescent moon. Drenched with innards, it took Enkid a few steps to realize there was no rain. No more wind, either, until a clap rang out and a gust knocked her off her feet. A call came from sternside, resonant like a lion's roar with a shrill undercurrent that raised her hackles.

Muhh-rarh-icks!

Wings, immeasurable in the night sky, flapped, sending another flurry her way. The creature hopped; boards splintered and groaned where it landed. Its head, large as the fish gut barrel, cocked. Enkid felt its burning, inquisitive stare before it jabbed a clawed spur into the nearest crewman's neck.

"A Laklor!" A shout rose up. Panic spread through the crew, and she heard screams and the splashes of men abandoning ship. Enkid had no idea what a Laklor was and no intention of finding out. She dashed toward the captain's quarters, more than mere opportunity spurring her speed now. Her ankle yelled from the landing impact after leaping through the cut-out square in the deck, but she pushed through the pain and broke the captain's doorlock with a swift down-punch.

The room was empty. Enkid climbed into a chest and pulled the lid over her head. Moments later, the captain stumbled inside, latching the heavy metal bar on the inside. He slid to the floor with a *whomph*, leaving his crewmen to fend for themselves.

Imbecile. Drunkards had always disgusted her; sharp instincts were vital to survival. Snores filled the room, loud enough to hear over the continuing horror above. Enkid waited, biting down on a leather belt when her ankle throbbed. The ship rolled like a die over Enkid's fingers. The shouting died out, yet the captain's snores continued. Except for a deepening lilt, the boat steadied. Still, Enkid bided her time. Only when water seeped into the chest and soaked her trousers did she open it.

The water lapped partway up the captain's protruding belly. She'd have to be quick. Holding a rag over his mouth to stifle any noise, she plunged her dagger into his chest and twisted it. A dark stain spread over his burlap shirt while he struggled. When his body went slack, she unfastened the vial, lifted the moneybag on his belt, and returned to deck.

Feathers, longer than she was tall, lined the ship along with half-chewed fingers and kneecaps. The sharp tang of blood and the stench of emptied bowels reminded her of a moldering chicken coop, stinking worse than she after the entrails. Nothing moved; all hands had been thrown into the sea or torn to bits by the Laklor. Enkid did not wish to wait and find out if the Laklor would return to pick over its kill. Plus, the cold seawater would numb the throb of her ankle.

Enkid climbed the gunwale. A wind burst dropped her to her feet as wings flapped overhead. She held onto the rail with all the strength she had left. Searing pain engulfed her forearm as giant black claws sped past her peripheral vision. Before the Laklor could circle back, Enkid released her grasp.

Let the fates do as they will. The sea engulfed her.

§

She woke coughing pink-speckled sand. Matted, jade-colored hair shook as she tried to expel the salty mass in her mouth. There was too much, so she thrust her index finger between her lips and shoveled out the grains. Not until she could breathe did she feel shivers pulsing up and down her body. The breeze was icy and her clothes were wet. At least it muted her ankle pain.

"Hallo there!"

From the dunes, a man approached on a horse almost as big as a gangmare. Too exhausted to wield her dagger, Enkid chose to play dead and pray the rider moved on quickly. She shut her eyes. When the horse was close enough that sand misplaced by his hooves pummeled her face, she took a deep breath and held it.

The muffled *clip clop* ceased.

"What do we have here, Nessa?"

The horse whinnied.

"Another shipwreck?" The man cupped his ear over Enkid's mouth. "Not breathing." He picked up her wrist. "But she's warm."

The ruse was over. Enkid gasped noisily for air and braced for the blow that would come. When it didn't, she opened her eyes.

"You're alive." The man clapped his hands together. "Let's get you to a healer." His eyes were agate, his hair coral-colored, his skin warm clay, and he appeared . . . concerned?

85

Enkid was flummoxed. She was defenseless. He should have lopped off her head and taken the captain's moneybag the moment he knew she was alive. *This must not be Creftland.* They'd sailed farther than she thought, which meant . . . *Trilonea.* A name whispered over ground fires, invoked as a banishment threat. Creftish people did not return from these lands.

"Here." The man swaddled her in a blanket like a child, not a stranger. "Think you can make it to the guard station? It's not far."

My head must be full of seawater. "Wha–what?" She recoiled with pain; her throat felt speared by a thousand sea anemone spikes. She was thirsty, so thirsty. Her ankle and her forearm pulsed.

"Nessa and I will get you there. You aren't bleeding much, but you need to be checked on the inside as well."

He's helping me, she realized. *And his beast has a name.* She mulled that over as he maneuvered her onto the horse. It was her last thought before the animal's rhythmic pace lulled her back into unconsciousness.

§

Enkid woke dressed in an amethyst-colored shift and covered with a blanket of woven, dried seaweed. She grabbed at her neck, relieved to find the vial there, though the leather rope that held it was stiff from salt water.

A gate grated over packed sand, and she lunged upward at the sound. Blood rushed through her body like molten lava and exploded at her ankle. She cursed, knowing she couldn't run and hide, not yet.

Peeking out the window, she watched two people approach the hut. One was the man who hadn't killed her, dressed in a lightweight, beige kaftan and sandals. His female companion wore an emerald-toned shift and a white water dahlia on her arm.

The visitors reached the hut faster than Enkid could have sliced a man's throat. *Good, the distance to the gate is short.* It would not be hard to escape when she was able.

The woman entered her room and smiled. "You're awake. That's good news."

Enkid said nothing. Better to let her do the talking.

"Do you remember me?"

Enkid made no gesture.

"No, of course you wouldn't. You've been asleep these past three days."

Three days? The length of time surprised Enkid, but the dulled ache of her ankle confirmed it. Dark claws flashed in her mind, and she twisted her forearm around.

"Yes," the woman kept her eyes on Enkid as she drew her finger over a crimson spot of puckered flesh on Enkid's arm, "you have recovered speedily from your surface injuries. Vijuan must have found you soon after the accident—your skin had not frosted."

The woman sat on the cot. "My name is Tera, and I have been with you daily, so you were not alone." She placed a hand on Enkid's shoulder, who tried not to shirk at the touch.

"I am a healer," Tera paused, "and a matchmaker." She cocked her head toward the man, Vijuan, who grimaced. "The two fields are one here." Tera rested Enkid's arm on the blanket. "Would you share your name with us?"

"Filor." Her mother's name rolled easily off her tongue. Giving her own was no option. What if word got back to the Creftish guards? There may be other survivors who'd seen her stealing across the deck. She was not safe here.

"What a lovely name." Tera took Vijuan's hand, pulled him closer to the bed. "We would like you to take Vijuan as your bedmate when your body is well. He is especially suited for your needs and you for his."

Enkid laughed. She hadn't found anyone "suited" for her in her thirty-four years. She'd swallow this Vijuan whole.

He groaned but smiled as he spoke. "I do hope you'll stay with me." His voice was rich, confident, as it had been when he'd found her. "If only so we can prove Tera wrong together."

He winked then addressed the matchmaker. "I think this is enough for now. She'll decide what she wants to do."

Tera nodded, and the two of them left. Enkid counted one . . . two . . . three . . . four strides to reach the gate. Not far at all, she thought, taking in the room. It was small, consisting of a bed and chair where her dagger lay along with the captain's moneybag, sandy and coated with crusted sea foam. If these people hadn't already robbed her, they likely wouldn't now—Triloneans were stranger than the stories of them.

She counted the coins, more than she'd ever possessed at one time. *Might be worth it to risk home again.* She knew a pair of gamblers, half-blind old men who spent every cent they earned distilling liquor on her dice games. Could she stay out of sight of the guards?

Enkid fell asleep running sleights of hand in her mind.

§

She needed time. Time for her ankle to heal. Time to decide where to run once she could. And Vijuan offered her that. In his return trips to the healing hut, he'd laughed off the matchmaker's attempts to get Enkid to speak. Yet, he ended each visit with one question: "Will you stay with me when you are well?"

Once the mark disappeared from her arm and she could handle her ankle with light grimaces, Enkid said yes. She needed time, and if the man was dimwitted enough to trust her in his dwelling, why shouldn't she take advantage?

So they walked, Vijuan gathering wood from the shipwreck and leaving it in piles as they traversed the few miles down the shore to his home. The small smile he had given at her assent remained on his face, though she had not spoken again, merely followed him at a polite distance. She knew no men like him in Creftland.

"You will want to work on that scowl."

Enkid colored at her own negligence in schooling her features, not realizing he had stopped.

He laughed, then stroked her cheek so briefly, she barely registered it before he went on ahead again. Another log clunked hollowly as it joined a pile of driftwood. "The Triloneans will wonder if you are adjusting. Most people do, in time, but still, they will wonder."

"I am not the first shipwrecked person here?"

"Oh, no." He met her eyes with a twinkle. "You may have noticed the Laklor?"

She shuddered. "How do you feel safe with it so near?"

He shrugged. "It is no danger to us."

"No danger? That creature nearly took my arm off." Enkid spoke more passionately than she'd meant to. The man's easy manner disarmed her. She needed to be careful around him.

His brow raised. "That's another thing you'll want to avoid making the Triloneans overly aware of, that it targeted you. Perhaps you raise too many warning flags. Time will tell."

Unnerved she'd said too much, she let him get a few paces ahead. But she had to better understand him if they were to share such close quarters. "Why are you so willing to house me if I am as hopeless as all that?"

"You are my bedmate." His eyes lit up with mischief as she matched his stride. "Or so Tera would have us believe."

He slid his hand into hers, and she found she did not wish to pull away.

"I will require that you stop wearing that dagger, though."

Always a catch. Her fingers went to where it hung on the mesh belt underneath her dress. "It reminds me of who I am. When I feel the dagger's weight, I know I am safe."

"When I feel its shadow on you, all I know is the blood and viscera it's caused."

"What would you know of such things here, if you are as peaceful as you claim?"

"Who said I was from here?" Vijuan dropped her hand to gather more wood, leaving her in stunned silence. Maybe they were more akin than she had thought.

"And what should I do with my dagger? Toss it in the sea?"

"If you like," he called back. Something drew his gaze toward the water. "But leaving it in the house will suffice."

Muhh-rarh-icks!

Enkid stumbled to the sand, fear enveloping her. Her eyes focused in on a dark, shifting oblong far off on the horizon, circling.

"Filor." Warm arms wrapped around her, combed fingers through her hair. "You are safe here with me. I promise you that. The Laklor will not hunt us."

"Okay, I will leave the dagger beneath our bed," she promised, wanting to believe his words. The Laklor was a threat she could not control.

She felt his smile in the lips that pressed against her forehead and the hand that brushed sand off her skin. Soon, Vijuan led her up a walkway of packed sand toward his home hidden within pink dunes. The Laklor had disappeared.

Inside, Enkid made a show of depositing her dagger beneath the bed. What did it matter? She still had the hemlock at her neck. And time.

§

Trilonea *did* have its benefits. Her mornings were spent guiding a sniffer, a beast that hugged the ground and wriggled its foot-long, scale-covered snout to suss out roots and berries from the meadows. Her afternoons were consumed with Vijuan, relaxing inside or in the shade of a dune during the hottest hours of summer that came upon them. She had never slept with just one man for longer than a fortnight before. But she grew to appreciate the familiar lines of his body and the scent of his skin, of almonds and wet sand.

"What do you dream about?" Vijuan stirred beside her one such afternoon. He'd fallen asleep after sex, which would have been fatal had they been in Creftland. Here, Enkid picked pink specks from his hair while staring out at the beach. One month and there had been no other survivors, not a body washed onshore. She felt safe among these people who claimed companionship more rewarding than wealth. The flutter she felt when thinking of Vijuan was almost enough to believe it true. But a life spent hungry and scheming and running gave her little trust in good fortune.

"Times past."

He was too distracted rooting around in his bag to respond. A moment later, he opened cupped palms to reveal a water dahlia armband. It shone like a ruby-studded brooch in the sun.

"Would you wear this tonight? I plan to give thanks at the Balancing."

She nodded. It would be her second Balancing since arriving in Trilonea. The townspeople gathered monthly to share their appreciation for each other and what life had given them. She'd find it inane, if it weren't so...so charming. Vijuan bound the flower band to her forearm, over where the Laklor's deep gash had once been.

"What will you give thanks for?" she teased. "The clear sky? A new caftan?"

He whispered in her ear, "For you, Filor."

Her cheeks colored with flattery and shame, the latter a new emotion for her. She could not trust him with her real name—did the shame mean she wanted to? She threw a handful of sand at him to hide her blush, which he threw right back with a chuckle.

They rinsed off in the ocean, the water brisk but warmer now than it had been when the waves had tossed her onto shore. Enkid roasted azure-toned tubers for supper while Vijuan swept the hut's floor. The vegetables oozed a viscous liquid a shade darker than their flesh. She took a moment to breathe in their floral scent. Cooking and feeling the texture of food between her fingers were pleasures she'd never felt back home, all her meals bought in a tavern and scarce resembling anything but mush.

"It's ready," she called. They sat outside, pausing to offer a bite to the ground as was his custom. A rodent banded with orange and tan stripes snatched the offering before they finished the meal.

At nightfall, they walked to the Balancing, hand-in-hand. It was so simple, this new life of hers. So easy to feel content and calm. The townspeople had assembled at the Black Pillar, a craggy obelisk whose top disappeared into the dark sky around it. The bonfire's warmth drifted her way, soaking into her skin. Her hair would smell of ash tonight.

"Welcome, VijuanFilor!" The people greeted them, combining their names as one. Vijuan led her to a tree stump, brushing off insects with pearlescent shells. A few more families trickled in, and Tera hushed the giggling children.

"Let me share with you my thanks tonight for Masi, my lifemate," Tera said.

A woman Enkid recognized from the meadows rose at the name, but she stumbled when a rush of wind filled the air with a rancid stench. A shadow spread over the group as a nasal bray sounded.

Muhh-rarh-icks!

Enkid dove for the bushes, praying this was one of her vivid nightmares. Insects tickled her skin, but she dared not shake them off.

Under the darkness of wings, Tera clasped her hands together. "The Laklor has seen fit to grace us with its presence!" The children jumped to their feet to cheer. Necks craned skyward, and people lifted their arms, standing on tiptoe as though they could reach the monster circling the obelisk.

Are they insane? Claws clicked against the Black Pillar as the Laklor roosted on its tip. Something grasped Enkid's wrist and she stifled a scream.

"The Laklor is a sign of great fortune," Vijuan whispered as he guided her out from her hiding place. "It is an honor to have it appear at a Balancing."

She shook her head fiercely. "I've seen the honor it can do. It will kill us all."

"No." He placed a hand over her shaking one. "It harms only those it finds lacking. Triloneans do not fear it."

"It harmed me."

"And you've healed. Have you not?"

The monster fluttered its wings closed, and the moon returned, dimming the bonfire's glow. Vijuan flicked the vial at her neck, and she gasped.

"Only you can know how hard you cling to what you were before, Filor," he chided. "If you're here, truly here with us, you are safe."

He caressed her cheek before sitting. Enkid took in the complete lack of fright on the townspeople's faces as they chattered with pleased amazement. The creature preened on its perch, making soft clicks.

She tried not to gag at the smell. Vijuan rubbed her shoulder.

"Let us return to our thanksgiving." Tera took her lifemate's hand. "Masi gave me a berry from her morning forage. I bit into it, and the sweet juice delighted me. My thanks, my love."

Both women sat down, eyes only for each other. The crowd murmured its pleasure before falling silent, mulling over whom or what they might offer as praise. When Vijuan stood, Enkid considered fading into the shadows, feeling the heat of the Laklor's jacinth gaze, but once she heard his voice, the desire to flee lessened.

"Let me share with you my thanks for Filor, our rescued traveler and my well-chosen bedmate."

She rose in acknowledgment, though her throat tightened when the bird made a harsh trilling sound. Clumps of feather fluff spiraled down like dandelion heads.

"She is a blessing to me," Vijuan's face flickered orange from the fire's flame, "a partner in sleep and wake. She has taken my life alone and made it full of her. I give thanks for the match," he bowed in Tera's direction, "and thanks to Filor for rising above the talon's prick."

The wound healed itself, Enkid considered, the necklace hanging heavy against her skin. *I had naught to do with it.* Vijuan raised one hand toward the Laklor as though thanking it also, then braced himself against the pillar, breaking off one of its jagged spires.

Enkid's eyes widened at what Vijuan's action exposed: a glowing hollow full of jewels. All thoughts of the monster above them fled. The obelisk's slick surface liquefied around the cavity, creating a viscous slime that filled it and hardened.

Vijuan held out the rock chunk for her to take. She stared at it agape. Black opals covered its broken edge, their iridescence a swirling mix of mother of pearl, amethyst, and garnet flecks in an obsidian sea. Vijuan kissed her while the crowd babbled its approval, but Enkid's mind weighed the rock, not his lips on hers. She'd never held such a fortune.

"To you, Filor, my thanks."

She regarded the smiling Triloneans with new respect. *Do they know how rich they are?* The chunk held enough jewels to keep Enkid provisioned for life. Imagine what she might do, what life she could make for herself in Creftland if she broke off just a few more. She leaned into Vijuan's arms, taking care not to glance at the obelisk too lustily. But she kept one hand on her rock while a child gave thanks for an orange as big as a rabbit and passed slices around. When the Laklor left, Enkid could not say.

§

That night, Vijuan asked if she liked her gift, and she threw her arms around his neck and yanked him down for an extended thank you.

"Perhaps you are becoming Trilonean." His fingers marched down her hip. "It is customary to give part of the Pillar to whom you wish to pledge your life. Bedmates have always done so when they were certain their matches would work. I hope you feel the same as I, Filor."

He played with the dahlia on her arm. "Stay with me always. I cannot imagine life without you."

"I don't know what to say." Though she could not see him in the dark, she could picture the look he gave, his eyes soft and smile easy. It made her feel things she did not know how to explain. Things she might want in another life. Things she did not believe this one held. But a tangible fortune that fit in the palm of her hand and would provision her most her days? That she could believe in.

"Will you stay with me?" His hand brought pleasure and comfort, but she felt something else, too, a craving that had burned ever hotter these last few hours.

"Yes," she lied, wishing she knew another way to be, but knowing there was none for her. She was Creftish, and Trilonea was forbidden ground. She understood that now.

Enkid pressed herself against Vijuan, saying goodbye with her body while being grateful the act also passed as hello.

§

The next morning, she rose to find Vijuan gone and a bouquet of gavol buds in his place. The paper-thin seed pods resembled silver-dusted lanterns in the sunlight. They brought a smile to her lips but paled in comparison to the rainbow of colors emanating from her jewels. She slung her foraging sack on her back, not so large to be noticed but big enough to make her richer than she'd ever thought possible.

Desire sped her actions. Her rock went in first, then the cloth-wrapped bundle of food Vijuan left for her each morning. Her dagger came out from under the bed, and she tied it onto her belt where it belonged. Then she left for the meadows, knowing no one would miss her until afternoon if she reported there first. She waited long enough for the other foragers to disappear from sight. Her hand lifted to pat the sniffer goodbye, but she laughed off the impulse. *It's only a beast.*

She kept a casual pace as she passed Triloneans working off-path who averted their eyes or clucked tongues in seeming disappointment. Enkid banished the worry to stay calm. *If they knew I was about to rob them, surely they would stop me, not scowl.* The obelisk's zenith loomed higher each step. She walked into its shadow and jabbed the dagger into it, prying fist-sized pieces off. Each time, the emerald and pink tourmaline glints from the opals merely made her want more. The clink they made as she tossed them in the bag brought immense satisfaction.

Stopping felt like sacrilege, but when the sack was full, she did. The black ooze that seeped over each new hole also encased her hands. She didn't have time to rub it off; she wanted to be well east before Vijuan came home. The sack's weight would slow her down, but she wouldn't take a single shard less. She had earned them, spending weeks among these people with nothing to show for it. Her heart ached when she thought of Vijuan, but her mind cleared when she peered into the sack. She could buy the affection of a hundred men like him with those stones.

Enkid headed east, picking her way through branches and scratchy bushes to avoid the paths. Her hands itched, so she flexed her fingers. The hardened black slime cracked, exposing a dusky coloring on her skin beneath it. Far off, the Laklor's call sent shivers up her spine, but it was too distant for it to have noticed her. Another boat keeping it at bay, she hoped.

The sun had been set a couple hours before Enkid thought it safe enough to stop to eat the rye crackers and candied tangerines Vijuan had packed for her. She walked through the night, shifting the sack from shoulder to shoulder as the weight of it wore a groove in her skin. A moldy smell followed her as she went, and she cursed the wet forest floor.

Early the next morning, she spotted a man fishing a small pond. He wore a golden caftan, but more importantly, he was alone. This far from Vijuan's village, no one would know who she was, and she needed an idea of how to pace herself. Besides, the dagger on her belt and hemlock at her neck were all the protection she needed for one man.

"Excuse me," she said as she reached him. He smiled in response. "I'm on my way to Creftland. Could you tell me how much farther it is?"

His expression changed to one of censure, and he glanced at her hands before she could hide them. "Nobody returns there. Why would you want to?"

An excuse leapt to her lips about a sick mother, but she suppressed it. Lying produced more traps than it avoided. "Please, I need to know."

He pointed off to the side of the road. "It's only half a league from here, but there is no path. No Trilonean roads lead there."

"Thank you," she said, keeping her anger in check at his insolence. "Thank you so much."

All this time, I've been only a day's journey from home? As soon as he was out of sight, she kicked up her feet and ran despite the heavy sack. Energy pulsed through her body, anticipation propelling her forward. She was so close to what she'd always wanted, to the security only prosperity could provide.

There was no sign, but when her foot struck the ground in Creftland, she knew. The woods dimmed and a concentrated rot stifled the air. Enkid shook off the oppressive feeling. She'd made it back! Now she needed to stay out of sight, find a good hiding place for most of the stones, and start amassing more riches with the rest.

It took a few steps more to realize her shoulders did not ache. She swung the sack around. It was light—far too light—and slack. Her arms shook as she inspected it, finding no holes. All the anticipation drained out of her like blood from a headless fowl. Panic rose as she forced her blackened hands to loosen the tie and peered inside.

Empty. Nothing but fine, pink-speckled sand and a few chunks of hardened slime. No rocks, no gems. She turned the sack inside out, grabbed at its edges, but they weren't there. The black opals were gone.

She tossed the bag away and felt ill, fell to her knees and yelled, a hollow, gurgling sound she regretted as soon as she felt a lashing wind at her back. Whether the rumble came from the pounding hooves of Creftish gangmares or the flapping of heavy wings, she did not care. Enkid closed her eyes and tried not to breathe.

The Weavers

Maxine Kollar

*A*erwyn's eyes fluttered open. Startled by the orange sky, she struggled to quiet her rising panic. She'd slept later than she meant to, but told herself there was still time. Her legs quickly swung over the side of her hammock and she looked at the fabric's beautiful pattern, so intricate that it must have exhausted her. Both hands waved over the hammock and the fine silky material untied from the trees and flowed back into her palms.

*D*ayad, her constant companion, must have been beside itself with terror at the vanishing daylight, but had no way of alerting Aerwyn. When the hammock was fully recoiled, she picked up the white, fluffy creature, stroked its long ears, ran them under her nose, and inhaled deeply. This simple act calmed them both.

"Sorry, Day," she whispered. She glanced back at the knoll. After a grueling week of studying and tests, she had needed a retreat, and this rare solitary trip was a reward from her parents. *Would they ever let me go off by myself again?* she wondered.

Aerwyn stepped gingerly into the stream, holding Dayad in one arm and the hem of her dress in the other hand. Damp clothing sticking to her body was well beyond an annoyance to her, and she glanced around modestly as she wound the garment's hem around her left forearm a second time. Still cradling Dayad in her left arm, she managed to keep her right hand free for the weaving.

Anchored to a tree first, the spins needed to be thin, light, and tight, plus she had to be careful not to get lost in the intricacies. Weavers created their threads in a variety of thicknesses and textures, depending on the need. As she watched the sun melt into the horizon, Aerwyn wished she could spin faster, but this was still a single-handed task for her. And it took so much concentration to make sure her creation was waterproof. She remembered enviously how her father, using both hands, had woven much larger and more intricate boats in mere seconds while talking to her mother.

Her boat finished when there were just slivers of sunlight left, Aerwyn was already practicing apologies as she carefully boarded the vessel. She untied its tether to the tree, and fell back as the boat sailed upstream. Moving her weave against the flow of the stream took additional effort, but she could manage. From childhood, Weavers would float toy-sized boats up and down streams for practice and play.

She was nervous, but she knew *they* needed moonlight to see her. Maybe, there wouldn't even be moonlight tonight; the sky had been so clouded over. Then, the stream turned westward and the first glints of moonlight touched her boat. Her fear became as solid as her boat. *They* could see her now. *They* could find her. But surely she had time to reach home. Didn't she?

There was movement up ahead in the bushes beside the stream. Not wind, but maybe forest creatures. No! Trouble was ahead. Aerwyn raised her hands to stop the boat, but it was too late.

"Now!" someone shouted from the riverbank, and a net rose out of the water and came overhead, splashing her with cold water.

"Oh, Day," Aerwyn's voice quivered as she folded herself to spare them from wet clothes and wet fur. *Silly thoughts, silly worries*, she thought as the reality of the situation set in. *They* had her. She looked down into Dayad's wide, trusting eyes.

"No! They don't have us yet!" She slid Dayad off her lap, and bolted upright with both hands extended in the sharpest weave of her young life. The point of a knife formed in her left hand. The boat weave was still in her right hand, and she could not yet issue two weaves from a single hand. The blade-weave grazed against the net, while her heart pounded like the Volka Drums at Festive Time.

But the half-woven knife clattered to the floor of the boat, and Aerwyn looked at it curiously. Even after she felt tight fists around her forearms, then a strange softness surround her hands, she could not believe she'd been captured by men.

"You can't spin through those, Weaver!" called a gravelly voice from the shore.

Aerwyn turned her head and recognized the staff from her lessons on Wizerns—but the beard took her by surprise. It was dirty gray instead of flowing white, but it was more than the beard color that was off-putting. When the Wizern moved, the angles of his boney form jutted out against his robes at odd angles. Unlike the pictures she'd studied of Wizerns, this one's body and beard were scraggly, sparse, and angular.

How did he dispel her Mezmer? Maybe she couldn't hide from the Wizern, but the Mezmer should have protected her from the sight of men.

He laughed as Aerwyn's sack-covered hands were bound in front of her. "We'll want to keep an eye on those, won't we?"

The men dragged the boat across the stream and plucked her out. Aerwyn's head was reeling, but she was shocked back to awareness by the coldness of her dress dipping into the stream, then wrapping around her legs. Anger and disgust heated her face, if not her legs. She weighed less than half of just one man. Couldn't a group of them keep her dress out of the water?

When they hoisted her ashore and placed her at the Wizern's feet, a gleaming ball of fur bounded from the boat and onto her lap. The men bristled at first, and then calmed when they recognized the fuzzy creature as a pet. The Wizern, too, seemed unconcerned with the shining hareball.

"Recoil your boat…and your useless blade, Weaver. I need you whole for our work," the majick-weilder told Aerwyn. Then, to the men he barked orders to hold her arms steady.

"I know you are just a child, at least for your race," the sharp side of the Wizern's staff pressed into the pulse of Aerwyn's neck as he continued "But know before we free your hands that I will not hesitate to end your life if you attempt an escape or an attack."

His eyes were as cold as his words, and Aerwyn did not doubt him for a moment. The Wizern appeared unimpressed, but the men watched with a mixture of wonder and fear as after removing the cloth sacks, the solid looking boat unraveled and withdrew into her palms. They had, no doubt, heard stories of Weavers, but witnessing one at work was different.

The Wizern's gaze returned to Aerwyn after her bindings and the sacks were replaced. "You are not what I was hoping for, but you will have to do. The High Commander is making demands that due to the shortness of time, I cannot fulfill. now, we have work to do, you and I." A misplaced smile crossed his face for a moment.

"What of the creature?" asked one of the guards as they lifted Aerwyn into a small cage on the back of a cart.

"Let her keep it, for now," answered the Wizern. "Best to keep her calm."

§

The journey through the forest and into the Fortress Bal'Carn was rough and slow. Aerwyn had never been this far north, and watched through the bars as grassy hillsides and flowered fields melted into rocky roads and spiny flora. There were reasons, she had heard, why men preferred the craggy mountain regions over the lush lowlands. The ores in the mountain were so precious to them that they chose to live out their days scratching and clawing in the ground.

The men rode on gelpins, sure footed, strong-backed beasts they captured to use in their work. The cart that held Aerwyn's cage was also drawn by two gelpins, with the Wizern seated next to the driver.

Yelling above the clattering hooves, the Wizern bragged, "I could get us to our destination much quicker, but it was I who laid down a dampening field around the fortress. Any majick used in that area will be subverted." Then, he added for Aerwyn's benefit, "I believe even your kind would not be able to weave properly here!"

§

The High Commander scowled as he stood at the tower window and watched the returning party. He turned to his High Guard, "A majick dampening field! That's what I get when I need help from the physical attacks. The Nil'Carn has a Wizern who is a skilled alchemist, not a useless conjurer. Our foe vastly outnumbered us and our spies report advances in their technology."

"The tales of powerful explosives that can shatter stone walls are true. Even so, I trust our men," advised the High Guard.

"Trust our men?" laughed the High Commander. "They are coming after us because one of your ranks is not to be trusted. How else could the Nil'Carn have known that we hit upon such a trove of glacxion?"

The High Guard looked distressed. "I still don't believe it was one of my men. Their Wizern is also said to be a powerful Seer. Besides, if our Wizern captures a Weaver, then it could shore up the defenses while our men work on the offensive."

"True," admitted the Commander. "But who knows what he's found. He was picking pretty flowers for his silly potions when he thought he saw a wisp travel down the stream. I still cannot believe I allowed him a contingency of men and gelpins in the hopes of capturing a reflection of the water. Still, it might give me an opportunity to ask the Wizern for his head."

§

As the Weaver-hunting party entered the courtyard, the Wizern pried his gaze away from the figure in the tower, pushed a guard aside, and helped Aerwyn down from the cart. Though his little-used muscles quivered under her slight frame, but he held her tightly by the shoulders as they walked to the door.

"We are not so different, you and I, Weaver. What do men know of our connection to the majick of this world? They only want to use us for their own bidding. After these affairs of man, you should take me back to your people. We could learn so much from each other."

The quiet words hissed into Aerwyn's ear and slithered around searching for an opening. Aerwyn felt him, like fog under a door.

Men, although a bother and a blight on the land, were of no concern to Weavers. Wizerns however, were a concern. While they considered themselves above men, they were dangerously jealous of the Weavers. Aerwyn's people believed Wizerns to be men infused at conception with dark majick. That same darkness made them very adept at spotting the light cast by Weavers. Moonlight made it easier for them to see a Weaver, but even in the day, they could sense the presence of their light.

The Wizern fell away, and two men lead Aerwyn up steep broken steps to a bare room; just a slab to sit and lay upon and stone bench where a guard already sat waiting. The high ceiling tapered into a conical opening where just hints of moonlight entered. She was forced to wait well into the night for the Wizern, but she did not mind as she had quite enough of his slithery words and his putrid breath. Meanwhile, Dayad jumped about her, wriggling its ears and thumping its heavy feet against the sacks and the binds on her wrists. The loving efforts made her tears spill over.

When the Wizern finally entered the chamber, he had slaves with him who brought trays of fruit and milled grains. Aerwyn stomach revolted. She knew he wanted her alive, but for what? And then, what?

"Weaver," he began, trying to sound gentle. "I am saddened I did not capture an older member of your tribe, one who knows more of this world. I am under the will of a High Commander who needs this fortress protected, at all costs." Here, he let out a dramatic sigh.

"This fortress," he continued, "is the last intersect. Our enemies are your enemies. If they wipe us out, they will come for your kind next. Things are changing. There are ways for men to see Weavers now, just as these men can see you. It is just a matter of time before they come for all of you."

Although she knew the truth was like molten ore on his tongue, fear for herself and her people was building inside her.

"Lend me your power, young Weaver, and help stop our mutual enemy."

If what the Wizern was saying was true, wouldn't the village leaders know? She felt confused.

A guard walked through the door, and apparently, Dayad hopped too close to the egress. The man grabbed the little creature by its ears, and swung it up in the air. Aerwyn screamed and railed against her shackles.

"You put Dayad down you..."

"Wizern," the guard interrupted, ignoring her completely. "We can't let this thing escape. It might go back to her people and guide them here to rescue her."

"Maybe," said the Wizern thoughtfully, "Or maybe it could lead us to more of her kind."

"No!" shouted Aerwyn. "Dayad is bound to me! Even if it could leave me and lead you to my village, it would not, as it has intelligence and morals, unlike you beasts!"

A hungry look crossed the Wizern's haggard face, and Aerwyn recognized it at once. "If you touch my Dayad," she began in a low growl. "I will weave such bitterness into whatever you plan to extricate from me," she continued, raising her voice and body slightly, "that it will melt like the flow from the Kan'Al Mountains, burning my soul and your plans and this entire fortress!" She ended in an impressive controlled crescendo.

A slight quiver of his lips belied the unimpressed expression on his face as the Wizern took Dayad from the guard and placed it gently in her lap. He patted both of them condescendingly, and turned to leave.

"How did you catch me?" asked Aerwyn, despite her resolve to say nothing to him that she did not need to say.

A thin smile crossed his face. "I can recreate moonlight, Weaver," he lied grandly. "I discerned that the stream would be a favored method of transport for your kind, and I have been watching it for some time. You came downstream very fast, young one. But as we all know, what goes down, must come up." He laughed at his joke and walked out of the room.

Aerwyn felt foolish. It was a practice of Weavers that whenever they left the village, they never traveled to and fro by the same method or the same path.

"Stupid," she chided herself. She had meant to spend time weaving the wings she had failed at on her test. She wanted to prove to herself that she could do better, and then, she would have gotten home faster flying over the Mazon Fields instead of sailing up the same stream. But she had panicked when she saw the setting sun.

Aerwyn could not tell how many hours later the Wizern ambled back into the room and wordlessly sat next to her on the slab. He blew a fine gray powder into her face, grabbed her chin, and peered into her eyes. He held her like that for a long while trying to pierce her thoughts and slither inside. He searched for the openings that doubt and fear stirred by his words should have created in her mind.

She resisted him with all her will. What she felt, but could not understand, was why he tarried so long on the Volka Drums. But worse, like a voyeur, he watched her in her quietest moments, warm and serene. He watched her stroke Dayad and run its long silky ears under her nose, breathing its scent in. He watched again and again, searching her mind for an understanding that he was drawn to but couldn't capture...

When he finally left, the sun was overhead and pouring through the ceiling opening, but Aerwyn felt like she would never be warm again. Having him pry into her mind was like wearing darkness—a wet dress sticking to her soul. She lay down on the slab and let the sun beat down on her while she rested. She needed a plan. Resisting the Wizern's will was working for the moment, but what of tomorrow? What if he persisted for a month?

Aerwyn heard a sound and opened her eyes. She watched a Grey Dorin flying overhead. It was carefree one moment, then under attack from a Sargen the next moment. Instead of fighting the larger bird, the Dorin simply yielded to the air and fell so far so quickly that it was able to escape the sharp claws of its attacker. A cunning idea sat her upright. She knew she would not get out of here with Gernet sacks chained to her wrists. She was bound to do the Wizern's bidding, but she needed to keep him from destroying her mind in the process.

She started weaving the chamber.

§

It was evening when a guard was ordered to alert the Wizern to the approach of the enemy army. The guard knocked at the chamber door, then waited for a long while. When he heard strange humming and the sound of rapid footfalls within, he burst into the room to find the Wizern dancing. The dance was wild and capricious with his bony knees jutting far out of the robes while the thin gray material swirled around him.

They exchanged looks, but no words, as the Wizern walked over to his potion-filled table and grabbed his newest masterpiece, a bag filled with a dark powder. He waited for the guard to stumble over words of armies and advancement, and then, he took a pinch of powder out of the sack and blew it into the man's face as he walked past. He paused until he heard the sound of the man's body hitting the stone floor, then headed to the Weaver's room.

Walking into Aerwyn's chamber, the Wizern quickly blew the black powder in her face, and her vision became foggy until the magick-weilder rippled in front of her like an image on a pond after a pebble was thrown in.

She wove the walls of the chamber.

The Wizern started chanting in an ancient tongue that Aerwyn did not understand, but it made the ripples change directions. He took her wrists and untied the sacks. She felt the air but her fingers felt as though they were on borrowed hands.

She wove the ceiling.

The Wizern's words were telling her what to do, even though she could not understand them. Aerwyn was confused and disconnected from her body, still she fought to finish the chamber. She watched her hands rise in front of her. The palms turned upward and there, one then the other, her strands poured out of them, lingered in the air a moment before shooting up and out of the hole in the ceiling. She followed the wispy whiteness in her mind and watched them drift across the courtyard, over the outer wall, and dive into the ground, becoming hard as iron.

She wove the door of the chamber.

Aerwyn wove and wove, tighter and tighter. So much of her life force was going out, but she could not stop it. This was no shield, it was a wall! He wanted her to surround the front of the fortress with her weave, her life. The fortress backed up against a mountain, but the exposed front wall was still very large. How did he expect her to survive such a large weave?

She locked the chamber.

The Wizern, aware of the risk, kept one hand near her face to reinforce the spell and another hand on her back to monitor her life force. "You are stronger than you know, young one. I can feel you ebb and flow under my hand, and I will keep you alive as long as I can."

A guard rushed in with news. The shield, the Weaver's wall, had met the other side of the mountain. The Wizern let out a sigh of relief. It would all have been for nothing if she died—her life force was the shield and the shield was her life now.

The guard motioned to the pale, stone-like child on the slab with single threads floating up from her hands. "Is she...alright?"

The Wizern laughed. "Of course she's not alright, fool. Most of her being is in front of the fortress guarding it from an enemy you are too weak to defend against. This shell is still alive though, and we must keep it that way. Be sure to have a slave come in every hour and try to get a bit of water down the throat of our shield." He left to receive his well-deserved accolades from the High Commander.

A few minutes later, the High Commander entered the tower chamber with the pleased Wizern in tow.

"This!" sneered the High Commander. "This child is our secret weapon."

"This child is older than both of us," the Wizern said calmly. "This child is a Weaver." He knew he needn't elaborate on all the fabled talents of the race, and silently allowed the High Commander to soak in what this treasure was worth.

"You believe a child's weave can withstand the coming assault by the Nil'Carn. Their Wizern is refining ways to use alchemy to break through anything we have, and you are working on ways to refine child labor. Excellent!"

The High Commander circled the stone slab with a look of scorn on his face. Finally, he begrudgingly said, "Through no fault of your own, you may have stumbled upon a majickal being that could turn the tide for us. If the shield can hold, the guards will be able to destroy the Nil'Carn forces. The battle begins soon."

Both commander and Wizern left for their respective war rooms.

The first blast hit Aerwyn's shield, and she awoke and covered her eyes. The blinding whiteness all around her was surprising, but she quickly recognized it as her chamber. This is where she sealed enough of herself away; away from her own weave so that the Wizern could not drain her of not just her life force, but also of her will. She briefly peered out of her own eyes, and she realized her body was still sitting on the slab maintaining the shield weave. Part of the plan had worked; for she had been able to seal herself off. But now what? How could she to get her body back and escape her captors?

The door opened, and Aerwyn watched a slave girl come in. The girl was probably not much older than herself, in relative years. There was a mug in her hand, and terror in her eyes as she watched the weave lingering above Aerwyn's stone-like hands. Inching closer, looking for signs of life, the slave tried to pour a dram of water into Aerwyn's slightly parted lips. At that moment, a loud volley of explosions shook the shield and the fortress. The poor girl screamed and dropped to the floor, spilling the cold water all over Aerwyn's dress. The slave fled, and the guard cursed and went after her.

Even inside her chamber, Aerwyn recoiled at the feel of her wet dress sticking to her thigh. The water was still trickling down her leg when Dayad came over to her.

"Yes! Please, stir. Please, call out." Aerwyn had always been very annoyed at her powerful revulsion to wet clothes. When she was very young, an unexpected squall had left her screaming. Her mother had peeled the damp clothes off her while she stood as fast as stone, unable to help herself. Now, that same powerful reaction was enough to rouse her even in this weakened state.

Out of the parted lips, barely above a thought came, "Dayad, enter." It was something the poor creature had to be invited to do.

Dayad leapt up on the slab and began to glow. It put its long ears on Aerwyn's chest, just below her neck, and its whole body slowly began to unravel. The creature became as thin and wispy as the weave coming from Aerwyn's hands.

At that instant, the door opened and in came the guard with the slave girl's hair caught in one fist. "Get back in there, and make sure the body gets water you…"

The guard stopped talking and the girl stopped squirming when they saw the billowy whiteness of Dayad around Aerwyn's face. The guard raised his sword, even though he had no idea what he was going to do. In the same moment, the terrified slave found the strength to kick the guard and run. The whiteness that was Dayad rushed into Aerwyn's nostrils. Her head was thrown back and her whole body arched violently, curving her like a drawn bow, as life force entered and coursed through her.

Aerwyn left the woven white chamber and joined back into herself to face the guard. He knew he couldn't hurt her, the all-important weave was still coming out of her hands, but he had to do something. He grabbed one arm, his other hand raising the sword in a useless gesture, and shouted for another guard to get the Wizern.

"He'll know what to do with you, witch!" he barked.

Aerwyn still had one arm free, and in a quick motion, she severed the tie with the shield, and deftly wove a single thick strand. "I'm not a witch!" she shouted back at the guard. "I'm a Weaver!"

She went up on her tip-toes, and buried the steel-like, razor-sharp strand into and through the guard's neck. Blood poured out of the man as his angry face became peaceful. Aerwyn recoiled at the pain of taking a life, but straightened herself and pressed on.

She looked up at the ceiling opening and began to spin wings onto her back. This had been her test in school last week, seemingly a life-time ago. Then, she had woven so slowly and carefully, but the wings had been flawed. Now, with her life in her hands, the wings she wove at adult speed, aided by ancient memory, were perfect.

Wings complete, Aerwyn flew to the tower's opening and just out of sight to those entering the chamber. Then, quick as she could, she recoiled the fortress shield.

Below her, she witnessed the enemy pouring into the fortress and the volleys of weapon's fire. By soaring over the mountain to the back of fortress, she avoided the Wizern's majick-dampening field. Once clear of the majick-wielder's defenses, she turned south and headed for home as quickly as she could.

When she returned to her frightened parents and alarmed village, Aerwyntold her tale again and again. The search teams were recalled, and the village let out a collectively held breath.

"They saw me," Aerwyn said sadly to her father and the other leaders of the village. "The Wizern said they have ways to see us now, and soon men will come for us."

"It was your own fear that revealed you, Aerwyn," her father began. "It broke down your Mezmer, but we have nothing to fear here. The village Mezmer is as strong and solid as ever. Men are not coming for us, but racing after what they have always pursued, riches. The current fight is over an immense vein of ore discovered in the mountain behind the fortress where you were held. The uneasy truce between the two opposing sides disappeared with that discovery."

Aerwyn blushed as she recalled how alarmed she had become in the boat when she saw the glints of moonlight. How could she have believed anything the Wizern said?

Aerwyn crept into the Room of Honor. Her mother was already kneeling below a woven likeness of Grandmother.

"Years ago, when you were still in swaddled clothes, your grandmother lay dying. She might have lingered weeks or months longer, but that was not what she wanted. She asked to have the remnants of her life force woven into Dayad so that a small part of her could stay with her only grandchild. Grandmother loved you so much. She believed you to be a gift from the Infinite Weaver, because the Sha'lin had said my womb was arid. Their kind was never wrong, and yet, there you were."

Aerwyn was stunned. She had never heard this tale before. Dayad was always there, and she would never have thought to question who or what it was. "Mother? Did Grandmother still know herself. I mean…was it really her?"

"Aerwyn, a being, any knowing being, is like a tapestry. We are so intricate and carefully made, with colors and textures beyond our sight. The hands that we are spun from are not for our knowing. You loved Dayad, but such a creature is but an echo of the whole being, just the last fervent hopes and dreams, but it was enough to save you. And that's all that matters."

"How did I know to call Dayad into me?" Aerwyn asked.

"How does one know to gasp for air when drowning, to grasp for branches when falling? We know, because we are meant to know," her mother answered.

Then, the Weavers gave thanks, and settled into their work and play.

One Day in the Hills of Milan
Jeffrey G. Roberts

"For once you have tasted flight, you will walk the Earth with your eyes turned skywards. For there you have been, and there you will long to return."

~ *Leonardo Da Vinci*

*A**m I playing God? he wondered. He continued to gaze up at* the skies of Milan. The soaring of the birds high overhead was hypnotic; their fluid movements a source of endless fascination to him. From the veranda of his villa, the great inventor could observe and sketch every movement and aspect of their wings, and add them to his *Codex of Flight.*

Pondering this moral dilemma, he soon settled the ambiguity which often vexed him. *No, there is no conflict here. God did not give man wings, it is true. Instead, he provided us the brains to fashion our own. And that is what I resolve to do.*

And back in his workshop, the grand machine began to take shape in Leonardo da Vinci's prodigious mind. He would add his current observations into his voluminous *Codex,* to improve, modify, and perfect it.

"May I see it, Maestro?" his young apprentice Bartolomeo, asked.

"It is not yet complete, my friend. But since you shall be an integral part of the greatest experiment in human history—come, and I will show you history in the making!"

It was like nothing Bartolomeo had ever seen. In fact, it was unlike anything *anyone* had ever seen. Was this a wooden bird of some sort? A wooden bird with wings in excess of thirty-three feet? A giant, bat-like contrivance, with spars and ribs supporting the huge wings. There were ropes, pulleys, and a rudimentary rudder. Underneath it was a crude sort of leather harness, with hand cranks and foot stirrups. The wings were covered in silk, and they glistened in the shafts of sunlight from windows high overhead.

"I am still not one hundred percent convinced human muscles possess sufficient propulsive power to imitate the birds of the air. But I am pondering an alternative solution to that potential problem. Do you wish to see what it feels like, Bartolomeo?"

"Oh, very much, Maestro! This is beyond anything I could have imagined!"

"It is quite beyond anything *anyone* has imagined, my apprentice. An inventor's is a lonely life, yes? We are ridiculed for what has never been done. As if the mere fact that it has not been accomplished precludes it from *ever* being accomplished?"

"Oh Master, *no one* would ridicule you!" The apprentice was adamant in his fierce loyalty to the great Leonardo da Vinci.

"Perhaps not for my other accomplishments in art, anatomy, and military inventions. But I fear what closed-minded men in positions of power will say or do, when they see *this* in the skies of Milan."

"They will shout your praises, and accolades shall surely pour in from across Italy."

Leonardo smiled at Bartolomeo's youthful naiveté and unshakable optimism.

As he showed his apprentice how to attach the straps and belts in the contraption's harness, he helped Bartolomeo adjust the loop around his head which controlled the rudder as he moved his head left and right.

"How do you feel, Bartolomeo?"

"Like I was never born a man! That to be a bird—*this* bird, was my destiny. Teach me, Maestro, and the dream will live!"

"That is precisely what I intend to do, my fortunate friend. But first we must eat to keep up our strength."

In the weeks to come, Leonardo and his apprentice worked more closely together than they ever had—the great inventor finishing the construction of the wooden bird, while improving and perfecting its operation, while Bartolomeo spent hours each day in the harness of the machine, practicing his movements, and building up his muscles for the first flight. The apprentice now knew how to control the machine under any condition and aerial situation. And he would repeat them over and over, until they were second nature to him.

Ancient man had discovered fire. Now, it was Leonardo da Vinci who would introduce to the world humanity's second greatest achievement—flight.

They carted the great wooden bird up to one of the majestic and verdant hills which surround Milan. They received quite a few stares on the trip, but they had expected this. After all—a flying machine? In 1505 Milan?

Soon, the contraption perched on the edge of a large hill, Bartolomeo securely strapped into it, as his Maestro steadied its wing in the light breeze.

"You look frightened, Bartolomeo. Are you having misgivings, my boy?"

"No, Master. Not in the slightest. Your genius is not what I fear. It is a beautiful machine! I am well trained and prepared. What I fear— are the French. Their incursions into Milan are what I fear. The next one may cause the defeat of our beloved city."

"My young charge, this has been on my mind as well. Fear not. I've been formulating a magnificent plan for months. I fully expect there to *be* a further French invasion—and they shall receive the shock of their life. Truly I tell you, Bartolomeo, the world shall take notice. The French shall be soundly defeated, and never step foot on Italian soil again!"

This seemed to greatly please his apprentice; and the young man appeared to trust his Master implicitly.

And when Bartolomeo was ready—he pushed off. It took a minute of furiously pumping the foot treadles connected to the wing's hinges, for him to realize that the Maestro was indeed correct: humans didn't have the muscular power to flap giant wings such as birds do. But the machine was so expertly engineered that the thermals did the job for him. And the great bird soared. And the angels on high looked down at the glowing silken wings of Da Vinci's creation, sunlight glinting off the machine, on this beautiful day in Milan. And they smiled.

"Dare I say I am one with the Gods?" the apprentice shouted. And he began singing in exultation. And he soared and dipped and banked with the birds, who chirped and squawked at the impudence of man invading *their* domain.

Throngs below began staring up, pointing excitedly. Townsfolk, farmers, shepherds in the fields, and peasants all observed the aerial wonder; as Bartolomeo landed in a field, without injury or incident. But they were not *all* who saw it. The friars of the ancient Basilica of San Lorenzo Maggiore also witnessed the spectacle of the ages; the dream since time immemorial—now realized.

Two weeks later, Leonardo was summoned to Rome by his Holiness Pope Julius II. To congratulate him? To bestow praises upon him for this crowning achievement of human flight? Somehow Leonardo did not think so.

The trip was arduous, but one did not refuse an audience with the Pope; even if one is convinced that the requested meeting would not be of a positive nature.

"Your journey was a pleasant one, Leonardo?"

"As pleasant as a 574 kilometer journey can be, Your Holiness. But it was—uneventful."

They stared at each other for a few moments. Both were quite aware of the serious circumstances of the meeting—niceties aside.

"Your achievements, your devotion to the Church, are undisputed. Without question, your place in the human panoply of art and science is now enshrined for all time. However..." the Pope paused, and Da Vinci knew what was coming, "...I have received disturbing reports from the Basilica of San Lorenzo Maggiore. At first I dismissed these accounts as merely misinterpretations, by tired eyes and elderly citizens, or perhaps the imbibing of too much wine by friars with too little self-control in such matters. Yet, these strange reports kept coming across my desk."

The Holy Father walked to the window, and gazed up at the sky, his back to Leonardo. "Our Savior is a stern God, who will not be mocked, Leonardo. Do not tempt the Lord thy God."

"Your Holiness, I..." Leonardo began. But Pope Julius II held up his hand for silence, admonishing Da Vinci to listen, not speak.

"You presume for yourself the mantle of God, Leonardo, in your attempts at human flight?"

"I did not *attempt* it, Your Holiness. I succeeded."

Pope Julius II whirled around from the window and slammed his fist onto the desk. "Then, you do not deny you attempted to play God?"

"With all due respect, Your Holiness, I admit I utilized my God-given mind to create my *own* wings."

The Pope was becoming impatient. "I see your legs are strong and muscular still, Leonardo. Not as bird-like as candlesticks. Would you agree?"

"I would, Your Holiness."

"And I see you do not possess feathered wings, nor—I'm assuming—you were not born with such wondrous structures?"

"No, Your Holiness. I was not."

"Ah, yes. And who, may I ask, created such marvelous creatures of the air?"

"The Lord God, Holy Father."

"Yes. The Lord God, Leonardo. *Not* you! If our heavenly Father had meant us to fly, we would have been *born* with those very anatomical parts I can see quite clearly you do not possess. Nor do I. Nor does anyone else I know. And do you know why? It is because He knows what is best for us. There is delineation, a hierarchy of creatures that are separate in God's domain: fish swim, birds fly; snakes slither, while the savage beasts of the jungle stalk and kill. *None* presumes the ability or aptitude of the other. Because God, in His infinite wisdom, wishes it to be so. Heed my warnings, Leonardo. Destroy that flying machine before it destroys you! The devil himself, the king of hell—*he* is the one who shines his countenance upon you—because it insults God! Neither Rome, nor my office, shall abide by your machine's continued existence as an affront to God. Man does not fly! Repeat that in your mind on your long journey home. I do not believe it is necessary for me to expound on the consequences, should you *not* heed my warnings."

"No, Your Holiness. I am well aware of such consequences."

"Then, we will not speak of this matter further. God speed, my friend. And safe journey home."

All the way back to Milan, Leonardo was torn with indecision, self-doubt—and outright fear. He knew perfectly well the consequences of disobeying Julius II—imprisonment. Or worse.

No One, not even the Holy Father, has the right to deny a man his life's work, his dreams, his God-given right to create for a better world, he kept thinking. *The devil indeed!* But he began to tremble—and he didn't quite know why.

Bartolomeo greeted him warmly upon his return. "Your meeting with the Holy Father went well, Maestro?" But the lad knew perfectly well why Da Vinci had been summoned to Rome.

"As well as could be expected. It was, at least—civil. But he made his position quite clear concerning the flying machine."

"What will you do, Maestro?"

"I do not know, Bartolomeo. I simply do not know. We will see. Time will tell. Ironically, I still believe God is on our side."

"Did you tell that to His Holiness?"

"Surely you jest, my friend." And they both laughed nervously, if for no other reason than to ease the tension of a decision they knew they must inevitably make.

§

About a month after returning home, Da Vinci received a visit from a worried Captain Ludovico de Pazzi.

"Captain, you have the look of a troubled man."

"Indeed, Leonardo. The world knows of your magnificent contributions to military engineering, but a threat shall soon descend upon Milan that I fear even the great Leonardo da Vinci may not be able to defend against."

"Sit, and tell me what you have heard, my friend."

"As you know, I have scouts, as well as spies, in France. They periodically report back to me on any threats the French might be planning. This morning, I received disturbing news from one of my couriers, that the French are indeed massing an attack on Milan—yet again!"

"Do you know when?"

"They shall be ready in a month. Perhaps two. And I fear our depleted military forces may not be able to successfully repel them this time."

Leonardo gazed at the horizon—he had a plan.

"I have seen that look before, Maestro. Do you have an idea?"

"Indeed I do, my friend. But it will require sacrifice, and great personal risk. So let me ask you: are you aware of my recent audience with Julius II?"

"That disease riddled old fool? Of course."

"Even with the power he still wields, are you willing to risk imprisonment, or worse, in the defense of Milan?"

"I am a military man. I have pledged my sacred honor to defend my fellow citizens, and this blessed land. Let Pope Syphilis do his damndest! He is not threatened in Rome by the French. *We* are."

"Excellent! And I agree. Now that I know where you stand, I want to show you something." And he took him to a secret room in his workshop. "You have seen my flying machine?"

"Indeed. With Bartolomeo flying it last month. Magnificent!"

"Thank you, Captain. But you have not seen *this*; for I have made many improvements." And he pulled back a curtain.

"Good God, Leonardo! This one *does* look different!"

It was sleeker, lighter, and more aerodynamic.

"But where are the foot treadles, to flap the wings? And what is this strange copper sphere atop the machine?"

"Ah, that is the greatest change of all, Ludovico. I knew from the first flight with Bartolomeo that human muscles were simply not strong enough to efficiently flap those huge wings. Sustained flight times were thus limited to the thermals. But *now*—you don't have to. And I owe it to a Greek genius named Hero, who lived well over one thousand years ago, in Alexandria. He was the greatest mathematician and engineer of his time. And *his* claim to fame was that he built a little metal sphere filled with water. The sphere was mounted on a spindle, and it had two small tubes pointing in opposite directions, for steam to escape when the water began to boil. The result was the sphere spun round and round, ever faster. Ergo, work could be performed—using steam power. And so it could be made to do what, my friend?"

"Flap wooden wings!"

"Precisely, Ludovico! I have modified it, of course. There is a small metal tray beneath it, filled with coals. Tiny holes in it allow oxygen to keep the fire lit, but will not allow sparks to escape, endangering the wooden bird. The steam from the boiling water is then channeled, not through tiny tubes, but into valves of my own design—powering the wings to flap. The pilot need do nothing but steer; the steam fire lasting approximately thirty minutes. And since the pilot will not be required to use his arms or legs as much as in the previous machine, he can utilize them for something else."

"Such as what?"

"Such as firing weapons, like matchlock pistols, or arrows!"

"Again, magnificent, Leonardo! An aerial weapon of war! But incredible as this new weapon is, how can one machine defeat the invading French?"

"One cannot. But fifty can!" And he led Captain de Pazzi to a large hallway, where fifty wooden birds, in varying degrees of completion, were displayed!

The Captain was speechless.

"But I need your help, Ludovico, if we are to finish them, and train men to fly them—*before* the French invade."

"You leave that to me, Leonardo. They will be completed on time; I have men more than willing to work and train day and night. We will be ready. And the world will soon change!"

Forty days later, the promise was kept. Fifty beautifully crafted steam powered Da Vinci flying machines were ready, their fifty handpicked aeronauts fully trained and prepared for the defense of their beloved home.

And Milan's military intelligence proved true as three days later a force of 250 French soldiers were spotted marching South East towards Milan. There was little time to lose, as the strangest sixteenth century convoy the world had ever seen trundled slowly, in modified oxcarts, toward the hills on the outskirts of Milan.

§

The French soldiers could not have imagined what awaited them: a line of fifty giant wooden birds with thirty-three foot wings, perched atop a hill—waiting—and a man strapped into each one, with puffs of steam intermittently coming out of the tops of the machines. They must have looked to them like angry dragons doing men's bidding. And they would have been correct.

At first the invaders must have thought the Milanese soldiers to be cowards. Had they surrendered without a fight? How easy this battle would be! Surely victory was assured—until they looked up. And had their worst nightmare realized. The lined-up contraptions launched themselves off the edge of the precipice, and straight at the approaching Frenchmen.

Below them, the Milanese soldiers could hear their enemies:

"Captain Vasseur!" one of the soldiers screamed. "This cannot be real unless the accursed Milanese have made a pact with hell itself!"

"What deviltry is this?" an officer cried out. "The Italians have made a deal with the devil to release dragons against us! Glowing monsters, with men atop their backs! Mon Dieu!" He was about to frantically confer with the man earlier identified as Capt. Vasseur, when a musket ball went through his head.

"Lieutenant Gaudin, the devils of hell are flying with them!" another soldier screamed. He had turned to run, when an arrow pierced his heart.

"We cannot defeat dragons from hell!" Capt. Vasseur shouted. And he ordered a retreat, even as an arrow tore through his leg. And as if to confirm the French soldiers fears, the skies darkened.

"Surely, this is a sign," screamed a wounded soldier.

"What defense have we against dragons?"

Below Leonardo's steam-powered machines, the Frenchmen began to flee in a blind panic from what they saw continuing to come out of the skies at them. They needed no further inducement to return to their homeland.

§

The French never attacked Milan, or anywhere else in Italy, again. Under threat of severe penalties, no returning French soldier was allowed to speak of what they saw on that ill-fated day. And no one ever did. After all, who would have believed them? The 'devil worshipping' Milanese might now be a pariah—but they would be left alone—lest the dragons of hell be unleashed against the French once more.

The flying machines were stored, and guarded, their pilots sworn to secrecy concerning the engineering of them. Da Vinci, at one point, seriously considered petitioning the government of Milan to institute a new branch of the military—the Aerial Defense Corps. But a vague uneasiness troubled him which he hoped was all in his mind, and borne of fatigue and age. It wasn't.

And Leonardo, Bartolomeo, Captain de Pazzi, and all involved in the winged onslaught against the foreign invaders waited apprehensively in the days and weeks following the aerial battle, for the expected and decidedly unpleasant consequences of their actions, from Pope Julius II. Yet, it never came.

An explanation finally came one day when the Maestro was wandering the grounds of the Basilica of San Lorenzo Maggiore. He overheard one of the priests speaking to another, in great distress.

"I only heard of it this morning, after prayers. It is most sad. The disease which has afflicted the Holy Father has unfortunately accelerated. He has literally lost his grip on reality and spends his days mumbling gibberish to himself. All that can be done is to make him as comfortable as possible, and see to his needs. I do not see His Holiness surviving much longer in such a state. Most sad, my brother."

Da Vinci was dumbstruck. Though his faith in God had wavered in the past several weeks, it was utterly restored *now*, in light of this new development. *You often meet your fate on the road you take to avoid it,* he thought as he breathed a great sigh of relief, and listened to the bird's songs with more joy than he had in quite some time.

The next day, Leonardo met with an old friend

"Ludovico, I have called you to my workshop, because something has been weighing heavily on my mind of late, and I wished to discuss it with you."

"What problem could possibly be weighing on your mind, Leonardo? Did we not decisively defeat the French invasion, advance engineering by centuries, and despite the Pope's threats, do so with God's blessing? What could possibly trouble you still?"

"What you say is all true, Ludovico. And yes, my joy at achieving human flight is indescribable. God has truly shone His countenance upon our efforts. But I fear it is this very achievement in science that might be our undoing. Yes, Julius II is no longer a threat to the success of my flying machine. But the world is filled with small-minded, suspicious, and superstitious fools who cling to the ancient ways, and who would destroy all which they do not understand. All in the name of God, of course. How convenient. And some of them possess great political power. And if not the Pope, then maybe the Inquisitore, the feared branch of the Dominican friars. And if not them, then other powerful groups waiting in the wings, convinced too, that human flight is akin to playing God. Perhaps this knowledge of my flying machine is far too advanced and theologically perilous in these times. Perhaps such ideas are for the centuries to come. I do not know. But, in the dead of night, staring up at the stars, I fear the consequences still."

His friend Ludovico frowned. "I must admit, I too have had my moments of worry. Yet, I did not wish to lessen your joy in accomplishing such a monumental feat for fear you might accuse me of vain imaginings. Now, I see we share the same vague uneasiness. What do you propose, Leonardo?"

"I now have my plans, my drawings, and my *Codex of Flight;* written in a special code that only I can read. As unpleasant as it sounds, I propose destroying all the wooden birds but one and hiding the diagrams where no one will ever find them."

"And what of the townspeople who witnessed it all?"

"We must have secret meetings with them! They trust me. They trust *you*. We saved Milan. They *must* remain silent concerning what they saw. If asked, they can blame the sun in their eyes, or failing eyesight. Perhaps, they can say it was giant condors in the sky that day.

For what else could it have been? In time, the story of the great wooden birds will be relegated to legend. Hopefully, many years from now, our great-great-grandchildren will know nothing of it. Our reputations will be safe, as will our honor and that of our families. Flight will be for another time, Ludovico. Another century, perhaps. But *we* will know it worked!"

"I concur, Leonardo. You speak wisdom."

2017
Leonardo da Vinci National Museum of Science & Technology, Milan, Italy

There were few who could read the strange code which Da Vinci utilized in his drawings and engineering diagrams. Dr. Ian Palmer McCullen of Oxford was one of those who could read it. He had studied the great inventor's achievements all his professional life, and bemoaned the failure of Da Vinci's greatest dream—the flying machine. It had failed, and he abandoned the dream as beyond him; beyond 1505 technology. History recorded it as such. *If only*, Professor McCullen often thought. *If only.*

He frequently wondered what unbelievable heights aerodynamics would have reached, had it been kick started five centuries earlier than it was! And now, in Milan, on one of his rare opportunities for travel, he stood staring at the only example of Leonardo's great wooden bird, proudly on display at the museum which bore the genius's name.

Ian had to capture this. As he raised his cell phone to focus on the machine, he saw something he hadn't noticed before. There, under the right wing, next to the hinge point, was a tiny inscription, faded and now barely readable after 512 years. But he recognized it for what it was—Leonardo da Vinci's special coded writing! Why had no one seen this before? Excitedly he focused in on it, and snapped a photograph.

When he had returned to Oxford, he anxiously blew up the image, and with the help of his computer began to decipher the inscription. And when he had translated it in its entirety, he turned pale for this is what it said:

I, Leonardo Da Vinci, successfully fought the first aerial battle ever, defeating the French invasion of Milan on August 4th, 1505, with fifty of my great wooden birds. The world was not ready for such wonders, and we buried the machine's secrets—lost to history. To he who reads this: may your century be more conducive to the marvels of flight.

The Sapphire Circle
TJ Perkins

*W**here was he? I hovered over a glass-roofed building* and peered inside. Nope. Not there. My ears picked up scuffling and the sound of empty drums falling over and rolling across concrete. I was close.

Click!

My heart caught in my throat—the sound of a switchblade! I couldn't waste anymore time. I frantically fluttered from rooftop to rooftop looking for him, but the growing mist and fog billowing in from the ocean was making it difficult to see.

Glass shattered, shouts went up, and Nick came tumbling out of the building directly below where I was perched on the roof—beaten, bruised, and with a bloody nose.

"That's it kid! I've had enough of your lies!" A man dressed all in white slowly approached as Nick crab-crawled backwards in the hopes of putting distance between them. But Mr. White Suit's thugs weren't having it. They fanned out and flanked Nick. The kid wasn't going anywhere any time soon and within seconds his back met the concrete wall of the adjacent building. He stood, eyes nervously darting back and forth, trying his best to guess the gang's next move.

I could swoop in now and scare the crap outa those guys. The mist would make me look ominous, like a demon. Way scary. Nick would be relieved, laugh off the situation he got his self into—then go right back out and do something else he shouldn't. I thoughtfully flicked my forked tongue over my one extra-long fang and waited. Maybe Nick needed to get a reality check. Maybe he needed to feel what it would be like if I wasn't there to save him all the time. Maybe the fact that he was in danger would sink in, and he would be cautious with his life, his choices, and stop being so reckless. I growled low in my throat and snorted, silently chastising myself. I knew I should've never befriended a human. Everyone in my clan warned me, but I didn't listen. Deep inside I wanted to leave; yet couldn't. The bond between Nick and me was too strong.

So I stayed where I was; perched on the topmost edge of the building looking down on the unfolding situation. Even when one of the thugs moved forward and grabbed Nick around the neck, pinning his arm behind his back, I didn't move.

"I say we take his fingers, eh boss?" The tall, skinny mustache guy holding Nick sniggered nervously. The twitch in his shoulder and arms told me he had issues.

"Go for the nuts! Go for the nuts!" Short and jittery, this other guy hung in the back of the group excitedly watching the outcome and constantly rubbing his hands over his face and scratching at his neck. Yeah, he was on something, too.

"Nah, nah, nah, this one's messed with the wrong Dealer. Liars get their tongue cut out, but those that steal, well, you know where I'm going with this." He snapped his fingers; mustache guy moved out of the way and two muscle-bound thugs grabbed Nick by the arms. "Don't ya, Nick? You've slipped out of my grasp once before, but saw what happened to your buddy." The switchblade was put away as the man in the white suit slowly approached. "Get the cement mixed and bring over a barrel."

Several of his gang sprang into action while Nick struggled against the grip of the two men holding his arms. Still, I didn't interfere.

"Wait! Don't do this," Nick pleaded. "I didn't steal your pot. I swear."

Ugh! I told him not to get mixed up with that again. He won't listen to his dad, his sister, or even his friends, but you'd think he'd at least listen to me. Sure delivering drugs was quick and easy money, but you're going to attract the wrong kind of attention sooner or later. Plus there's the whole moral thing to consider. When was he ever going to learn?

I spread my wings to swoop down and save him—again. But instead, paused and watched.

"You stole it, sold it, and pocketed the profits!" the man in the white suit was nose to nose with Nick, never taking his eyes off of him as he held out his hand and a butcher knife was placed at his disposal. "You did this to me once before and I never said nothing about it. I let you go, but your friend got cement shoes. Now, it's your turn."

"I didn't! Seriously! It wasn't me!"

"It wasn't me, it wasn't me, hahahaha!" the jittery guy chimed in with a maniacal laugh.

"Yes, you did. But pot isn't what I'm worried about. Sapphire—that's what I really want. Now, what did you do with it kid?"

"I, uhhh, wha—?" Nick flashed him that silly what-the-hell look. It always made me laugh, but this guy was not amused. "I don't know what…"

"Don't lie to me!" White Suit shouted and put the knife blade to Nick's throat, drawing a tiny speck of blood. "The vials of blue liquid!" He latched onto Nick's neck and jaw, squeezing with a vise grip as he pulled a tiny glass vial out of his jacket pocket. "See this? This is my liquid gold! You—yes, *you*, took an entire crate of this stuff a few nights ago." He jiggled the vial of luminous blue liquid in Nick's face. "And destroyed my lab!"

"Lab? What lab? You don't have proof!" Nick shouted back, while struggling to swallow.

"Oh, yes we do. Paco!"

A dark-skinned man stepped up, opened a laptop and pressed play. I had to shift my position slightly to get a look at the screen; the scrapping of my clawed feet should've drawn attention, but the men were so interested in Nick that no one looked up. I held my breath as my eyes zeroed in on the image on the screen.

Sure enough, clear as day, there was my buddy Nick sneaking into a warehouse dressed in black from head to toe. I was a bit impressed as I watched him trash the tables of chemistry sets, beakers, and small vats of the dripping blue stuff with a baseball bat. Was he getting a conscience? Did he want to stop these guys and protect the public instead of making a profit his self?

"See that? Huh? See? That's you, punk!" White Suit was getting all fired up now, pointing from the screen to Nick and back again.

"Looks nothing like me!" Nick protested.

"Really? Keep watching."

And sure enough, the culprit in the video turned to face the camera—full on and clear—before bashing it to pieces. Yes. It *was* Nick.

"Who's that, huh?" White Suit turned and looked at his men, smiling, hands out to his sides. "You guys agree? It's him?"

Of course, his men chuckled, nodded their heads, and settled glaring eyes on my bud.

Head hung, shoulders slumped, Nick took on the profile of someone that was found out, beaten, and out smarted. He should've been scare to death, instead a whole new personality emerged. One I hadn't seen before.

"That's right, Julian, it was me," Nick said still staring at the ground. "And I'm here to stop you." He raised his head and glared defiantly at White Suit Julian. I'd never seen him more serious, more intent on what he was saying. "Pot is one thing, but this is seriously bad. Ingest too much Sapphire and you die. A regular dose and your customers are hooked, can't function with out it, can't think for themselves—for life! There's no doing a hit of this stuff every once in a while. Sapphire has the potential to condemn the entire human race, weakening us, and leaving us little more than zombies commanded by morons like you!"

Julian punched Nick in the gut so hard, even I had to squint my eyes shut. Nick doubled over and coughed. I said a silent prayer that they didn't crush the nacho chips in Nick's backpack. I could smell them a mile away. *Mmmm*, nacho chips!

"Who are you to decide? Huh? People have free will—they do what they want. And if they have the money for a Sapphire high, then who am I to deny them?"

"One hit of Sapphire and their free will is gone!" Nick struggled against his captors. "Sapphire takes them over and they become human shells with no zest for life. They just sit around, staring, but as soon as they're shown more of the blue stuff they come to life and claw your face off to get to it!"

Julian laughed and shook his head while pacing in a circle close to Nick.

"You think this is all a game?"

"NO! This is business!" Julian jabbed a finger in Nick's chest, then turned as a barrel, heavy with wet cement, was rolled close by. "And so is this." Julian gestured to the barrel and its contents.

"Have you tried Sapphire yourself?" Nick blurted out as two of the thugs pushed him toward the barrel. "Of course you haven't, or you wouldn't be able to think, much less do all the things you're doing right now."

Julian stopped and turned to look at Nick, his hands held out to his sides. "And why would I care?"

Nick stopped fighting his captors, almost defeated. "It can't always be about the money. If it were *your* younger sister hooked on Sapphire, you'd do everything you could to destroy it."

My long, pointed ears pricked up. Sister? Did he mean Rebecca? *No!* Not beautiful, model material, I'm going to be a rock star Rebecca!

"So you're some DEA agent now? Because you got a family member hooked on Sapphire?"

"Not my own. Someone close. I see what Sapphire does. I've been to the hang-outs where the junkies are." Julian turned his back on Nick as the kid stated his case. I hoped he might be getting to Mr. Hot Shot Dealer. Even the hardest, toughest of criminals have a soft spot for family. . "Julian, you have to listen to me..."

"I don't have to do crap !" Julian spat on the ground in front of Nick. "I don't hold a gun to their heads. People use Sapphire all on their own. " Julian jerked a thumb at the mixture-filled container and walked away. "Get him in the barrel before the cement hardens."

You're making a big mistake, Julian!" Nick dug his feet in, trying to stop the forward motion towards the barrel as he was manhandled. "Sapphire makes you a zombie!" They drug him closer to the barrel and stirred the cement a bit more with a nearby board. "And your brother is one of them!"

Everyone froze in mid-motion, and all eyes turned to Julian, who paused and looked at the ground. His body trembled with anger at the accusation, but instead of turning on Nick and rushing to beat him to a bloody pulp, Julian collected his thoughts, cracked his neck and sighed. This may not have been a good thing. I feared the nacho chips where in particular danger.

"What did you say?" He didn't turn around. He didn't pull out the switchblade. He just stood still, hands on hips, shaking his head and smiling with a look of amused disbelief.

"It's true. I saw him in the alley next to the abandoned building where all the Sapphire zombies hang out. He's there. You've got to save him."

Julian slowly turned around and approached Nick. "*My* brother, huh?"

The kid nodded, hopeful that Julian would believe him and allow him to lead the way for a rescue. But I wasn't sure that's how this was going to go down.

"My brother is in California, running our club! You're a liar, Nick." The crack of a swift backhand echoed in the dark.

"Your *younger* brother!"

"Get him outa here, now!" Julian turned away. "Squirrel, go check." Julian thumbed for the jittery guy to go see if what Nick said was true, and I'd have thought he would wait and see if the information panned out before condemning Nick to the cement barrel. But, no.

Tired of the struggle, the thugs picked Nick up under his legs and lifted him high enough to drop him in.

That was it. Time to step in.

I took flight, circling high above the men, and knocked out all the nearby streetlights with my talons, plunging the alley into darkness and causing confusion among the gang. Though they couldn't see what was going on, I could see everything perfectly.

A cry of alarm rose up as Nick tried to break away, but the men weren't easily fooled. One guy seized Nick as the others pulled out machine guns. I flew from rooftop to rooftop; my leathery wings catching on poles and pieces of metal making them wobble and twang. The scraping gave away my position several times, and the thugs were quick to zero in on me.

Gunfire rang out. I rebounded from the sides of the buildings using my strength and clawed feet to grip, then push away as bullets ricochet off cement or embedded in brick, wood, and metal. I felt the skin tear on my upper arm as one of the projectiles grazed it, and I roared in pain and anger.

I was going in.

The men shouted and screamed as I slashed through their group, huddled together in the darkness. They may have thought there was safety in numbers, but for me it was like fish in a barrel. Speaking of which—I grabbed the nearest thug by his machine gun and slung him into the barrel, tipping over its thick oozy contents and sending him over the edge of the pier and into the dark water below.

A smash to the back of my head with a shovel barely fazed me, and I quickly turned on the idiot who'd thought that was a great idea. I grabbed him by the arms, lifting his feet from the ground and roared so powerfully his hair and skin blew back. I'm sure he got a brief glance of my face before he became airborne, sailing over the nearest roof and landing, well, somewhere—in pieces most likely.

Even with all the damage I had done to his men, Julian wasn't going to give up. "Stay back!" He wrapped one arm around Nick's neck, choking him, and put his gun to the kid's head. "I'll kill him, I swear I will!" Wild eyed and sweating, he waved the gun from side-to-side, fired off a few shots into the mist to let me know he meant business, and then returned the gun barrel to Nick's head. "Back off, or he dies!"

"Not on my watch," I said, as I stood to my full height of seven feet and walked on my hind legs toward him. Growling deeply, I opened my wings wide, and allowed the natural red in my eyes to glint in the dim moonlight. I stopped about seven feet away from them, partly shrouded in the fog, and tried to look as ominous as I could.

Julian, well, I thought he would pass out at the sight of me. He stood fixated, body uncontrollably trembling and mouth hanging open as terror enveloped him.

"I am your demon, Julian. You made me and I live in your mind." I growled more, and snarled for effect. "Your lust for Sapphire has brought me to life !"

"No! Go away!" Julian started to back away. Nick was now forgotten.

"I will be with you until the day you die unless you stop dealing!" I revealed my front talons, erupting with a scraping *sching!* like pulling a sword along metal.

"Ahhhh!" Julian fell and tried to crawl away, messing up that sparkling white suit and cutting his hands on broken glass as he went.

"I am your creation, like Sapphire, like all the people whose lives you've destroyed!" I roared.

Julian jumped up and ran—a wet spot evident on the front of his pants.

Sitting on my haunches I relaxed and folded my wings. Nick got up, dusted his self off, and found his backpack. I greeted him with a brotherly hug.

"You okay?"

He was like a child in trouble, and didn't look at me. Finally, he lifted his chin and faced me. "Yeah." He ran shaky fingers through his hair. "Thanks Goji. Guess I really got myself in a mess that time, huh?"

"Dude, this has got to stop. But I'm proud of you."

"Yeah?"

"Sure! You were trying to be a hero, trying to stop the bad guys zombifying people. You know, putting your life on the line to save others." Silence fell between us for a few seconds before I loomed in close and bared my fangs at him. "That doesn't mean you can do it again, cool?"

Nick smiled, reached into his backpack, and handed me the bag of nacho chips I had been anxiously waiting for. I ripped open the bag and looked in. "Awww, man." I turned the bag over and tiny, mashed up crumbs poured out. "Crushed? Crushed! Noooo, they're crushed!" I tried not to cry.

"I'm sorry, Goji."

"Seriously? And they were cool ranch flavored! I've been waiting for these all day. How am I going to get my nacho chip fix? The sun is about to come up in like, what, an hour, hour and a half? Even the convenience store on the corner isn't open!"

"I know that's a bummer, but I have a little something to fix that whole turning to stone during the day thing." Nick dug in his pocket and pulled out a dark stone laced with red. "A bloodstone."

"The stone of my clan!" I beamed with astonishment and pride. "You clever little thief, you." And I flashed him a toothy smile.

"Yep. Took me a while to acquire, but it was worth it."

"How's this gonna work?" I was too excited to think straight. "Do I wear it, or eat it or put it up my—"

"NO, not that extreme! The sun comes up. You turn to stone. I use some of this cement to attach it to your chest. Then you wake up—forever."

"Forever?"

"Yeah. You sleep when you want to, just like any other mammal." Nick picked up a soda can and used Julian's knife to cut off the top, and then, scooped up a bit of the wet cement.

"And the Bloodstone?"

"Ah, well, I dunno," Nick tried to avoid my eyes and shrugged. "I guess it stays attached to you, wherever I put it." He flashed me a lopsided grin. "We'll find out, Goji, you and me. Don't worry. And no matter what, I'll stay by your side just like you've always stayed by mine."

I returned the grin as we fist-bumped. "Come on. We don't have much time left."

I got on all fours and stooped down low enough for Nick to get on my back. Once he wrapped his arms around my neck, I blasted into the nearly dawn sky. We had to hurry and find a safe place for me to stone-sleep until he could fix me up. Yeah, fix me up!

"This is gonna be great," Nick laughed.

"What's gonna be great is you getting me a new bag of uncrushed cool ranch nacho chips, man."

"No problem."

"Nick. Seriously. I'm not playin around."

"Dude. You're going to get your nacho chips. I promise."

But even as we joked around and celebrated my impending freedom, I knew we both thought about Sapphire and wondered if there was another lab, another dealer.

Up Where the Clouds Are Red
Adam Millard

"Flight without feathers is not easy." – Plautus

His first lesson of the day was with an eighteen-year-old kid named, of all things, Everton, after his father's favorite soccer team. As Al completed the pre-flight inspection on the Skyhawk, Everton followed him closely around the plane, asking questions enthusiastically and generally getting in the way. It was Al's job to teach this novice everything there was to know about this plane, and yet the constant beating just behind his eye-socket and the pain gnawing at his temples prevented him from going into too much detail. The sooner this one was over with, the better.

"Empennage, fuselage, power-plant," Al said, motioning to each section of the aircraft. "These here are your ailerons, and that right back there is the rudder. Without these, you wouldn't be able to turn. You'd just keep on going until you fell of the edge of the world." It was a non-joke, but Everton laughed anyway. Once the kid had settled down again, Al went on. "You'll notice on this particular aircraft that the wings are on top of the fuselage. That's because it's a high-wing plane."

"Makes sense," Everton said. Al could see he was losing the kid. It was best to just skip the formalities and get the show on the road; kids these days had the attention span of a fruit fly.

Once inside the Cessna, Everton seemed to brighten, and even more so when Al began taxiing across the runway. The migraine, like long, icy needles scraping at the inside of his skull, had begun to wither, and for that Al was eternally grateful. There was nothing worse than hitting nine-thousand feet with a thumping head, and it was always embarrassing to upchuck into the cockpit whilst you had a student up there—which had happened only once in recent years, following a weekend of ill-advised debauchery.

After a little back and forth on the radio with Joe, who informed him that the weather was just fine and he was good to go, Al ran through the instrument panel in the cockpit.

"That there's your attitude indicator, and over there you have what we like to call the 'Six Pack'—"

"Have you ever crashed?" The question came out of nowhere, but with an eagerness which suggested Everton had been dying to ask it for some time now.

With a shake of the head, Al said, "Not once in over eight-hundred-thousand hours of flying. And, you know, you shouldn't really think like that if this is something you're serious about. You'll see how easy it is once we're up there, and do you know *why* it's so easy?"

"Computers?" Everton said, which was pretty much the answer to everything these days.

"Nope," Al said. And then, "A plane is designed to fly. It *wants* to fly. That's its only purpose."

"Why do they crash all the time, then?" asked Everton. "If they want to fly, why do they sometimes drop out of the sky like—"

"Why do cars sometimes crash and trains sometimes derail? Shit, Everton, do you even *want* to learn how to fly, or is this some sort of prank? I've got better things to be doing than answering your dumb questions."

Everton held up placatory hands. "Hey, I was just curious, is all. I admit, I don't know jack about planes, but I'm willing to learn."

And then, Al saw it. It was in the eyes; a look of pure fascination as they darted around the cockpit at the myriad instruments, the throttle, the yoke. The kid *did* want to learn; he was simply overwhelmed. Al had been just the same when he'd climbed into his first cockpit back in '87.

"Hey, I'm sorry, okay?" Al didn't know what else to say. The last thing he wanted was negative feedback on the website, for he knew the UK CAA checked up on it, from time to time. Too many bad experiences on record would result in a visit from one of the Civil Aviation Authority's suited automatons. "Just, do me favor, will you? No more talk about crashing."

Everton nodded. "Got it," he said. "Like how you can't say bomb on a commercial jet, right?"

"Something like that."

Two minutes later, the Cessna was barreling along the runway, Al having advanced the throttle and checked the mixture rich.

"Power available," Al said, even though it meant nothing to the kid sitting adjacent to him. "Airspeed alive. Now, Everton, I want you to watch that dial there, okay? When it gets to 55 KIAS, I want you to slowly pull back on the yoke. Don't just yank it back like you do in your mom's Fiat; ease it slowly back. Got it?"

Everton looked nervous, but he nodded anyway. "Shouldn't you do it?" he asked with frank incredulity.

"If you do it nice and slow," Al said, "there's very little that can go wrong."

"Okay."

And so, when the KIAS climbed to 55, Everton did as he had been instructed. The nose of the Cessna lifted, and within one minute they had climbed to 1,500 feet. Al took a little off the throttle—down to 75 Knots—and settled back in his seat. It was, he couldn't help but admit, a near-perfect take-off.

"We're going to continue to climb slowly now for a few minutes, so ease the yoke back in just a… that's it, right there, and just let her go." Al enjoyed this part of the flight. The ascent. Truth be told, he just liked the fact that he was putting distance between himself and the earth. All his problems were down there. Up here, they couldn't touch him. Up here, he was free, if only for a moment.

A blithe god amongst the gossamer-thin clouds.

Upon turning, Al saw the beatific smile stretching across Everton's face as he stared down at the world passing by beneath them.

"Beautiful, isn't it?" Al asked. "Take out the motorways and ring roads and you'd have a pretty wonderful vista."

"I can't believe... I'm actually flying!" His knuckles had turned white as he gripped the yoke with both hands. Al knew that, should he check, the lad's palms would be clammy with sweat. It was natural amongst beginners, for taking to the skies in a light aircraft was a wholly different animal to jetting to Magaluf on a 747 with three-hundred other souls on board.

"Okay, we're fast approaching our maximum altitude for today," Al said as the Cessna moved up through a sea of fine white stratocumuli. Most introductory sessions topped out at five-thousand feet, but Al wanted to take the kid up above the blanket of clouds. "I wouldn't want to take her any higher than seven-thou. Gets a bit choppy up there." He levelled the plane out and pulled the yoke to the right, pushing the right rudder pedal to the floor. The Cessna began to slowly turn back.

"What do you think?" Al said. "Think it's something you could get used to?" His headache was completely gone; either the altitude had relieved some pressure or the pills Joe had given him were of a decent quality.

"I don't *ever* want to go back down," Everton said. "Is that wrong? I don't think that's normal, is it?"

"Perfectly," Al reassured the kid, straightening the Cessna once again. Beneath them, the clouds grew thick. The ground was no longer visible through the blanket. "I remember the first time I came up here," he went on. "I was eight years old, and my father used to bring me along on his lessons, provided the student didn't mind. My father—"

might be dead right now

"—taught me how everything worked up here. I spent most of my early life naming clouds and, when I was older and my father trusted me enough, navigating from airfield to airfield." He paused, remembering everything so vividly, wishing away the stuff that followed, spoiling all that came before it. "It was, of course, no surprise when I became an instructor by the age of twenty. I worked with my father for nineteen years, and then—"

he should be dead by now

"—he got sick. Too sick to continue with the business. He sold up, and I started working here." Why was he telling the lad all this... this *stuff*? He hated talking about it to anyone, couldn't even run it by a counsellor for that very reason, and yet here he was, spilling his guts as if it were nothing more emotionally grueling than reciting a shopping list aloud or lying to Joe about weekend conquests that simply had not happened.

He could see he was making Everton uncomfortable; the poor sonofabitch was staring fixedly down at the yoke as it rattled slightly left and right, for anything was better than looking into the eyes of the stranger whose sad story meant nothing to him.

"I'm sorry," Al said, straightening up in his seat, for he had slipped down into it somewhat. "How very unprofessional of me. Do you think you could tell me how we drop down to 3,000 feet?"

Everton patted confidently upon the yoke. "Push this in?" he said.

"You've got it!" Al said. "So slowly do that, and we'll..." He trailed off there as something off in the distance caught his attention.

Perhaps a mile in front of the Cessna, something red hovered above the pale white bed of clouds. Al leaned forward in his seat, squinted against the sunlight to his right in an attempt to better identify the anomaly.

"What is that?" Everton had also spotted the strange scarlet entity.

"I have absolutely no idea," Al replied. Could it be a trick of the light, the sun limning the tops of the clouds in such a way that it transformed them into something wholly beautiful? Whatever it was,

Al found himself inexorably drawn to the object, could not take his eyes off it for fear it might disappear, never to return.

As it drew closer, and as Al became more and more breathless with fascination, Everton said, "It looks like a cloud. A *red* cloud."

That was precisely what it looked like. Al could see right through it now; its opaqueness had merely been apparent from a distance. Up close it was smoke, like the tendrils of a flare.

"I've never seen anything like it." Al slowly dropped the Cessna down a few hundred feet, so that the red cloud was directly in front of the plane. A cursory glance out of the window to his right brought with it even more enchantment. "There!" he gasped. "There's another one over there!"

"And my side, too," Everton said, pointing down and to the left. When he turned to face Al, his countenance was riddled with fear. "What if it's some sort of chemical thing?" he said, his mouth ostensibly dry. "Like, I don't know, a dirty bomb, or something?"

Al shook his head. "I don't think so. Look, it's moving." He pointed to the object directly in front of the plane. It was indeed moving. Shifting, expanding, crawling through the sky. *A sentient cloud?* "It's just nature's way of reminding us the world is a beautiful place," he said, if only to put his student at ease.

"We're not going through it, are we?" Everton's eyes were wide now. A thin sheen of sweat coated his forehead and aquiline nose.

"We're already inside of it," Al said, motioning to the pink miasma beyond the cockpit window. "It's just a cloud, is all." *A red cloud,* he thought incredulously. *One of many, scattered all across the sky.* "We'll be through it in a moment, and then we'll get back to the airfield."

Relief seemed to wash over the kid. "Cool," he said.

As they flew onward, the red cloud became thinner and thinner, until it was no longer visible, but Al knew if he were to turn the plane around it would still be there, along with the others.

Part of him was terrified, and yet he knew not why. "Okay, kid, take us down to 2,500. We'll be back on solid ground in five minutes' time. I don't know about you, but I'm gasping for a cup of coffee."

Everton eased the yoke in, sighing heavily as he went about it.

§

Joe was waiting in front of the hangar when Al brought the plane around front. His hands were filthy with grease, as were his blue coveralls and the silly train engineer hat sitting atop his head. As he approached the Cessna, he worked at his grimy palms with an equally oil-stained rag, but Al was more interested by the frown his friend wore as he came across the runway to where the plane came to a halt.

"You did good up there, kid," Al said. "A lot of people think they have it in them until they get up above the clouds, and then they tend to freak out. But, no, you've got the right attitude."

"It was awesome," Everton said unclipping his belt. "Just wish I'd learned more."

"If you come back next week," Al said, "I'll show you how to lean the mixture at 3,000 feet."

The kid laughed nervously. "I have no idea what that even means," he said, "but I'm definitely willing to learn."

Al undid his own belt and shoulder harness before pushing open the door. And that was when he saw Joe standing there, staring up at the plane as if it were a baked potato with cheese for wings.

"What the hell you been *doing* up there?" Joe asked, his mouth agape and his eyes unblinking.

Al climbed down from the Cessna. "Saw some really strange things. You ever heard of red clouds, Joe?"

"Can't say I have," Joe said, seemingly staring past Al toward the plane. "But I can see you went straight through one. Either that or you hit a flock of pigeons on your way down." He lifted a huge arm, extended a sausage-thick finger toward the Cessna.

Al turned just as Everton came around the front of the plane, both of them transfixed by the strange red... *substance* coating the aircraft. "Holy shit, what is that?" For Al was no scientist, but he was familiar enough with the skies to know that clouds seldom clung to a plane like window putty when you past through them.

And yet, the Cessna was enveloped by the stuff. Before Al knew what was going on, Joe was already running a hand along the fuselage, sniffing the crimson matter. For the briefest of moments, Al thought his buddy was going to lick a little from his palm. A dangerous Pepsi-challenge, even by Joe's standards.

Everton, too, was mesmerized by the red ooze, for that was what it was. A gelatinous substance of unknown origin, and the kid was haphazardly poking and prodding at it on the underside of the Cessna's wing. "I should go home now," the kid said. "I really want to go home now." He turned his back to the aircraft.

And then, he screeched and the pigment disappeared from his eyes in an instant. Al didn't know what was going on, but took a few steps away from the kid all the same.

That was when Joe unleashed a guttural roar off to Al's left, and when Al turned, he saw that Joe, too, now possessed milky-white cataracts. His face was contorted with pure rage. The viscous red substance dripped from his knuckles and fingertips.

Al backed away even further as he suddenly realized the red stuff on the aircraft was the cause of all this.

Whatever *this* was.

Another plaintive screech from Everton elicited the same from Joe, and then they were both running for Al, staccato grunts emerging with each stride they took.

Post-haste, Al turned and raced across the airfield. He wasn't as fit as he used to be—years of alcohol abuse and bad diet had added twenty years, not that he would have complained under ordinary circumstances—but he managed to put some distance between himself and the two lunatics in pursuit.

As Al reached the airfield office, he came to a stop at the door and glanced back across his shoulder. There, out in front, was the kid; Joe's age and cumbersome build meant he couldn't quite keep up with Everton.

"What in the name of…!?" Al said as he flung open the office door, closed it behind him, turned the key, then proceeded to drag a filing cabinet across to barricade the damn thing.

He was taking no chances. Whatever had happened to Joe, to Everton, had happened because they had come into contact with that red stuff. It might have had the consistency of squashed cherries, but it had the propensity to turn even the most loyal of friends into some sort of mindless shrilling psychopath.

Al recoiled in horror as something heavy slammed into the barricaded door. Then came the racket as first two hands beat upon the wood, then four, their frantic hammering punctuated by lethargic groans and wet choking laments.

This isn't happening! This can't be happening!

As Joe and Everton continued to beat upon the barricaded door—it shook violently with each new attack—Al rushed across the office to where the ATC radio sat upon a waist-level cabinet. He switched the machine on and began searching through the frequencies.

Each new voice coming from the speakers was filled with terror or dread.

"…some sort of… red slime!"

"… all over me, man! It's all over me and it burns!"

"… do not land. I repeat! Do not land, N61848!"

"… Argh! Get it offa me! Get it the hell offa me!"

Al slumped to the floor as the voices came through on a wave of static. This was not a local crisis. Those red clouds, whatever they were, had affected every single light aircraft in the county, which meant more of those things were already out there.

"… this is Delta flight DL9344 arriving from Amsterdam in a little over ten minutes. We appear to be experiencing some sort of red mist on our descent. Any news? Over."

Al closed his eyes, caught his breath, and urged himself to waken from this nightmare. He thought for a moment of his dying father, lying there in that cold hospital room while machines beeped incessantly all around him and the nurses arrived on some sort of indiscriminate schedule to empty his catheter bag.

He thought about his father, and he envied him, for his father would never know of the horrors that would ultimately bring the world to its knees. He would never see a red cloud, up there above the ivory white ones. He would die blissfully unaware, as he would have anyway.

The door to the office crashed inward, toppling the filing cabinet, and then Joe was scrabbling over it, over the kid Everton.

To get to Al.

Cemetery Angels

Trisha J. Wooldridge

I ***knew cemeteries were safe, because that was the only place*** Mom never locked the car.

She did everywhere else, and I mean *everywhere*, even when she was going into the Dairy Mart one street over to get scratch tickets and milk. And then, she'd make sure the doors were locked while she balanced the scratch tickets on the rim of the steering wheel so she wouldn't accidentally honk the horn. She needed to know right away if she won.

Cemeteries also had angels. I knew they were only disguised as statues. They winked at me once in a while, and sometimes I could hear them shifting, their wing "feathers" scraping against each other, sounding like how only cement feathers can sound.

Daddy was in the cemetery, because he'd died of a heart attack two years ago. Mom's parents and grandparents were there, too.

We visited once a week. Mom said Dad and she had waited ten years to adopt me, so he'd make sure to be there to see me even though I couldn't see him. If someone's birthday or anniversary happened on another day of the week, we'd go an extra time. And for holidays, like all the military ones because my Daddy was a veteran in Iraq, and for Christmas and Mother's Day and Father's Day and Grandparents' Day.

It wasn't sad, either, like people always think. Not only because of the angels, but because Mom wouldn't be sad. If we had a long day of errands, we'd pick up McDonald's or Wendy's and grab the blanket that was always in the back (because, Mom said, what if the car broke down in the middle of winter?) and we'd have lunch with Daddy.

We'd visit Mom's grandparents and parents first, because they were closer to the entrance, where the stones were not as shiny but had better statues. Bachi and Jaju's stone had a Virgin Mary face that would look up from the Baby Jesus she held and smile just for me. Mom would water the planters of carnations, geraniums, and green stuff from Memorial Day to Labor Day, when we were allowed to have planters. She always kept 2-liter soda bottles of water in the trunk in case the radiator needed it, or we were stuck in a snowstorm somewhere and needed water (we'd have to melt it, of course), or if we were at the cemetery and the plants needed watering—which is what it was used for most of the time. Mom told me her mother, my bachi, had taught her to come regularly to clean the stones, water the plants, and visit.

Mom would say an "Our Father" and a "Hail Mary" and a few other prayers, then tell them newsworthy items, like if I got all good marks on my report card again and how her deliveries were going and how tall I was getting. Then, we'd go down a few rows to where her grandparents were. They had an angel on top of their stone. If the angel wasn't on the stone, I think she'd be about as big as me, a normal-sized eight-year-old. She had the face of a grown-up, though, and usually her eyes were closed. Except for when I'd rush through "Our Father" and "Hail Mary" and I'd be stuck waiting because Mom had only gotten to "lead us not into temptation… but deliver us from evil"—which she always repeated a few extra times—and hadn't even begun her "Hail Mary." While I was trying not to be impatient, because I didn't know my grandparents, much less Mom's, the angel would look at me or shift her weight or adjust her wings.

This last visit, I must have been acting especially bugs-in-my-pants because she gave me a particularly dirty look. So, I stuck my tongue out at her. Who did she think she was? Mom caught me, though, and told me that was disrespectful and what if her grandparents saw that and their feelings were hurt?

I tried to tell Mom about the angel's dirty look, but she said that was ridiculous. "It's a statue, Lil. It doesn't make faces."

She turned and walked away. I was stunned. I'd always talked about the angels protecting us and keeping an eye on us. She agreed then! Why was this different?

I didn't press. This hadn't been the first incident of her changing things on me. She always used to agree with the stories I would tell her, too, but now, especially if we were out on errands or if I had homework to do, she'd be upset at my stories. There was no use arguing, and my breath was tied up jogging after her fast pace.

Daddy's grave was in the newer part of the cemetery, a long walk from my grandparents with several rows of stones between us and the car. Usually, we'd walk slowly, and Mom would tell me how to say the pretty Polish names that magically turned all the hard letters into flowing, curvy words. Walczak: Fahl-chak. Szczepanski: Sh-cheh-pahn-skee. Gryzbowski: Greejh-bow-shkee.

Walking to Dad's grave, we passed lots of pretty angel statues and stones. The planter flowers might be dry and dying, but the carved roses on the stones would open and bloom even bigger when I looked at them. The grown-up Jesuses always seemed to have the happiest smiles of all when I passed. Mom said that Jesus liked kids.

On this trip to Dad's grave, Mom kept glancing back towards the car. She seemed to step more stiffly, crunching harder on the yellow grass.

"What's wrong?"

"Nothing, sweetheart."

I didn't say anything because she said "nothing" the same way I said "nothing" when I didn't want to talk about something. Usually, though, it was because I'd done something wrong and didn't want to get blamed, and that didn't make any sense for Mom right now. Maybe it was the kind of "nothing" that meant something hurt, like when I got into an argument with my best friend Millie, and I needed to think about it more. Maybe Mom was upset because she'd snapped at me and had to think about it.

Except something just felt weird. It was colder, and the angels weren't moving as we walked to Daddy's shiny black gravestone. I glanced back to the car and saw that someone had parked behind us. The other car was what Daddy would've called a Bondo-mobile and had mismatched fenders. It was the kind of car that I usually saw in the neighborhoods Mom double-made-sure we locked our doors in— even when we were driving. I didn't see anyone at any of the stones, either, and two guys looked like they were arguing in the front seat.

When we got to Daddy's grave, Mom gave me the soda bottle of water. At Daddy's grave, I was responsible for doing what she did for her parents' stone: brush off the dirt that collected on the headstone's flat surfaces, water the flowers, pull off dead leaves. Mom took extra long at Dad's grave this visit, though she didn't say much besides her prayers. She had me talk about school and my friends and how we were planning my birthday party for two weeks after school started. She even had me recite my whole list of what I wanted for my birthday.

Daddy didn't have a statue or a face on his gravestone. He just had a cross with ribbons, a flag, and carved borders. Mom had said he didn't want more. Sometimes it looked like the flag and ribbons on his stone would flutter along with the small flag stuck above the bronze plate that showed his military service, but they were stone-still now.

"All right," Mom said, sounding like she was trying not to grind her teeth. "Let's go, Lillian."

"What's wrong?" I asked again. She hardly ever called me Lillian.

"Nothing. Just…stay with me and do what I say."

"But—"

"No buts."

She hardly ever used the "No buts" with me, either. Usually we could talk about things, but her voice closed the conversation as hard as her hand closed around my arm and marched me back to the car. Her other arm clenched over her purse.

"You don't like that other car? You think they're Bad People?" I knew there were Bad People in the world, people who would hurt other people—especially kids. They lived in those neighborhoods Mom had us double-check the locks in. Anyone anywhere could be a Bad Person, and Mom wanted me to be careful of everyone, even people I knew. Even teachers and priests could be Bad People. I didn't think about it most of the time, but Mom was acting worse than she normally did when we were in a situation where we might run into a Bad Person.

"It…could be nothing." She bit her lip, pulled out her cell phone, and hesitated a moment. "Better to be careful, right?"

As we approached her car, she lifted her chin and narrowed her eyes, slowing her steps. (You always check the back seat when you are approaching a parked car somewhere, even your own driveway.) She froze.

But only for a second.

The world blurred from how fast she spun me. We ran around the front of Mom's Buick. The back door of our car swung open. A hand with a knife grabbed the roof, and out came a large, ghost-pale man who was tangled in Mom's blanket. I saw this in glances as we crossed the road to put more space between us and the man.

Mom let loose one of the words I can't repeat as I felt the sickening swirl of falling to the ground. I scrambled to my feet and felt her give my butt a shove. I looked behind me, and she was also just standing up from our fall.

"Go, go, keep going!" she shouted. I paused. Tears streamed down her face, and I heard her swear again as she tumbled back onto her knee. Her left ankle was swelling and loose pieces of gravel stuck in bloody bits up her shin. She always told me to watch where the pavement ends on the grass; it's uneven and could trip even the most graceful people.

"For God's sake, run Lillian!" She swatted at me with her purse as she got back up. The man still had one leg stuck in the car. The back-seat blanket tangled him, like a plaid costume-ghost was eating his legs. He jumped, shaking our whole car, to kick it off.

I ran.

Behind me, I heard Mom shout and swear more. I heard thuds. I heard a man's voice swear, too, and cry in pain.

I dared glance back. The pale man was holding his head and leaning on a gravestone, but the hand he leaned on seemed to keep slipping off the stone. Mom was running toward me, but slowly, and she was limping. Our empty soda bottles bounced like toys on the grass behind her. There was blood on her turquoise-and-white tote bag.

"Keep going!"

I did as I was told and headed toward where the road curved around this lot. There was one more square of graves before the roads funneled into the main alley terrace that passed the statues of St. Michael, St. Stanislaus, and all the priests who had worked at the Polish church.

The Bondo-mobile squealed around the corner to the road I was headed toward. I stopped myself so hard I fell backwards. My butt crunched dry grass, but I was back on my feet really fast and changed direction.

"Lillian! Where are you going?"

"Daddy!" was all I could say. He was always there, watching, right? He wouldn't let these men hurt me or Mom.

I went by Bachi and Jaju's grave. The Virgin Mary whispered to me, "Good girl, keep going."

I did.

I got to my Mom's grandparents' grave and my lungs were burning. I stopped and looked for Mom. She was behind me, but still slow. There were two men running now. The pale-guy's face was bloody from where I guess Mom kicked him or whacked him with her purse. He was lagging behind, but the second man, who looked like a skeleton in clothes, was catching up. He seemed to keep almost running into gravestones, while Mom slipped between them as if they parted for her. I heard the rustle of cement feathers. Mom's grandparents' angel gave me a look as stern as Mom would have. I nodded and ran.

Then, Mom screamed.

Then, I heard *all* the angels awaken.

The sound of cement wings is like nothing else. When they adjust or shift, it's a soft and rough scrape and sigh. When they open in flight, the movement is a low, gritty growl. When you have a cemetery full of flying stone angels, it's a roar that shakes the ground.

"Keep running!"

Jesus, two stones down, was not smiling. He looked quite angry, but not at me. His thorn-crowned heart was beating as fast and as hard as mine.

The uninjured skeleton man was right in front of me! His eyes were wide, bloodshot, with the pupils so big, they were almost all black. Even though all his veins stuck out over his face and neck and arm bones, he looked every bit as ghostly pale as the other guy. He snorted like a bull-demon through his flaring nose and stank like oniony B.O. I yelped and fell. He grabbed for me. I flailed, hoping to hit or kick him. He backed up enough for me to run.

I ran to Daddy.

The dust from stone and cement wings rose to the sky, dimming the sun. I fell at Daddy's grave. My fingers scraped over the bronze plaque. Tiny drops of blood stung my palms, and I gasped for breath.

"It'll be all right, my angel."

I felt arms around me. Daddy's arms.

I tried to look up, but the angel wing dust stung my eyes and made me cough. He hugged me tighter. I squeezed my eyes open just a little so I could see through my lashes… I could see his ghost.

The car the men had come in was flying up the road. It couldn't seem to go straight, but it aimed up the veterans' path. I couldn't detect any breathing or heartbeat from Dad, of course, but he seemed calm. One hand smoothed my curls, like he used to when I had nightmares.

The angels above us separated, uncovering more sunbeams that made Dad's ghost more invisible. Then darkness and a roar of cement feathers blocked the light for one brief moment.

A whistle of wind introduced a thunderclap as the biggest angel landed his bare feet upon the battered Bondo-mobile's hood, spearing the engine with a giant stone sword. The two front tires popped like gunshots, and the front end's metal screamed as it collapsed. I gasped but wasn't frightened. I recognized Saint Michael the Archangel from the third branching of the main cemetery road. He held the Earth in one hand, his sword in the other—the sword he now pulled from the mostly-cracked-in-half engine.

Inside the car, a third man yelled lots of swears and shoved at his door. St. Michael stood at his full height, much taller than any person I knew, and watched. He pointed his sword towards the man, who started slamming his head into the driver side window till it shattered. Blood covered most of the man's may-as-well-be-a-ghost face and blossomed over his T-shirt and jeans as he fell onto the steering wheel and stopped moving altogether.

I saw the other two men stop and stare at the car. At their slumped friend. At Saint Michael who now pointed his sword at them. They had cuts up and down their arms and legs; their clothing hung in bloody tatters; and the cement dust of circling angel wings above us started to coat them—as if they were transforming into cemetery statues.

They fell to their knees and started babbling—like babies and not sounding like any language I'd ever heard. Then, both of them collapsed.

I heard sirens.

Saint Michael turned to me and Daddy, and nodded. With a crunching whistle, the stone archangel leapt into the air and spread his massive stone wings. The car flattened and broke into pieces from his jump.

The rubbing of cement feathers lessened and disappeared as more sun slipped through the dust and angels. I couldn't see Dad any more, though I could still feel his hand on my head and my head in his lap. More scrape-flapping let me know another cemetery angel approached. It was the me-sized one from Mom's grandparents' grave. Obviously, stone angels are strong, because she carried Mom in her arms all by herself. She stood Mom up, and Mom stared open mouthed at me and Dad. She took a few limping steps toward us.

Toward me.

I don't know when Dad left. I was sitting on the ground, confused, cold, and hurting. Mom closed her eyes. Her grandparents' stone angel floated away, but wind, or maybe Dad, pushed Mom's hair out of her face. Tears came to my eyes, and I couldn't stop them. Mom let herself fall onto her butt beside me and pulled me in her lap. We both cried until the police came.

The two men who hadn't been in the car got resuscitated. One left in an ambulance with a police officer; the other was healthy enough to get stuffed in the back of a police car. The guy behind the wheel was covered with a sheet over his face and left in an ambulance without a siren. I wish I didn't know what that meant, but I did. And it made me sad, even though I knew the man might've killed me and mom with the car.

The police said the men were high on drugs and one had overdosed. The two not-dead druggies were babbling about cemetery statues coming to life. The officers, of course, attributed their "nonsense talk" to the drugs. Mom and I had looked at each other and silently decided not to tell them otherwise.

"We've been looking for these guys for a few weeks," the policewoman explained. "They robbed an old couple at Our Lady of the Rosary last week, and another couple at Oak Hill Cemetery before that. You both should be proud of yourselves."

"I didn't see that in the paper or news." Mom sounded like she wanted to scold the officer for not keeping people informed of such things.

The policewoman shrugged, and then, her voice sounded like she was talking to me more than Mom, so I looked at her. "You did a good job taking care of yourselves and calling us right away. I know it's hard right now, but if you need anything…" She handed Mom a business card.

"We'll call," Mom said.

"Do you want a ride to the doctor's? An escort?"

Mom shook her head and promised to get us to the doctor's. After all, she had a sprained ankle—she'd told me that even before the medics said so. Mom told the policewoman that we just needed some alone time.

The policewoman nodded, but she and her partner insisted on at least walking us back to the car. Mom hesitated a moment before getting in, but then got that stubborn look on her face that people say I got from her. When we pulled off the cemetery road to the main street, Mom let out a deep, ragged breath. Keeping one hand on the wheel, she fished around with the other in her bloodied tote bag. Between her thumb and forefinger, she held up a stone feather.

"My mom always had me take good care of graves," Mom reminded me. "You water the flowers, you take care of the stones… take care of the memories."

I nodded. "And they take care of you?"

"My mother never told me that part. But, if I ever catch you sticking your tongue out at an angel again, so help me, Lillian…"

"Yes, Mom. I'll be good." I slouched into the seat. Looking at my cut-up hands and still feeling my Dad's arms, I could hardly argue.

She snorted a sound between a laugh and a sob. I looked at her. She was blinking, but her lips curled in a little smile as she tucked the stone feather into the side pocket of her purse. "Think this will make a good ticket scratcher? I think the hospital gift shop has tickets. I betcha it's good luck."

Of course Mom had to be practical after all.

An Afternoon in the Park with the Coyote Brothers

Michael M. Jones

I'll come home when my shift is over," I explained to my mother over the phone. "Yes, I know I promised to help Aiko with her homework this week but—it'll be a few more hours. Yes, but—look, you pushed me to get this job, so you can't complain when—I...I'm sorry, I didn't mean to yell. There will be plenty of time to help her before bed."

It took some more apologizing and cajoling, but my mother finally ended the call. I put the phone down on the counter, and then rested my head in my hands, groaning. There were days when it seemed like dueling responsibilities would be the death of me, and they all stemmed from obeying my parents. Get a good education. Get a part-time job. Help my little sister. Don't talk back. Behave. When would I have time to be me? I needed a break. Or something.

The door jangled, and I jerked my head up, plastering a welcoming smile on my face. "Welcome to Desiderata," I greeted.

It was the Coyote Brothers.

I knew who they were, because Izzy had posted their pictures on the staff bulletin board. Underneath, she'd written, "Coyote Brothers. Extreme pains in the ass. Do not buy anything they try to sell you, do not eat anything they offer you, do not make any promises you absolutely cannot keep. Above all else, do not offer them crash space, gas money, alcohol, drugs, or shiny things. Seriously. I mean it."

Seeing as how Desiderata was part antique store, part pawn shop, existing to buy and sell odds and ends from just about anyone, it seemed unusual for Izzy to call people out for something other than passing bad checks or shoplifting. I'd even asked her when I first started working here what these guys had done, and she just sighed. "That's an entire collection of long stories. Someday you'll find out first-hand, and I apologize in advance." When pressed on the matter, she shook her head and sent me to do inventory instead. Now, it looked as though my first-hand experience had arrived.

As the two men approached, I glanced from them to the bulletin board and back again. They matched their photos: two men of indistinct age, both with tanned skin, rugged features, and gold-flecked eyes. One looked kind-of-Caucasian, the other kind-of-Hispanic. They were dressed identically in faded jeans, dusty boots, red plaid flannel shirts, and cowboy hats, looking just like a couple of workers fresh from the farms outside town. They were smiling, but in that "We need to make a good impression because otherwise you're not going to be happy with us" sort of way.

"Is Izzy here?" one asked, the darker-skinned guy whose picture identified him as Raoul.

"I'm afraid she's not in today," I said. "I'm Suzume. How can I help you?"

The other one—Merle—looked me up and down with an arched eyebrow. "You're a little young to work here, aren't you?" He sounded curious rather than judgmental, his drawl just a little more pronounced than Raoul's. "Since when does Izzy hire children?"

Indignant, I puffed up, trying to appear taller than my 4'11 ½". I stepped back into my sandals, gaining an extra inch or so, bolstering my confidence. My Japanese heritage made me short for my age, and it hadn't done much for my figure either. With my lack of curves, people always assumed I was a lot younger. "I'm seventeen!" I insisted. "I usually just work weekends. I'm only here after school today because Izzy had plans she couldn't get out of."

Merle and Raoul exchanged a look. "Plans she couldn't get out of," said one.

"A hot date is more like it," replied the other.

"It's about time. She's always so wound-up when we appear. I've been saying for ages that she needed more action. You think this means she's back with Therese?"

"That would be what, their third break-up and reunion this year alone?"

"Third time's the charm!" They fist-bumped one another, before turning their attentions back to me. "Well, you'll do. Maybe. See, there's a problem."

"Just a little one."

"Tiny."

"Minuscule."

"Hardly worth mentioning."

"In fact, why mention it at all? Tell Izzy we said hi, and we'll catch her next time we're in town. And if she asks anything, we didn't do it."

The rapid back-and-forth made it impossible to keep up with the speaker—after a few minutes, they were indistinguishable, like two sides of a coin, even though they were supposedly brothers in name only. They sidled towards the door.

I cleared my throat and gave them a pointed glare, eyes flicking from the shelf nearest Raoul to his bulging pocket. Without so much as a sheepish look, he put a Russian nesting doll back where it belonged. I switched to Merle. He shrugged, before returning an old deck of cards, a baseball, and a small teddy bear to their spots as well.

"Damn," said Raoul. "She's got The Look down pat. Her stink-eye is better than Izzy's. Reminds me of this nun I knew back in grade school."

Merle nodded in agreement. "Eyes like a hawk." He furrowed his brow, trapping me with an intense, golden stare. "What are you?" he asked me.

"I-what?" I responded.

"What *are* you?"

I narrowed my eyes in return. I couldn't believe these two scruffy weirdos had the audacity to ask me such a rude question. "I'm American," I insisted. "Born and raised right here in Puxhill. My grandparents were Japanese, but they moved here before my parents were born."

Merle blinked, crestfallen. "Aw, no. I didn't mean like—shit, girl, I'm sorry. God, I bet you get a lot of that racist crap, don't you."

Raoul reached over to smack his companion on the back of the head. "Language! Asshole." He offered me a smile. "I'm sorry for Merle. He has no manners. We just meant: what do you become?"

"Pardon?" I asked. This was quickly leaving my comfort zone. Under the counter, my hand inched towards the alarm button which would summon the cops, in case it escalated into an actual problem. Their amiable exterior seemed to be slipping, offering a hint of something serious underneath for a fraction of a second. My skin prickled. How long would it take the police to arrive if I summoned them? What good would it do?

"What do you turn into? What's your other skin?" He waved a hand. "Y'know, your second spirit."

I stared at them, lost for a response.

Merle and Raoul exchanged looks. "She doesn't know."

"She hasn't shed her skin yet."

"She hasn't found her second spirit."

"We need to help her!" They fist-bumped again, and then beamed at me, faces full of good-natured mischief.

I didn't like the turn this was taking. "You're not helping me with anything. In fact, I think you had the right idea when you were leaving. I'll let Izzy know you stopped by."

They were undeterred. "Just tell us something," Merle insisted. "When you dream, is it consistent? Are animals involved?"

"Or birds?"

"Do you dream of running across the plains?"

"Or stalking through the woods?"

"Do you dream of Nature, red in tooth and claw?"

"Or of the tyger, tyger, burning bright?"

"Do you dream of flying?" Merle leaned in, his face almost in mine, as if to find his answers in my eyes.

I froze under his inspection. "Everyone dreams of flying," I murmured. Somehow, they'd struck a chord, deep down, in half-remembered childhood fantasies. Under the counter, my hand, poised on the silent alarm, locked into place an inch away, unable to make the final movement.

"But not everyone dreams of flying as a bird," he said. "Spreading your wings, soaring through the air, dancing in the clouds… how long has this been going on?"

"Since always," I whispered. "How did you know?"

Merle pulled back. "We have a knack for sensing cousins. Though Izzy tends to hire family, so it wasn't too wild a guess. I'm just surprised she hired you with your eyes still closed."

"That's Izzy for you," said Raoul. "She's all responsible and stuff. Comes from being the Raven. I betcha she was working around to it slowly." He shot Merle a wide grin. "Just imagine how grateful she'll be if we help Suzie find her true nature."

"My name is Suzume," I reminded them.

"A pretty name," Merle drawled. "What's it mean?"

"Sparrow," I said. I'd learned the definition when I was barely old enough to say my own name; my parents had emphasized its importance, that it ran in the family. "It means sparrow."

"Suzume, here's what we're gonna do," said Raoul. "You're gonna lock up the shop because this is far more important than buying gewgaws from folks off the street, and we're going to teach you how to fly."

"Oh, and we're going to need beer and barbecue. It's a moral imperative," added Merle.

Given that this proposal broke most of Izzy's rules for dealing with the Coyote Brothers, I shook my head. "No, no, and hell no," I told them. "Not happening, guys." I couldn't explain why, but I no longer feared them; I no longer wanted to trigger the alarm for whatever good it might have done. I held up both my hands to emphasize the repeated "No."

"Call Izzy," suggested Raoul. "Tell her that the Coyote Brothers want to teach you how to fly. Tell her... we'll respect Cousins' Honor." For a moment, I saw past the jokes, to a bone-deep sincerity that blew past my defenses and convinced me they were, at least somewhat, legit.

So, what else could I do? I picked up my phone, and dialed Izzy's home number, the one she'd given me in case of emergencies. She picked up after four rings, sounding quite grumpy at the disturbance. I apologized, and then filled her in. At first, she seemed frustrated, even annoyed. But after I told her what they'd said, repeating Raoul's words, her tone became a mixture of amusement and relief. Her instructions... were unexpected.

I hung up and looked to my two visitors, who were draped against the counter, wearing identical expressions of hopeful anticipation. "She said...she said I should go with you," I informed them, a little dumbstruck. "And to take the petty cash."

"Yes!" They high-fived as they stood up. "Beer! Barbecue! New friend!"

"By the way," Merle told me as I ushered them to the door (once again shaking them down for illicit goods, relieving them each of several small items), "You might not want to ride in the back of the truck. That's Skeeter's spot."

"Who's Skeeter?" I asked.

Skeeter was their cat. Thirty pounds and then some, he was short-haired, mostly white with streaks of grey, black, and silver, huge blue eyes, and a black-ringed tail. When he saw the Coyote Brothers, he started purring like a rusty chainsaw. He shared the back of their pickup truck with an assortment of junk, including shredded lengths of rope, old carpet, and a bolted-down scratching post. The sight of him woke a primal reaction deep in me; I wanted to run—no, fly—away, as quickly as possible. I'd never felt comfortable around cats. They always seemed to be eying me funny and planning something. Skeeter was no different. He yawned at me, displaying huge fangs, and I resisted the urge to flee.

Instead, I ended up riding shotgun, with Merle driving and Raoul keeping Skeeter company in the back. The inside was just as cluttered as I'd expected, the floor under my feet littered with crumpled fast food bags, cigarette butts, and unpaid parking tickets. I scrunched up a little, trying not to touch anything more than I had to. Sometimes it actually paid to be short and slight. Despite the mess and general oddity of my companions, I felt safe. Like I was with family. Okay, really weird family, but the kind that looks out for each other.

Half an hour later, armed with copious amounts of takeout from Bobby Q's Rib Shack, we settled around a table in a nearby park. The Coyote Brothers dug into several racks of the dry rub special, tossing the scraps and bones to Skeeter with wild abandon, while I nibbled on a piece of cornbread and some coleslaw. "You'll need food," they told me, "because it takes a lot of energy to shed your skin. Plus, it's only proper to feed Coyote. Think of it as a sacrifice to avoid accidents. I'm not saying anything *will* happen, but better safe than sorry."

"You're not reassuring me. Could you please just tell me, in a straight-forward manner, what this is all about? This wasn't just an excuse to mooch a picnic off me, was it?" While still wary, I'd begun to relax around Merle and Raoul. I couldn't help it; they had a goofy, charm that grew on you after a while. It didn't hurt that this whole excursion felt like I was playing officially-sanctioned hooky from my obligations, leaving the store behind for this bizarre adventure. It was exhilarating, an unpredictable break from my routine. I'd always wondered what an adventure would feel like.

They exchanged another one of those looks. "Izzy's a lot better at explaining the cosmological stuff," said Merle. "We're more of the cosmo-illogical side of the equation." He flicked a half-eaten rib to Skeeter, who swatted it out of the air with an over-sized paw and set to gnawing it clean with a loud purr that made me twitch. I did *not* trust that cat one bit.

"Once upon a time," Raoul said, "humans and animals lived in a kind of equilibrium. There was a balance in the cycle of life. But stuff happened, and things fell apart." He used both hands as he talked, gesturing wildly to illustrate the story.

"No one's really sure why," interjected Merle. "There's a lot of stories, but it all boils down to someone screwing up. I don't reckon we'll ever know the truth after this long."

"Thing is," continued Raoul, "humans and animals stopped understanding one another, and here we are today, all messed up. However, some folks are still connected to the animal realm. They have an extra spirit. A second skin. An affinity." He finished his beer, crumpled the can, and made a perfect shot into the back of the pick-up truck. "Three points! The crowd goes wild! Er, anyway, that's how you got stories of shapeshifters in every culture and mythology. Explaining them all would take a hell of a long time, mainly because no one's ever been able to identify all the ways in which this connection manifests. Merle and me are Coyote-kin. Coyote gets around, and leaves lots of babies in his—"

"—or her—"

"—wake. It's a Coyote thing, so of course it's complicated," Raoul added, seeing my dubious expression. "I reckon you don't have much background in this sort of thing. You'll learn. Now, take Izzy. She's the Raven. The symbolism varies from place to place."

"Around here, it means she cleans up other peoples' messes."

"Like ours."

"Even when it's an accident. Which it usually is." Merle grinned. "She's like a troubleshooter." He made guns with his fingers and shot them at Raoul, who keeled over dramatically for a second. "Sometimes literally. Once filled my ass with buckshot. Can't blame her. I *was* on fire at the time…"

"So, what exactly does this have to do with me?" I asked, tilting my head. I stuck my plastic fork into the coleslaw, where it stood straight up, like a signpost. "You really think I'm…connected to some animal?"

"Little Cousin, we have no doubt of that. Like we said, we can sniff out our family, however far removed."

"Usually, it's so we know when to start running," interjected Raoul. "Coyote's not what you'd call popular. We have trouble with rules." So, I'd gathered. "Given the evidence at hand, we're pretty sure you're related to Sparrow."

I opened my mouth to say something, but stopped. I had no idea how to respond to that. A sparrow? When you think about shapeshifters, you think of werewolves and stuff. Predators with fangs and claws. I'd read a few paranormal romances, enough to know that no one was impressed by rabbits and mice and little chirpy birds.

They must have seen the disappointment in my eyes. Merle said, "It's not as bad as it seems. Sparrows are important. Some folks consider them to be psychopopes."

"That's psychopomps, you nitwit," Raoul corrected him. "Carriers of dead spirits, basically. On the other hand, Jewish lore says sparrows bring the souls of the newborn to Earth."

"The Indonesians think a sparrow flying into the house is good luck. Although in Europe it's been considered a sign of impending death," Merle added. "Oh yeah! There's even a Japanese fairy tale about sparrows which reward the kind and punish the greedy. That's a good one. A real classic."

"How do you know all this?" I asked them, trying to keep up with the flood of information.

Merle shrugged. "Raoul and me, we get around a lot, talk to all sorts of people. We pick things up along the way. Some folks write everything down, we just store it in our noggins. We're nosy and you never know what'll come in handy." His grin was wide, even infectious. I returned it without thinking. "We kick ass at Trivial Pursuit, too."

"Point is," said Raoul, "you might be a harbinger of death or a bringer of life, a symbol of luck, or an ill omen. It's up to you to figure out your purpose."

"But first," Merle told me, waving a half-eaten rib for emphasis, "you gotta learn how to spread your wings."

"And how do I do that?"

"Easy. Get a running start," Raoul suggested, "and start flapping your arms as hard as you can, while thinking bird thoughts. It'll come to you naturally."

"If it helps, we can have Skeeter chase you," added Merle. At the sound of his name, the giant cat looked up from where he'd been sharpening his claws on the legs of the wooden table, and acknowledged them with a lazy mrowl.

I shuddered. "You can leave your pet mountain lion out of this," I said. "I've seen him eying the wildlife." I looked to Raoul. "It's really that easy?"

"Yup," they both said.

Backed by the Coyotes' contagious confidence, I decided to give it a shot. I kicked off my sandals for better footing, pointed myself at a long stretch of grass, and took off at a sprint. I ran as fast as I could, while flapping my arms like I had as a kid, and tried to think bird thoughts.

Feathers. Wings. Wind. Chirp. Tweet. Umm... *soaring through the air. Freedom from the ground. Dancing in the clouds.* I could do this. I could. Something deep within me responded, stirred, answered the call in my heart. I ran harder, flapped harder, leapt for the sky...

...and landed on my ass.

In the distance where I'd left them, the Coyote Brothers were doubled over with laughter. I stalked back, glaring at them, my feathers-in-metaphor-only ruffled. "You assholes," I growled.

Once they'd stopped howling in amusement, they patted me on the shoulders and offered me a beer, which I turned down in disgust and annoyance. "Sorry, Cousin. Just having a little fun," said Merle. "You should have seen yourself."

I couldn't stay mad for long; I should have known the suggestion was too ridiculous to actually work. I might as well have thrown myself at the ground and missed. I just gave them both The Look again until they wilted. "So, can you help me, or what?"

"Close your eyes," said Merle, his drawl low and soothing. "You need to fully immerse yourself in being a bird. Your second spirit lies deep within you. Look inwards. Find it. Pull it out slowly. Bring it into the light."

"Think of an egg hatching, and your true self emerging for the first time. Feel it. Embrace it. Wear it. You have to let go of a lifetime's accumulation of human baggage; it only weighs you down. Believe you can transform." Raoul joined in, his voice soft and knowing.

I followed their advice. I stood still, eyes closed, letting the words flow over me. I could feel the two circling me as they talked, the words growing indistinct as they seeped into me, sinking into my very essence. Their warmth took root in my heart before spreading outwards, following blood and bone, unlocking mysteries from the world's younger, wilder days. I knew this, and now I'd always known it.

Even with my eyes shut, I could see them now, one a man, one a coyote, as they walked around me. *Join us*, their manner said. *Embrace your true self.* I dug deep for their meaning, looked for the truth. I found that tiny spark deep in my core, where my childhood dreams of flying had nested until I was ready for them to come true. Ever so slowly, I teased them free. I spread my arms up to the sky, fingers splayed, head tilted to find the late afternoon sun. I thought *sparrow—*

--and so it happened. A magnificent, contradictory feeling, it was like simultaneously taking something off and putting it on. I felt light and free, so tiny and yet larger than myself. I opened my eyes, and I saw the world for the first time. Everything had a new texture and vibrancy to it. It shone, and I felt whole.

And there were Merle and Raoul—first they were men, then coyotes, then men with the heads of coyotes, grinning at me with triumph and welcome. "You did it, Little Cousin," said Merle. Ever so gently, he reached down to pick me up and cradle me in a palm grown huge. He lifted me up. "Now fly!" he commanded, swinging his arm and letting go of me at the highest point. Startled, I spread my wings, and long-buried instincts took over. I caught the air, and I soared. I swooped and dove, flying in joyous patterns while my mind raced through a thousand thoughts in a heartbeat. It felt amazing. Fantastic. Bizarre. Unreal. It felt…right. All of my human baggage and worries had been left behind with my crumpled clothes and obedience to gravity.

Eventually, I came to rest on a nearby branch, trying to make sense of it all, trying to cope with the flood of new information.

The Coyote Brothers cheered and hollered. "That was awesome!" Raoul yelled. He wandered over to stand under me. "You're going to want to wear your skin for a bit, just to get used to it. We'll meet you back at the store."

I would have protested their sudden exit, but I hadn't yet figured out how to communicate in this strange new shape. Instead of words, I let loose with a string of angry chirps, which they ignored. They gathered up my discarded clothes, packed up the leftover food, and clambered back into their truck. Skeeter gave me a long, hungry look and licked his lips, but when Merle called his name, he jumped into the back of the truck; it shook under the impact of his landing. As I tried to get my body under control, they peeled out, leaving me to find my own way home.

By the time I reached Desiderata, evening had fallen. I'd gotten lost a number of times, distracted and confused by this fascinating, literal bird's-eye view of the city I'd lived in all my life. Things were different as a bird—my senses worked differently, distances were hard to judge accurately, and streets I knew intimately as a human became strange and disconcerting all over again. I oriented myself by using the sprawling grounds of Tuesday University, unmistakable even from this angle. I knew I'd have a lot of explaining to do when I got home so late, but I had quite a few questions for my parents as well, so we were even.

I wasn't surprised when the Coyote Brothers were nowhere to be found. They'd taped a note to the door which read, "Your clothes are in the package box. Thanks for the gas money. P.S. Tell Izzy we didn't do it."

At first, I was pissed that they'd left before telling me how to reverse the transformation. It took me a while to figure it out. I settled on top of a nearby newspaper vending machine, and concentrated, digging deep to find my "human" skin. I thought of human things and concerns. Work. School. The ache of a stubbed toe, the taste of the cornbread I'd eaten earlier, the feel of a book under my fingers. My sister, who needed help with her homework. My mother, with her expectations. I reached for the things which made me Suzume, and teased at the skin I'd worn for seventeen years.

Just like that, I turned inside-out and became a girl again.

A naked girl. On a dirty metal box. In public. I bolted for the safety of the store.

I'm going to kill the Coyote Brothers next time I see them.

Alchemy

Gregory L. Norris

He started with buttons—three, carefully removed from an old suit that had once been his father's. Buttons were a safe bet. Back in Prosperity following the time after planet-fall—what was now referred to as the Dark Age of Technology—gold buttons were a standard among many of the mining interest's barons and even some of the miners themselves, those lucky enough to stake claims before the K'Sel Ministry of Resources took full possession of the planet.

August Unger made sure the buttons were completely free of threads or any other contamination, also of any identifiers etched into the plastic by the manufacturers that would betray his crime. *Crime.* He snorted a humorless snicker through his nostrils at the notion. Was eating a crime, or keeping the fresh air utility flowing, or having enough to live on?

He clutched the three buttons pulled from a dead pauper's suit, only to think better of it. Donning old work gloves, he wiped the buttons free of fingerprints and entered the stonecutter's workshop at the rear of the crumbling mastaba built of volcanic brick on the eastern slope of Gigantis Mons. Three buttons wouldn't be enough to retire on. Augie laughed again, but the emotion darkened at the image of the lines etched into the doorframe, recording the height of the child he no longer was and hadn't been for almost two decades.

A gust of cooler, sweeter air greeted him beyond the workshop door. The relief owed mostly to the counterfeit jungle of potted plants strung in a green necklace across workbenches and storage shelves, fed on well water and the sunlight filtering down through the oculus. The atmosphere in the room, purified by the plants, stoked his resolve. Augie continued to the back. The row of stone statuary lined along the room's inner brick wall stopped him.

His late father's gargoyles studied him through vacant, wide eyes. Most were complete, in the classic form: hounds with reticulated bat wings, posed on haunches, mouths open to convey rain water from the roofs of cathedrals never built, those mouths open in a kind of sinister grin. Two of the statues weren't finished, and appeared to be frozen while in the act of pulling free from the blocks of volcanic stone.

The craftsmanship was exquisite. But Augie experienced the same chill he always suffered in this part of the mastaba. Blinking out of the trance those statues had cast on him through their scrutiny, he made it to the section of floor with the false bottom. He removed the first of two tiles. The Midas Machine rested under a tarp of green velvet cloth, which kept particulate matter from clogging its intake pores.

Despite his care, the device maintained its ancient appearance, its decorative spools showing a patina of permanent dark stains across etched symbols for which there was no translation available. He'd found the priceless alien tech under the shelf of dusty rock upon which the mastaba's volcano-facing outer wall rested. The scrap of velvet had once belonged to his late mother, part of a dress. That meant the Midas Machine had been in his father's possession, clearly never exploited according to their life in the Gigantis Mons Poortown. And, just as clear, the senior Unger had long ago buried the alien tech rather than give in to any temptation to activate it and potentially better their living situation.

He imagined the gargoyles staring at his back and quivered. For a week following his attempt to shore up that part of the house's sagging floor and the discovery that resulted, Augie had tried to reason the details. Where had his father acquired the odd contraption? Which, again exposed to the too-bright light of K'Sel's Grade-Y sun, began to come alive—*inhaling and exhaling*, he swore. Surely, back then the alien machine had been in a working state. As he pondered, the dual scrolls that formed a kind of dorsal backbone began to turn, like parts of an old music box. The melody was a not unpleasant whine, similar to that of an insect but more a sound of distant traffic or a passenger transport shuttle moving away through the sky. The sound left him with a curious sensation in his stomach, as well as that of a nonexistent breeze gossiping over his skin.

Augie set the three buttons before the device. It didn't matter which end—the mechanism seemed to work equally front to back. From one end of the alien symbols, two feeler-like appendages extended, each thin and straight, though bending at elbows as the tiny arms touched and tendered the objects placed near it. The hum from within the Midas Machine quickened, becoming the furor of an angry hive. The dorsal scrolls flapped like tiny metal wings. Then the noise cut out and the scrolls stilled. The feelers drew back inside the machine, and the magical transformation began.

As he watched, not daring to blink, the three buttons went from worthless plastic to shiny, valuable metal.

Gold, thought Augie.

He picked up the three buttons, expecting them to feel warm against his skin. To his surprise, they were cold.

§

K'Sel's primary planet, an unremarkable gas giant with rusty bands and six other moons, hung bloated atop the horizon. Augie closed the mastaba's shutters to filter out the late afternoon particulates kicked up by the southeasterly wind and dialed up the fresh air. The gold would pay enough for him to splurge on such a luxury. Let the meter run, and the utility company submit its usual barrage of warnings about paying for what he used.

He sat down to a simple meal but only ate a spoonful of the nutritional concentrate before he washed and dried the plate, a survivor from a set dropped and broken over the years. Augie carried it into the workshop. Minutes later, the Midas Machine's insect feelers caressed its surface, recording parameters. The spools turned and flapped in agitation. The elbows straightened and the slender arms pulled back inside the hieroglyphs. The plate, made of ceramic, had been alchemized into solid gold.

Presented in front of him was a small fortune. The problem, Augie thought, was that it was still *small*.

§

Six decades earlier, K'Sel Mining had made planet-fall on the gas giant's sparsely forested moon, and sent its surface strippers loose on sands and strata rich in platinum, tungsten, and gold. The juggernauts chewed through soil, separating troves of raw materials. In volcanic regions like Gigantis Mons, workers were brought in for mineral mining and the building of infrastructure, thousands seduced by the guarantee of shared riches.

Augie's father had been one of the duped. Cheap labor, relegated to company-built housing like theirs in Poortown.

The surface separators had uncovered artifacts and entire alien cities covered over by silt and windblown sand. Some of that tech, activated by Ministry of Resources Ministers and curious miners alike, had resulted in the Dark Age. To the dormant volcano's west at five hundred and eleven kilometers, a vast asterisk of ash and rubble still scarred the planet, the result of tampering with one such alien device. The Dead Bloom, as history referred to it, was visible from orbit despite half a century of particulate storms and cyclones.

Perhaps, his father had uncovered the Midas Machine during that time, when possession of alien tech became illegal, some offenses punishable by life sentences. Buried and mostly forgotten, he'd ignored the machine's ability to give his family the life that the Ministry had promised. Gold on K'Sel wasn't in short supply, except for the unskilled labor force brought planetside to dig it out of the volcanic wastes where surface separators couldn't operate with the same ease of human hands.

A plate. Three buttons. He needed to exercise caution. Even if the supply of whatever potion or material contained within the wing-spools was inexhaustible, suspicion for a Poortown stonecutter's son would also be in abundance.

§

Located in the proximal main of Poortown were a handful of Resource Ministry exchanges, where customers who'd come into possession of small amounts of valuable minerals or volcanic gemstones could be paid a fraction of market value for their tailings. Desperate neighbors often went there to barter to pay the fresh air bill or other utilities, or to waste the dusk in one of the slum's numerous watering holes, where tales of the Dark Age of Technology were still being shared through rounds of low-shelf drink.

Augie wandered down Benton Street, past two- and three-story buildings made from crumbling volcanic brick, to the official Gigantis Mons Exchange and Pawnery. The air that morning was unexpectedly light and effortless to breathe, minimal on particulate matter and sulfur. Surely, a good sign, he hoped. The shop window bore the scratches of years of sediment storms, as did the tile in gold paint with black letters. He knew the place well from many desperate past visits.

The Ministry agent who presided over this particular branch of the exchange was a miserable sand baron named Silber. The man's narrow, humorless face had always reminded Augie of one of the gargoyle statues lined up at the back of the stonecutter's workshop. Silber regarded Augie with a pinched scowl as he entered the exchange, his arrival announced by a mechanical bell that lacked all the charm posited by Edgar Allen Poe's tintinnabulations.

The exchange was laid out in an oblong geometry, with private office rooms and weighing booths off to one side and the protected lair where Silber lorded over the desperate behind a reinforced glass window with a tiny slot for communication.

"Can I help you?" the man asked, his voice sounding as unwelcoming as the bell.

Augie reached into his pocket—an action clearly warned against in the protocol signs posted around the room.

"*Slowly*," Silber barked.

Augie willed his fingers to steady and raised those of his free hand in surrender. "I have gold. Just here for a fair exchange."

Fair? The real criminals were men like Silber, who paid less than half of what the weight demanded at market value anywhere else. Forty-three percent, according to the same signs. If you didn't like it, you were welcome to walk out the same way you came in.

Three buttons, just like those on a Minister's coat. Augie set them in the little tray at the base of the window. "How much for these?"

Silber scooped up the buttons and examined them. Among the rules posted was the exchange's right to ask potential customers where they'd sourced their valuables. Silber did.

"Origin?"

"My father's coat," Augie said, which wasn't a lie so much as an omission of part of the truth.

Silber eyed him, the man's disdain clear, before turning toward the scale. The buttons barely amounted to anything, though their weight would bring in more than his stone art had garnered in months. Four months, Augie calculated given that forty-three percent algorithm.

The scale posted additional figures and sang out a mechanical warning. Silber returned to the window. Augie's heart galloped in anticipation, driven into its frenzy by the slippery grin at the corner of the other man's mouth.

"There's a five-point-two percent impurity," Silber said, seeming to bask in that pronouncement. "Anything more than five pays at a lower rate."

"How low?"

"Thirty." Before Augie could respond, Silber added what sounded like standard boilerplate, practiced to perfection. "Substandard material commands substandard payout. Take it or go."

Augie took it. By the satisfied look on Silber's expression, the Minister hadn't doubted he would. Silber counted out the bills and change from a register and returned to the window.

"I can apply this to past-due utilities or direct deposit to your Ministry bank account for an additional fee."

"No," Augie huffed.

Silber slipped the money into the slot. Augie pocketed it. He started to turn, their dealings assumed done.

"You got any more of this sub-gold?"

Frozen in mid-pivot, Augie pondered his response. "Maybe," he said. "Some."

"How much?"

Augie turned back to the window. "Why?"

"There's a client interested in gold. Don't care the purity—demand on Parker's Planet. Or maybe it's New Alaska. Don't matter. What does is that a decent supply would be well received, and at a better market rate if we were to come to an understanding."

Despite the heat holding his body prisoner, a chill teased Augie's nape. He fought the impending shiver, failed. It tumbled down his spine. Silber, looking so pallid and predatory in his sunless lair, wanted to strike a bargain with him? Of all the morning's possible outcomes, he hadn't expected this.

"How about you up this percentage first," Augie boldly said while rattling his hand in his pocket, enough to make the few coins there clink together.

Silber exhaled a sigh. Instead of returning to the register, he reached into his own pocket, producing a thick roll of bills. He counted out three notes and slid them into the tray.

"I'll be in contact," Silber said.

Augie took the money and instantly regretted it.

§

He paced the workshop, knowing he'd made a mistake in agreeing to Silber's offer. Even so, the Midas Machine had already transformed several useless, everyday things into substandard gold. The treasures lined one of the work tables, now cleared of art tools and art-in-progress: a number of loose bricks from the outside of the mastaba, cutlery, a stone cat he'd carved from a block of volcanic rock. The pieces reflected the glare raining down from the oculus at him, painful on the eyes.

The alien device was presently in the process of changing a simple drinking cup into a treasure made of gold. Given the upset in Augie's stomach, he doubted his morning tea would taste any better as a result of sipping it from a king's chalice. The thin feelers swept over the ceramic, recording details, pulled back, and unleashed their alien sorcery.

Another golden object appeared in a workshop that had mostly known poverty, dating back to the start when, promised riches, his father had worked to craft winged gargoyles for cathedrals never built. Augie gave himself permission to hope—with a windfall like the one Silber promised, he could live without worry, here on K'Sel or a dozen other planetary destinations. All that gold was going off world to be laundered—likely to fund conflict of some kind. Some corporate, political, or military war.

Guilt added to his burden at the thought. Like the gold, he could leave K'Sel, with its dusty, dead promises and short but miserable history. Go wherever he wanted. Be whomever he chose.

Steeling himself, Augie picked up the first of a handful of worthless volcanic rocks he'd collected from outside the house. Soon, all would be sizable gold nuggets.

§

He attempted to work, but distraction over waiting kept him from hammer and chisel. Also, the gargoyles seemed to study him more than usual. Augie knew their judging gazes were wholly in his imagination. Still, he returned the Midas Machine to its hiding place and tossed an artist's tarp over the spoils made from rocks, project castoffs, and basic household wares. Occluding their radiance gave the workshop a modicum of its former humble identity—a green oasis where not only Augie's dreams but also those of his father had flourished in spite of their lowly situation.

Neither had prospered with their art. For a time, his father had worked on a contract to sculpt sepulchers and gravestones out of volcanic obsidian. With the memory, Augie felt the gargoyles staring again. Cathedrals weren't built and churches went bankrupt on K'Sel because miners didn't want them. The vacant-eyed gargoyles watched him through the ferns, the potted cycads and ornamental puckerbrush—the most generous of all the oxygen-exuding flora in the workshop. The gargoyles seemed to both judge and implore his conscience. Wasn't he happy in here, using his vision to create, like his father had? And hadn't his father ascended temptation enough to bury the Midas Machine?

Augie again picked up hammer and chisel and returned to one of the stalled projects—a statue of a horse from Earth. For a brief time, work sustained him.

§

He convinced himself to not go any further, either with the alien device or Silber. He'd double his efforts at creating art. There were

Ministers living in expensive homes with large gardens beyond Gigantis Mons and Poortown—if he impressed them with his stonework talents, he'd do with art what Silber offered through gold. But hadn't his father said the very same thing?

A knock sounded at the door, and breathing ceased being easy or even involuntary. Augie sucked down a deep sip of the green-scented air and hastened through the house, where the atmosphere wasn't as fresh or filtered of particulates.

Silber stood outside in the new shadows just past dusk. He was a creature of the night, Augie thought, allergic to sunlight. Again, how much the man resembled one of the stone gargoyles registered, Silber's cloak adding an illusion of dark wings to the image.

Saying nothing, Silber made a move into the mastaba. Augie blocked him from entering.

"I don't think so," Augie started.

"Would you prefer to discuss our business out here in the open?"

Augie considered Silber's threat for the next few, tense seconds. The other man was no more eager to have the arrangement that had brought him so deep into Poortown made public than Augie, and clearly gambled that he'd cave. Augie did. Silber entered the mastaba, stirring the new night's arid dustiness. Augie choked down a dry swallow and tasted something foul, its source the man who'd stormed into his home.

With the door again shut, Augie said, "I've decided to hold onto the few bits of gold I've got."

Silber flashed a malevolent smile. "Oh, you have? Hold onto those few bits, have you?"

"Yes."

"I don't think so, any more than I believe you've got only a few bits, Unger," the gargoyle countered. "You're a stonecutter, like you're father—nothing more. Those gold buttons contained trace amounts of secreted resin from a form of life that went extinct long before the Ministry landed here."

Augie turned away.

"I know that you've laid your hands on some of that alien tech," Silber continued, forcing him to turn back to face the human gargoyle. "What we used to call a 'Gold Bug' or 'Midas Machine' before the Dark Age of Technology. What the people who built those cities under the sands created, we think, as part of their own terraformation plans before they died out. Only three have ever been recovered—and of the three, only one was fully functioning, the life form contained within it still alive! Can you imagine the potential?"

"No," Augie protested.

He reached for the door, intending to show his unwanted guest back out. Silber aimed a bony finger at his face, hardly a threat. "I've already spoken to my client about you and the gold. Where he's taking it for exchange, they don't care about impurities, or that it's been spit out by an extinct race's terraforming tech."

"I don't have—"

"You'll make gold—*and lots of it*—or I'll report you to the Ministry. They'll tear this pit apart and find your Midas Machine, and you'll spend the rest of your life cutting stone, all right. In prison, if you don't do as I tell you, you worthless—"

Augie didn't realize he was still holding the hammer, or remember striking Silber with it, only the surge of rage, which rose red before his eyes, and the crunch of metal against bone. When the spell passed, the gargoyle was crumpled on the floor, gazing up at him through vacant, accusing eyes.

§

Three nights later, another knock sounded on the mastaba's front door. Calmly, resigned to whatever outcome awaited, Augie answered.

A man dressed too well for Poortown stood outside, flanked by men in black uniforms and helmets that hid all but their eyes.

"Mister Unger?" his visitor said, smiling widely and extending a hand adorned in rings of gold with fat squares of precious gemstones.

"Yes," Augie said.

The man glided into the mastaba. "I'm here to take possession. Oh, don't worry, we'll be discreet."

The uniforms followed.

"I would have called on you sooner, only our mutual friend seems to have taken an unplanned holiday. Never mind that, however…"

In the workshop, Augie removed the artist's tarp. Golden bricks and object d'art covered the table.

His visitor's smile widened. "Well, I like what I see."

"Then, you'll love these."

Augie drew down the second tarp. Several winged gargoyles made of gold stared blankly out.

"Magnificent," the man said.

The men in black uniforms entered the workshop. Their leader motioned toward one, who scanned the treasure trove with a wand. The uniform nodded. Another set a metal case on a corner of the worktable and popped the lid. The case was filled with money.

"We're good," his visitor said. "Thank you for doing business."

The uniforms formed a line and began to remove the gold, starting with the gargoyle statues. The well-dressed man started back in the direction of the front door, only to pause.

"That piece," he said, indicating one statue in particular, now being hefted out of the workshop by two men. "I swear it looks familiar, like someone I know."

Augie's already-racing heart attempted to jump out of his chest and into his throat. "That? It's just something I created. A gargoyle."

Then the man smiled, laughed, and continued on his way. Long minutes later, his hired hands and the gold were gone, too, leaving Augie alone in the mastaba, free from all eyes save those in his memory.

Instability

Steven R. Southard

*L*unatic, *Phyneas wondered, or heretic? Perhaps Brother* Eilmer was both. "Did you say you believe a man could *fly*?"

"Yes," the younger monk nodded. "Two have flown already—a Grecian man and a boy. I read an account of it. They made wings of feathers and flapped them with their arms."

Moments before, toting his rags and bucket, Phyneas had trudged up the stairs to the tower of Malmesbury Abbey for his hour of punishment. Expecting to find only birds, he'd discovered Brother Eilmer sketching the jackdaw crows that alit on the crenelated tower railing. The monk's odd drawings showed bird-like wings affixed to a man. When Phyneas had spied the pictures, he'd inquired, but didn't know what to make of Eilmer's strange answers.

"Birds fly because God gave them wings," Phyneas said. "He gave no wings to man."

"He gave us no fins and yet we swim." Eilmer smiled, his blond fringe of hair brightened by the sunlight. "He gave us a mind to figure out how to do things. He even left clues hinting that we should learn to fly. Do you know how many times the words *bird*, *flying*, *eagle*, or *dove* are mentioned in Scripture?"

"No."

"Nine score and four times! Why, the word *wings* alone is cited five score and ten times. I've counted them, in both testaments."

Frowning, Phyneas shook his head. "That doesn't mean—"

"You seek more proof? Look to Psalm Fifty-Five: 'Oh, that I had wings like a dove! For then I would fly away, and be at rest.' Does that not suggest God intends for us to fly?"

Phyneas stared at him, stupefied. "I don't know. It just seems so unusual."

"Exactly so!" Eilmer gave a wide-eyed smile. "Now is the time to try unusual things, new and novel things. We live in *Anno Domini* One Thousand and Four. One millennium since the Blessed Jesus Christ brought His new thoughts to the world. It is a new era, a day for new thinking."

As he talked, Eilmer had begun raising his voice, waving his hands, and speaking faster. Phyneas began paying more attention to the growing excitement than to the words.

"Your expression tells me you still reserve doubts," Eilmer said. "That is understandable, Brother. One day all your doubts will vanish. Until then, I must ask for your silence about this matter. Soon, I will tell the Abbot, all of Malmesbury, and the entire world. For now, however, it is an unfinished dream, too insubstantial to tell others about. I've not even begun to gather all the feathers I will need. Will you promise me to keep this secret?"

The mention of feathers sparked a thought, a way to get Eilmer to pay Phyneas' demeaning penalty for him. "No," he said. "Your idea is heretical, almost blasphemous, and it could get us both excommunicated if anyone else knew. I cannot give you my promise of silence."

Eilmer's shoulders sagged.

"But I can *sell* it to you."

Eilmer's eyes narrowed. "What?"

"I won't say a word to anyone about what you've told me." Phyneas held up his bucket and handful of rags, "if you'll collect the feathers and clean up the bird droppings from the tower roof for me."

Eilmer's face turned sour. "Bird droppings?"

Phyneas nodded. "Each week. For my silence."

With a sigh, Eilmer took the cleaning supplies.

But my duty to the abbey and to God, Phyneas rationalized, *is greater than any promise I make to Eilmer.*

§

Before taking his job, Abbot Beorhtold had imagined it differently. He'd pictured studious examination of the scriptures, and time to write scholarly analyses on Biblical matters.

The wall shelves in his gray office contained rows of books covering every aspect of Christianity, as well as astronomy, history, philosophy, and mathematics. These tomes sat pristine and unopened while his desk stood buried under the monks' work assignment schedules and performance reports, as well as tallies of egg production, document transcription status, bread baking statistics, and every other matter connected with abbatial administration.

He rubbed his naturally bald head near his remaining vestiges of gray hair, as if that could ease his stress or somehow make all the papers fly away.

When a knock sounded at the door, the Abbot groaned. No one ever came to his office with good news. "Come in."

Brother Phyneas entered, a monk well known to the Abbot, but not for positive reasons.

"*Pax vobis*, Father. Forgive me for bothering you, but I've just learned some disturbing news."

Never good news. "Sit down. Go on."

Phyneas related that one of the other monks intended to construct wings and fly from the abbey tower. The Abbot didn't believe a syllable of this preposterous story, but couldn't credit Phyneas with enough creativity to make up such a tale himself.

"Which monk intends to do this?" he asked.

Phyneas shrank back in his chair as if separating himself from the whole matter. "I shouldn't say."

"Tell me, Phyneas."

"Brother Eilmer."

"Eilmer?" The Abbot thumbed through papers as if trying to locate a report on this particular monk. In truth, he knew of the young man. Diligent, industrious, a fast learner in any skill, Eilmer possessed tireless energy according to reports from the Claustral Prior and sub-priors, with no black marks against him.

Reports about Phyneas, however, revealed an inferior monk. He was lazy in his work, critical of others, sloppy in his transcriptions, off key in singing, and often late to services.

The Abbot rubbed his head. Why couldn't monks just go about their duties, and spare him their troubles? Why couldn't they confine themselves to the two parts of the Benedictine motto, *ora et labora*—pray and work? The Abbot detested these mundane and trivial annoyances. He feared being found wanting at the gates of Heaven, kept out of eternal paradise for his incompetence in dealing with details.

He forced a smile. "I'm grateful you told me this, Brother Phyneas. I'll resolve this matter promptly. Thank you, again." He stood, and Phyneas took the hint and stood also, then left the office.

The Abbot returned to stare at his papers, dismissing the peculiar exchange from his mind.

§

"Take another feather, string them all together," Eilmer chanted, choosing a feather from a pile and binding it with thread to a growing sheet of them, the beginning of the first wing.

Above him, the sunny day deteriorated fast. A darkening shroud of clouds advanced like a blanket being stretched over the heavens. Far to the west, diagonal lines signaled rain in the direction of Bristol.

Eilmer stitched with deliberate haste, forming the feathers into a mat. He'd been working hard gathering jackdaw feathers (*and cleaning bird excrement*, he thought, with bitter remembrance of buying Phyneas' silence). According to the account he'd read, Daidalos and

Ikaros had used larger seagull feathers, but he was forced to use those of the small jackdaws that flocked to Malmesbury Abbey.

A drop of moisture struck his arm and he hoped it wasn't rain. He tried to stitch faster. "Take another feather, string them all together." Each feather was so tiny and needed extreme care to tie with thread to the others. At least he'd learned the lesson of Ikaros and was not using wax.

His discovery of the Greek manuscript itself had been a sign, a commandment that he, and only he, must claim the sky for mankind. There had been a previous sign, also.

Eilmer recalled the event from his childhood, fifteen Septembers earlier. The year would have been Anno Domini 989, Eilmer realized. His mother brought him outside that night and bade him look to the sky.

"You see that hairy star, Eilmer?" his mother had asked, kneeling beside him and pointing. "See it there? The one with the long tail?"

Eilmer had nodded, seeing it.

"The hairy star is an omen for you." She tousled his blond hair. "You were born in this month, five years ago. That star portends something miraculous for your future. I don't know what, but some miraculous thing awaits you when you're grown."

Now, years later, he knew with certainty that the miracle was to be his winged flight.

Still, his progress making the wings was slow. The jackdaw feathers had been tedious to gather, since the birds didn't lose feathers often and he couldn't bring himself to kill a bird. However, on a few blessed occasions a bird had died and he could pluck all its feathers to gain a fine handful at once.

Another drop splashed on his tonsured head. Definitely rain, now. He saw other round wet spots on the tower roof, and the clouds had darkened. In the distance, thunder rumbled.

He collected his small wing fragment, thread, and pile of feathers to continue his task inside. No sense trying to work in the rain.

Just as he reached the wooden door leading to the stairwell, the heavens opened and torrents of rain fell. He shut the door above him and sat on a stair. Meager light seeped through the dusty window.

Eilmer sighed, anticipating the difficulty of threading tiny feathers in such dimness.

He had so far to go. He'd calculated the wing area he'd need, knowing his own weight, that of a jackdaw, and its typical wing area. No matter how often he performed the mathematics, the result came out very large, with each wing extending outward over twenty feet. He hoped he could manage some degree of flight with wings smaller than that.

Looking at the single square foot of wing he'd assembled thus far, he began to despair. When he shut his eyes, a tear squeezed out from each as he faced he truth. At his present pace it would consume years, perhaps decades, to complete the wings.

As if God Himself concurred, a lightning flash blazed in the window, followed by a sharp crack of thunder that rattled the pane. Eilmer buried his head in his hands.

Between sobs, he heard a rustling in the darkness. Someone was with him, here within the tower! He looked, but saw no one on the stairs.

He heard the fluttering rustle again. It came from the square central shaft running inside the winding staircase. He peered up into the gloom.

Bats. A colony of the filthy, ugly pests hung from wooden rafter beams at the very top of the tower. Tiny eyes looked back at him, reflecting the muted light.

The wind outside shifted, and rain battered the window. Eilmer had an odd thought. *Bats fly, too. Without feathers.*

§

The piles of paper on Abbot Beorhtold's desk had grown. He stared at them in exasperation, then realized something. No matter how hard he worked or how much he strived, the piles would always remain. They'd be here on the day he died, probably higher. He had allowed these stacks of paper to control his time. When the final tally of his life was taken, no one would count up the reports he'd read or approved. He thought about their motto—*Ora et labora*. Pray and work. But praying came first.

Imitating Moses, he parted the sea of parchment to clear a central spot of bare desk wood, not caring when some pages slipped off the edge and fluttered to the floor. He gazed around his shelves of books. *Which of you shall be first?*

A knock at the door smote the mood. He sighed. "Come in."

The door opened, and Brother Phyneas peeked around the edge. "*Pax vo—*"

"Sit down. What is it this time, Phyneas?" The Abbot resisted the urge to rub his scalp.

"Actually, Father, I need you to come with me."

"What?" The Abbot frowned. "Why?"

"I must show it to you, Father. It is too horrible to describe in words."

"My time is scarce and precious, Phyneas. Try very hard to describe it."

"It's Brother Eilmer. He is possessed by a demon, or perhaps Satan himself."

"Possessed." The Abbot looked at Phyneas, who appeared solemn and sincere. "Do you have proof of this?"

Phyneas nodded. "That is what I will show you, Father."

The Abbot sighed and stood up. "Let me see your proof."

Phyneas led him past the offices of the priors and the chapter-house meeting room. After ascending a flight of stairs, they entered the dorter, the collection of cells where the monks slept and worked.

They arrived at Eilmer's cell. Phyneas opened the door without knocking or pausing, with what seemed to the Abbot like long-accustomed ease. Even he hesitated at the threshold of any monk's cell, whether or not its occupant was present.

The room looked like any of the others, only cleaner, with no ornamentation other than the cross on the wall. Nothing sat on the desk but an unlit candle and a capped inkwell. *I wish my desk was that clean*, the Abbot thought. The room was the perfect Benedictine monk's cell—simple and plain.

He glanced sidelong at Phyneas, who walked in and slid out the desk's single drawer. Along with two quill pens and a penknife, a thin wooden slab sat on several parchment pages. Phyneas withdrew the board and placed it on the desk. A bat's wing had been affixed to the slab, with measurement annotations scribbled on the wood around it.

Two things bothered the Abbot. First, how did Phyneas know the contents of the desk drawer in Eilmer's cell? Phyneas apparently compensated for his own deficiencies by sneaking around and observing others, hoping to exploit their weaknesses. Standing here in Eilmer's cell, the Abbot felt himself drawn down to Phyneas' level of behavior, complicit in his knavery.

"Leave me now, Phyneas," the Abbot said.

"Are you going to—"

"Leave me, I said." At the gonging of the church bell, he added, "It is now the free hour. Time for you to clean the tower roof."

"Yes, Father." Phyneas wore an unreadable expression as he departed.

The Abbot rubbed his scalp. The second bothersome item was the bat wing. He could not ignore Eilmer's peculiar desk contents. He reached into the drawer and withdrew the papers. Spreading them on the small desk, he saw many bore mathematical calculations; one showed a map of the borough of Malmesbury; but most showed drawings of bats, jackdaws, and men with wings. Some of the pictured men wore angelic bird-wings, while others soared on dark and leathery bat-wings.

Bats, the Abbot thought, those screeching and disease-ridden flying beasts of the night, companions of witches, demonic messengers from Hell. He'd seen images of Satan with pointed, bony bat-wings. *What has Eilmer been doing? Could he really be possessed, as Phyneas claims?*

The door opened and Brother Eilmer walked in the cell with his usual focused haste. He froze when he saw the Abbot, and his eyes shifted to the items on the desk. Recovering, he bowed. "*Pax vobis*, Father."

"*Pax vobis*, Brother Eilmer." The Abbot sighed. "Are these your possessions?"

"No, Father. By my vow, I have renounced all possessions. These things belong to all mankind."

The Abbot reached down and touched the drawings and diagrams. "I doubt they will be of much value to mankind." Looking at Eilmer, he saw worry and fear in his blue eyes, but nothing demonic. He showed none of the four known signs of satanic possession. His preoccupation with bats must be some temporary digression, some transient perversion. A stern warning should suffice to set him back on the virtuous and holy path. The Abbot walked to the window, where the light of day poured down from the heavens, lending brightness to the trees and the roofs of the borough.

"We are here, Brother Eilmer, to contemplate the infinite and eternal holiness of God and of our Lord, Jesus Christ. You may believe there is plenty of time in your life for that. But years will pass, during which you may become distracted by other, lesser things. One day you may find yourself an old man, wondering where those precious years went, whether you have labored on worthy tasks, how you will be judged," he closed his eyes, "and where you will be found wanting."

Eilmer approached him. "I beg you to let me explain, Father. I'm certain you'll support my effort to fly, and not punish me for it."

The Abbot turned and frowned at Eilmer, who must not have been listening. "Why is it *my* support you seek, and *my* punishment you dread? Worry, instead, about *God's* support, and fear *His* righteous judgment."

§

With the morning sun warming his back, Eilmer stood atop the crenelated edge of the abbey tower. His wings stretched out to both sides, a web of wooden spars with tanned leather cowhide stretched over them. He recalled reading the tale of Daidalos, which had excited his imagination six months earlier and brought him to this point.

Though his wing design differed from that of the ancient Greek, he would soon know the feeling only experienced by that long-ago inventor and his son.

He remembered also that day only a month ago, when the Abbot had discovered his drawings and his bat-wing. How terrified he'd been, until the Abbot had left his punishment up to God. In that moment, he'd passed from fright to exultation, for God had already shown him by omen and the Holy Scriptures that man *must* fly. Further, both the hairy star and the divine placing of the Daidalos text in Eilmer's hands meant he'd been ordained to show others the way.

He saw God's blessing, too, in the choice of this day. A chilly day, to be certain, with a wind that rustled his robe and shuddered his wings. But the fog had lifted and the sky had cleared. This must be the day, a bright day in the new millennium.

Looking down, he felt a wave of horror. The ground looked so far away, as if the tower had risen higher. Any failure of the wings would mean his death.

Eilmer shut his eyes and calmed himself by chanting words from Isaiah: "'Fear thou not; for I am with thee: be not dismayed; for I am thy God: I will strengthen thee; yea, I will help thee; yea, I will uphold thee with the right hand of my righteousness.'"

Opening his eyes, he smiled and knew God had banished his fear. He looked out to confirm where he would fly first. To the north and east there grew a dense forest; to the south lay the borough of Malmesbury. Straight ahead to the southwest, a grassy hill sloped down and away toward the river. He'd begin in that direction, then soar where he pleased, and swoop back here to the abbey's tower.

A sudden gust tugged at his robe and buffeted his wings. He flapped them as a test and saw them respond to his arm movements.

Door hinges creaked behind him. He heard the voice of Brother Phyneas, whom he'd come to dislike.

What are you doing?" Phyneas asked. "Come down."

That was all Eilmer needed. With a heart full of faith, he leapt.

He dropped with sickening swiftness, but the wings caught the air and upheld him as if borne by a divine hand. Eilmer glided on the breeze, the wind breathing on his shaven head. He was flying!

It unnerved him to see the hard ground so far below, but when he looked forward, it felt glorious. Birds and bats knew this feeling of freedom and speed every day, but only two men had ever experienced this ecstasy before him.

He glided toward the river, riding the air, the grassy hill passing by underneath. He'd been descending at a slant, and now tried flapping his wings. When he did not rise, he flapped harder. Flapping with all his strength made him pitch upward, and then plummet with greater speed until he could spread his wings and glide again.

At once Eilmer understood his peril and its cause. Moving faster and faster, descending lower and lower, unable to rise or turn, he would soon strike the ground. Instead of flying, he'd been merely falling at an angle. He'd forgotten to build a tail. Birds and bats have tails to keep their flight steady and straight. Even the hairy star had a tail.

As the ground drew closer, Eilmer could do nothing about it. He glanced off the foliage of a tree and slammed into a hedge.

§

Abbot Beorhtold sat in his chair, his feet up on his desk, his shoes crinkling several parchment pages. He sat with a book on his lap, a smile on his face, and thoughts of the infinite in his mind.

There came a knock at the door.

Just this one time, Dear Lord, let it be good news. "Come in."

Brother Phyneas peered around the door with a wide-eyed look of shock. His voice was panicked. "Forgive me, Father, but Brother Eilmer tried to fly and hurt himself badly. He's in the infirmary."

Together, they hastened to the small infirmary building separate from the main abbey. The doctor attended to Eilmer while he lay on a straw mat, mumbling. Upon seeing the Abbot, the doctor came over to him.

"A farmer brought him here on a cart, babbling some nonsense about tails and wings. Both his legs are broken, and he's covered with scratches and bruises. I'll do what I can, Father, but he may never walk again."

"Bless you," the Abbot said, "I know you'll do the best you are able."

He wanted to comfort Eilmer, but saw Phyneas standing expectantly.

"Brother Phyneas," the Abbot frowned at him. "You have beheld the mote in your brother's eye but ignored the beam in your own long enough. I will assign Sub-Prior Aquilius to watch after you day and night. He shall report to me every transgression in your behavior, every negligence in your work, every tardiness in your attendance. Now, leave me."

"But, Father—"

"Go."

Downcast, Phyneas left.

§

Eilmer saw the Abbot draw up a chair beside his bed of straw. "Father, I flew! I landed hard, but I know why. I lacked a tail. Bats and birds have tails. The next time I'll—"

"Be still now, Brother Eilmer." The Abbot shook his head. "You must never fly again; God has punished you." He touched Eilmer's arm. "But be of good cheer, for in His mercy He has spared your life. Your purpose here remains unfulfilled. I know not what it may be, but I pray He may reveal it one day." He smiled. "Rest and get well."

When the Abbot stood, his face shown half lit by light from the window and half darkened in shadow. "Your desire to fly...I know not whether you were commanded by God or tempted by Satan. Even after we burn your wings and drawings, one day someone else will try what you have tried. If he should succeed, will that be God's will? Or the Devil's?" As he walked away, he said, "I wonder."

Through the open window, Eilmer heard the caw of a jackdaw and the rustle of wings. He smiled, for he knew the answer.

The Raptor

Nancy Springer

*H**er husband, poor old child, bringing her home from the* oncology ward and setting up the rental hospital bed next to the picture window—in denial, he still thought she would get better. But she knew damn good and well that she had come home to die, and she had made up her mind to do it with integrity. Her entire adult life had been given to compromise, getting along in the community, making the marriage work, keeping both sides of the family happy—but during those bleak cycles of chemo and radiation she had realized that, when it came to dying, there were no compromises. As an invalid, she had realized that she could not with validity die as she had lived. Living was a juggling act, but dying was an absolute, Death the swordsman of the Major Arcana. She had to do it right, and she would not have a second chance.

Because she had always accompanied her husband as a Christmas-and-Easter churchgoer, blockheaded preachers had kept showing up at the hospitals to pray over her. It had never mattered so much before that she did not believe a word they said, but after the cancer came back, each *outreach* had driven her farther out of reach. She wanted no more goddamn prayers. Cumulatively, all those prayers had left her feeling like the steely rider portrayed on the Death card in her mother's Tarot deck, and of the poem her mother had taught her to go with it:

Cast a cold eye
On life, on death.
Horseman, pass by!

Cold.

Her hands and feet even more so than the rest of her were always cold nowadays, mittens and socks no help against necrosis. From her bed partly elevated, her pillows piled high, she looked through the window at the blue, blue Florida sky and the dancing tops of trees just leafing out in April. Atop one greening scrub oak she saw glimpses of another color: heliotrope. Then, tracing the color backward down the tree, she found more High-Priestess purple throughout the branches. Pretty. Wisteria had climbed the tree, making it beautiful, and the beauty, natural beauty, comforted her. The natural cycles comforted her. Foreseeing natural death comforted her: eventually the choking vine would kill the scrub oak tree—but more trees would grow.

She looked up again at the sky, casting a cold but serene eye, aware of death and cycling life, just at the moment when the great raptor swept across like a white, white epiphany, cleaving the air low to the ground so that she saw clearly the long, black V of its tail like a pair of shears to cut her last umbilicus, and in its talons a writhing black snake. She felt equally awe for the predator and sorrow for the prey; snakes had been her pets during her childhood in the circus, many years ago. Young and wild and free, she had worn snakes as circlets on her arms. As she watched, this one squirmed into the shape of a magic she had seen countless times over the head of the Magician in her mother's Tarot cards: the infinity symbol.

Oh!

"Oh, take me!" she cried to the white raptor. "Drop that poor thing and come take me!"

It gave no sign that it heard her. No one could have heard. Her cry was nothing more than a croak, because she could barely breathe, her lungs flooding with fluid, her body drowning itself. Yearning, she watched the great bird's flight, expecting to lose sight of it as soon as it soared above her home's peach-hued eaves. But no; with its widespread wings nearly motionless, it swept to one of the immensely tall long-leaf pines, head and shoulders above loblollies and wax myrtle, rain oaks and mimosa—but this pine stood skeletal and dead, struck by lightning years ago.

At about the same time she had been struck with lightning, figuratively speaking.

The great raptor landed at the apex of the dead tree, folded its wings, and turned black.

Startled, she peered. Silhouetted against the sky? No. The cancer had not affected her eyesight. She still had the distance vision that had prompted her fellow carnies, more than half a century ago, to nickname her "Hawkeye." The raptor perched with black, folded wings crisscrossing to frame the long, slender, black inverted V of its tail. Lowering its head, it sank its hooked beak into the black snake. Riveted by recognition, she watched the raptor eat the snake the way the cancer had eaten her; there went the first big piece of meat, the mastectomy. It pleased her that she could watch with such shudderless interest. What she looked upon was predation, one of the great patterns; the serpent's pain and dying was natural and right. *Not* punishment. *Not* inflicted. *Not* torture by some cockamamie deity.

Suddenly weary, she turned her head away, lifting one shriveled, necrotic hand to ease the oxygen tube along with it; the evil little prongs of the thing had clawed the insides of her nostrils so sore that they bled. She closed her eyes; if her husband came in, he would think she was napping. She felt blood trickling from her nose. No matter. Nor did the pain throughout her body matter. It was all part of the patterns—rain to river to ocean to sky, sunbeams to tree to heat and light—the many circles and symmetries, moth and butterfly, moon and sun, the images assembling in her mind, images now including a day-and-night black-and-white predator bird—

A shrill mechanical beeping noise insulted her, trampling her thoughts. The damn oxygen machine was complaining that she wasn't breathing deeply enough. She opened her eyes to see her husband come thumping in, all big bald beer-bellied six feet of him, his eyes bugging as he saw the blood dribbling down her shrunken chin. "Sweetie! Why dincha ring the bell to call me!"

Because she wanted to be let alone, that was why. Coaxing him to take her home from the hospital, she had trusted he would be a half-assed nurse, and sure enough, he was. But because he believed himself to be her hero, she managed a small smile for him as he silenced the histrionics of the oxygen machine. The cancer had eaten away her heartfelt love for him, but she wanted never to hurt his feelings. That was why she let his damn preachers pray over her, because he still believed exactly what he'd been taught when he was five years old. Never gave it another thought. But having been raised nomadic and free, she knew to her core that deity was not some poor bastard nailed to a cross. Crucifixion was mean, ugly, and cruel like nothing in nature. No proper father would ever do that to a son and call it love, and then to cover up by saying he and his son were the same person? So he tortured and killed himself? And this was supposed to *comfort* her?

Her husband flumped half his fat ass down on the edge of her hospital bed. "Honey, you gotta let me know when this thing needs changed," he said, easing the prongs out of her mouth and replacing them with an oxygen mask, a clear plastic ovoid half-shell that covered her nose and mouth, more comfortable but not conducive to talking or eating. Not that she wanted to do either of those things anyway. "Anything else you need right now?"

Mendaciously she shook her head, knowing that it would never occur to him to take her pulse or her temperature, let alone check her diaper or wipe away the blood on her face. There was a whole world of things he simply never thought about because they did not affect him or apply to him, and long ago she had loved his sturdy, ignorant pragmatism. She had married him in order to be a regular person, to have a normal life far from the freak show and the fortune telling and the flying trapeze. But now she knew she should have been more careful what she wished for.

He lifted the face mask so she could speak. "You ready for something to eat?"

"Can't keep anything down," she lied.

"Drink? Apple juice?"

She shook her head again. The more dehydrated she got, the better.

"Pain meds?"

No, no way. But instead of answering, she took the face mask back from him, then lifted her shaky, desiccated arm to point out the window, surprising herself with the gesture; she had not thought there was that much of a bond still left in her. But yes, just because he was her husband, she wanted him to observe the manifestation that had flown into her dying.

As if she had raised her hand to summon it, the great raptor launched from its perch atop the dead pine to glide toward her, enlarging in her vision until it filled her mind as it impended, a mystic symmetry, black above, white below.

"What the hun?" yelped her husband, lurching to his large feet.

"Yang and yin," she mumbled beneath the mask, but he seemed not to hear her at all.

The bird swooped, stalled, then perched in a wild cherry tree within ten feet of the picture window, looking straight at her. Her longsighted eyes and mind focused on its white, white face in which its ebony pebble eyes, charcoal nares and sharp, downturned beak formed a black V, another black V, smaller, but nevertheless mirroring the V of its great scissor tail. Everything about the symmetries, the dualities of this bird told her it was arcane.

Her husband let out a howl. "What for kind of crazy buzzard is that?" Typical man, he always yelled when frightened. "What's it doing so close to the house?"

"Beautiful like a two-tone Edsel," she murmured, echoing a nonsensical sweet nothing he used to say to her when they were courting.

Again, he seemed not to hear her. "I'm getting my shotgun."

"*No.*" This time she lifted the mask and made sure she was heard.

He stared down at her. "What the hun, Hon? You want that thing sitting there?

"Yes. I like it." Her shortness of breath required her to edit everything she said out loud, and what more could she have told him anyway, when there was all the beauty of death right in front of him and he could only see a buzzard? When he still couldn't say the C-word, when he was still telling people that his wife was laid up with double pneumonia? The big sissy, talking like she was going to get better when the cancer was perforating her vitals, eating her from the inside out.

"That ain't no buzzard," she said.

"Huh." His stare hardened but he made an effort to soften his voice. "You say so, sweetie. You're the boss." He turned away. "I got stuff to do." He strode out.

Placing the precious oxygen mask back over her face, she didn't give her husband another thought. At once she turned to face the raptor patiently waiting so close to her, perched almost at her bedside with only air and glass separating them. It gazed back at her with the frontward eyes of a predator, and just that way of looking forward giving it a face, made it a person. It gripped the wild cherry tree with what looked like hands, like in another poem her mother had taught her in which the raptor "grasped the crag with crooked hands." Its presence felt more intimate than that of her husband. In its stillness she felt it questioning her: *What do you want? Why have you cried out to me?*

"I beg you to take me," she told the bird from beneath her mask, making no sound and wasting no breath, but shaping the words with her lips to delineate the thoughts in her mind.

When she was a child learning to be an aerialist like her parents, she had perched in high places to soar, dangling by her hands, her feet, her ankles, her knees from ropes, swings, hoops, and swags of silk, loving every moment she spent detached from earth and in defiance of gravity. The ultimate goal had been for her to fly from trapeze to trapeze or to a parent's catching hands. Her family had left the circus and settled down before she ever actually did it, but readily she could imagine herself flying away with a winged thing.

In the cherry tree with its face and breast toward her, the eagle-sized bird looked pure white, like an angel. Eerily she felt certain it could hear her, understand her.

In the same silent way she said to it, "I don't want to lie in a hole and be prayed over."

Doomed to earth's clutches, prisoner of gravity, buried in the shadow of a cross? No, no, infinitely no. In all her life she had never borne a cross, had never wanted to bear a cross, had never perceived pain and debility as bearing a cross. Cancer was pain was death was natural. A good and daring life, trying to fly but ultimately falling, should mean wings. Readily she imaged herself being borne away by the winged mystery of death, a baby being delivered by a great black-white bird far more mystic than a stork.

Then her eyes widened. Watery, diminished eyes, shaped like minnows, sunk deep in their sockets, still they widened, because high and clear as hawk cry in her mind she heard the bird's reply. *What is this nonsense?* it begged. *What you ask of me is unnatural. How am I your savior? I am a hunting bird like any other hawk or falcon, osprey, eagle or kite. I fly over treetops and pluck frogs and birds, lizards and snakes out of their mazy leaves and branches. I glide on broad wings that scarcely waver, I change directions with a twist of my tail, I chase down dragonflies and eat them, then sit on a branch and poop. I am a bird, not some cockamamie deity.*

"Do you love flying?" she asked.

Of course.

"Do you love finding the birds' nests?"

Yes, I love seeking them out with my keen, keen eyes.

"Do you love the snakes?"

Yes, I adore the snakes, bright snakes and black snakes but most of all the shining green snakes that hang in loops, draped upon the branches.

"Like the shining green silk ropes upon which I used to swing before I forgot who I was."

If you say so. I do not know what this silk thing is, but I hear snakes in the sound of it, and I love them. I love their graceful sliding, the whisper of their hiss, their slithering tongues black and forked like my tail.

"You love the snakes and you eat the snakes."

Yes! This is the great pattern, is it not?

True. But she could not speak, for the moment hurt too much, the moment when she saw how she fit the pattern: she had loved who she was, and she had swallowed that self, hidden it in her deepest belly, almost killed it.

"I was a wild thing," she mouthed at last.

I am a wild thing, a natural thing. I am who I am.

"Meaning your name is Yahweh?" Did the circles overlap?

I have no name. What does it matter? What is your name?

"I renounce that name. I never want any such name carved on any tombstone. Take me with you."

The hawk clacked its beak at her, and its tone of mind heightened, wrought. *Are you a baby bird that I should take you from your nest? Are you crazy? What do you think I am?*

"I think nothing but I know you are *something.*" Something spiritous, she meant, this bird that talked with her mind to mind. Because nothing like this had ever happened in her long life, she knew death perched facing her and also on her frail shoulders. "Take me with you."

Behind her she heard the tramping of her husband's Red Wing work boots, heard him entering the room, but she did not look at him, only at the raptor in the wild cherry tree, V face above, black V tail below crooked hands clutching a smooth-barked branch the color of venous blood.

"That there buzzard's got no business hanging around so close to the house," she heard her husband growl. Years earlier she would have rolled her eyes at him and teased him about his irrational guard-dog attitude, asking him whether he went around the place to pee on every fence post each day. But now she barely spared a mental shrug for him.

"I'm getting the shotgun," he declared. "Period." She heard him go stomping out toward the garage.

Eerily, this did not disturb her, because she knew beyond a shadow of a doubt that the raptor was the Death card ascendant, top and center, and that this day, these events, this turning of the wheel was no mere game; it was the laying down of the cards, final, implacable, and welcome. Whatever her husband did was condign and fitting with one of the other Major Arcana in the deck.

Maybe he was the Fool.

She guessed herself to be Judgment. Judgment had wings.

Given the vast pattern into which she was passing, the utterly strange circling cycle that needed to take shape, she judged that the shotgun was justified and necessary, the shattering to take place was fated and ordained, given that the raptor was unwilling. The raptor was afraid, but she, the aspiring hierophant, was unafraid, having already crossed over halfway into the beyond, as evidenced by the fact that she was conversing with a denizen of the wild. Dying, she was finding herself again, her utterly wild and natural selfish self.

The great raptor brooded with folded wings; along the edge of each black pinion, she saw, ran a thin glimmer of the white lining. She said to it, "You are beautiful."

You are honored to see me so nearly. I do not know why I remain here, perched in this insignificant tree.

"For me."

You are nothing to me. Yet you summoned me and I obey.

"I have never in my life been so powerful as now, as you die for me and take me with you."

What! Like a gathering storm the hawk roused, hunching its shoulders, gaping its beak, erecting its feathers to look even bigger than it truly was, partly unfolding its wings. *What are you talking about?* Then, before she could answer, the black-white bird shrilled in her mind, *The gun! I see the hunter with the long gun stalking to shoot me!* Its wings shot up into a V. One downbeat, and it would be flying, fleeing, free, safe.

She commanded, "Don't go away."

The great bird froze like a pillar of salt just as it was poised. Its protest screamed in her mind, *You want me to let myself be killed?*

"Yes, you are to die and take me with you." She spoke with uncanny certainty and utter selfish authority.

No ordinary bird weeps, but this one did; it wept. Tears ran down the white feathers of its face. *I do not want to! Please, I beg of you, let me go!*

"No. All my life I have let things go. In death I will have my way. Stay."

But the agony, the blood, my perfect plumage ruined—

"It will be quick. Not torture."

You torture me now! It is horrible! YOU FORCE ME TO BE A SACRIFICE FOR YOU—

Instantly she recognized the truth of this, and the irony of the truth, and given time, she would have acknowledged wickedness, and she would have admitted herself to be cruel, no better than the rest of them. Again, given time, perhaps she would have changed the pattern, set the great black-white bird free, let herself be the sacrifice to the cruciform shadow of a deity who seemed to have no goddamn common sense. But because Death was what it was, she had no time. Her time ended in a concussion so loud it made no sound at all.

It was a shotgun blast and it was a cataclysm. The bird of prey did not so much explode as expand, looming huge and dark, dark, all that had been white about it now blood red wet and shimmering. It did not shatter, but the glass shattered, and the air, and the oxygen machine, and everything that separated the raptor from her. It was vast, so vast it dwarfed the world, dwarfed her life, shadowed her memories into nothingness, and grasped her easily in its great clawed feet, talons closing around her without piercing her, with more mercy than she felt she deserved.

With huge, lustrous, bleeding wings that, like her heart, did not beat, it soared up and away. Weightless and nearly soulless, she felt as if she had let go of the trapeze but there was no one to catch her, and she wondered whether she might have made a mistake. So as not to be prayed over, was she to be preyed upon? But within an instant it didn't matter. Death's crooked hands clasped tighter, and she knew no more.

Wheels and Deals

Todd Sullivan

*T*he angel's gaze swept over the human skins hanging in its closet. Like a businessman choosing the best suit for a power meeting, it sifted through the hollowed-out flesh, and decided upon a nineteen-year-old female to slip over its six wings and three faces. The skin stretched, then tightened on its bulky form, slimming it down until it appeared exactly as the university student, before the angel had kidnapped, strangled, and gutted her.

The angel dressed the female in a suede skirt, cashmere sweater, and fur trimmed hooded jacket, then studied itself in the full-length mirror on the back of the bedroom door.

"Today," it announced, "I am Kim Li An."

She stood a little more than one and a half meters tall, her long black hair falling neatly down her petite shoulders to the middle of her back. She smiled at the sharp contrast between the true form of her many wings and faces, and these two simple human legs and arms and the female's singular, oval face. Humans had truly been made closest to the Creator's image, and were so much less complicated without the exotic details of angels.

When the angel looked into the girl's elegant eyes, the smile twisted in frustration at the flaw threatening the illusion. Maintaining her gaze revealed the missing spark, the spirit long since departed

Most humans never noticed the lack of life lurking in the empty stare of her puppet's eyes. Those who did posed a danger to the angel, who was struggling for an identity that the Creator hadn't gifted it with at inception.

Her brow furrowed, and she repeated, *"I am Kim Li An,"* in a voice that trembled in doubt. With a low growl, she hurried out of the apartment to the elevator, and went down a dozen flights and out the glass double doors into the busy Gongdoek district streets. Towering skyscrapers shot up into the blue sky around the major intersection outside Li An's apartment building. Time neared noon, and taxis poured down the broad gray avenue in successive waves of yellow and silver and black. Mopeds and scooters zipped between cars, forcing them to swerve to avoid collisions. The helmeted riders, cigarettes dangling between their lips, ignored the sounds of wheels screeching on asphalt and horns blasting after them as they raced to fulfill delivery orders throughout the mega city.

Li An observed Seoul's chaotic bustle with hungry eyes. Earlier that week, a merchant had contacted the angel about a job to procure a pure soul at a fantastic price. The two of them had set up a meeting to discuss the details at the nearby Café Bene in the next hour. Li An decided to walk the three blocks to the café this brisk December morning. She exhilarated in the sensation of taut muscles contracting and relaxing in graceful symmetry in her compact body. She breathed in the crisp air, and flexed her fingers and toes with the pleasure of being substantial instead of luminous and indefinite. If this soul proved valuable enough, perhaps she could work out a deal to extend her time within mortal casings. At her current level of power, she could only inhabit human flesh a dozen or so hours a day before her true form threatened to cast off the lifeless body.

When she accidentally brushed against a young man in the crosswalk, he turned and looked her over with an appreciative eye. Li An ached to become closer to him, to listen to the minute details of his highest goals and deepest dreams as lazy afternoons of in-depth conversation lead into peaceful evenings in each other's embrace. The Creator had also not wanted this for angels, the ability to form such intimate connections with humans. But why? The mortal world was so beautiful, yet ultimately denied the angels as they existed alongside them on Earth.

The angel's curiosity had given it shape and power beyond those enforced upon it by the Creator. Yet everything in existence had a price, and the angel was set to pay it again no matter the cost.

Li An reached the Café Bene and stepped inside into the heavy smell of roasting coffee. She inhaled deeply, held the dense fragrances inside her lungs, then exhaled slowly in pleasure. The server at the counter greeted her, and she smiled brightly at him. He, too, seemed captivated by her appearance, and was eager to help when she stepped up to order an Americano, garlic and cheese honey bread, and a small bottle of grapefruit juice. When her drinks and dessert were ready, she took them upstairs on a brown platter.

She recognized the merchant at once from the first time they worked together six months ago. He sat alone by a row of windows looking out upon the city. He wore an expertly tailored gray suit over a prim, athletic figure.

Li An approached his table. He glanced up at her and nodded, his gaze briefly sliding over her before he directed his attention back to the window. She placed her platter on his table, and he sat back, momentarily startled.

"I'm sorry, may I help you?" He looked around the mostly empty second floor of the café. "I don't mind you joining me," he added with another quick appraisal of Li An's figure, "but there are plenty of other free seats available."

"There are," she observed. "But why be alone if you don't have to?" She sat down opposite him. Setting the slice of cake on its dainty dishware between them, she placed the platter on the table behind her, and took a sip of her Americano. "It's so delicious on this cold day," she said, the warmth of the hot coffee flowing down her throat sending thrills of pleasure through her. "Please," she added, motioning to the cake, "have a slice."

"You only have one fork," the merchant pointed out, to which Li An shrugged.

"It's okay. We'll share."

The merchant didn't hesitate. He carved off a piece of cake for himself, placed it gingerly in his mouth, and then cut a piece for her and delicately presented it for her consumption. He stared deep into her eyes, and as she leaned forward to take the fork between her teeth, the merchant issued a low gasp.

"It's you," he hissed, and dropped the fork in disgust. The clatter spread across the second floor and caused the only other patron to look over at them. The body the angel wore tightened in sudden rage. The angel restrained itself from reaching across the table, placing its petite but strong fingers to the man's throat, and throttling him. The merchants were only humans, after all, and mostly ignorant of the cosmic game in which they dealt in-artfully in. But this particular mortal had grown in enough understanding of the divine to see the truth in its eyes.

"My name is Kim Li An," the angel said. "It's a pleasure to meet you."

The merchant shivered. "You were a man when we met last time. And now..." He swallowed.

"Don't ponder too hard on it," the angel replied. It smothered the red-hot anger threatening to submerge what identity it had successfully created within itself. In their natural state in this world, all angels existed only as emotions of light influencing humans to do acts of extreme goodness. But occasionally, one of the more inquisitive ones forged personalities for themselves. In order to experience greater sense of individuality, the angels bartered pure souls with demons, growing not only in complexity but also power.

But their sense of self was fragile. Humans who peered through the camouflage threatened their existence. The angel had already lost the brightest of the light the Creator had gifted it with, leaving it only a glow of wings and faces when alone in its apartment in Gongdoek. If it succumbed to hate, it would lose what spark it still possessed and become an emotion of deep shadow without thought or reason, and with only one purpose left to it: influencing humans to do terrible acts of evil.

"Let's get on with this," Li An said, her voice frosty. The merchant blanched, and with a flick of his wrist, a small leather notebook appeared in his hand. Trivial tricks like this were what the human merchants received in exchange for selling souls to lords below in Hell. A bit of precognition, extra speed, strength, and youthful appearance that lasted longer than that of a typical mortal. For these slight abilities lasting eight or nine decades enabling him to gain more wealth and power easier, this man sitting before her would spend an eternity of spiritual torture in some realm below.

"The soul you're to steal tomorrow belongs to a Congolese girl," the merchant said when he'd flipped to the right page in his notebook. "Her name is Rose Kabaselle." He glanced up at Li An, but didn't meet her eye.

"She'll be a difficult catch, but the rewards will be high. She's a Catholic missionary living in the rectory in Shin Chon Church. Training to be a nun. Proficient in English and French, she's studying Korean at Sogang University. Be careful around her," the merchant added. "She's truly a pure heart, and will be a very formidable opponent to you."

Li An did not give the merchant the satisfaction of a reaction. "How and when is the girl estimated to die?" she asked.

The merchant swallowed hard. "Between 1:00 and 2:15 tomorrow. Sorry, that's the best I can do. You'll have to be near her body between those times, or else her soul may get away from you."

"I know what I'm doing," the angel informed him coldly, and the merchant flinched. He looked out the window, then at the door, and last at his watch.

"I should be going," the merchant hastily said, and closing his hand, swallowed the notebook in his palm. The angel grinned. So proud the man was for so little. It could slice the mortal open and empty him of his insides slowly so that he'd scream for hours until he'd lost his voice and mind to the torment. And even that would pale in significance to what waited for the mortal after his death. And also for this girl, Rose Kabaselle, once it secured her soul for the realms below.

§

Sogang University was only several blocks from the angel's apartment in Gongdoek. The next morning, it pulled on the flesh of a young Colombian man it'd acquired a year ago. Memories of the romantic encounters it'd shared with the male sent tingles of warmth through the angel as it slipped the flesh over its wings and faces. Standing solid instead of an apparition of dimming light in front of the mirror, the angel said, "My name is Carlos Hernandez."

Carlos had been a lover of American classic rock and an explorer of Far East cultures. He'd traveled far beyond his small town of Bogota to live in Japan, then Hong Kong and China, to finally arrive in Korea. His rhythmic, staccato voice floating between the notes of the bass guitar he played in the streets around the university clusters in Seoul had been a magnet to Korean women. Then, one late night a week before he was to continue on his adventure to Vietnam, he met Kim Li An. Everything about her had enthralled him. She'd taken him back to her apartment in Gongdoek, and for long moments in the dark he'd shared his innermost soul with her as he revealed the aspirations he wished to accomplish in that blink of time humans called life. When Li An realized she wanted to add him to her collection, she extended her six wings and the puppet of flesh peeled from her three faces before his startled eyes. The angel held him down with the force of its dying light. Skinning him alive, it swallowed his terrible cries within the darkness blossoming around it in the form of writhing, probing shadows.

Now the angel dressed Carlos in jeans, shirt, and suede jacket. He left the apartment and took the city bus to the Sogang University station.

The bus rumbled from block to block, its sudden stops and abrupt accelerations causing the passengers to lurch backward and forward as they fought for balance. Several times the bus almost sideswiped cars speeding around it, or rear-ended mopeds that suddenly appeared before the barreling vehicle. While the other passengers hung on tightly, Carlos exhilarated in the chaotic momentum, every experience outside his apartment a treasure to explore.

The merchant had emailed Rose's picture and class schedule. This was the end of the semester for Sogang's KLEC, the Korean Language Education Center, and the students enrolled in the program were taking three days of exams. Carlos arrived at the building minutes after 8:00 a.m., and waited outside beneath the pale blue sky stretching wide over Seoul. Teens in uniforms walked in clusters to the surrounding high schools, and men and women rushed down sidewalks to nearby subway stations on their way to work. Carlos sat on a bench outside the KLEC and watched the busy humans with intense envy. To truly be able to experience the everyday wonders of daily mortal life, to be a complete individual free to decide their own fate every morning when they opened their eyes.

After securing this soul, the angel would be able to bargain for a higher power from one of the lords below. The angel had heard rumors of the ability to transfer its essence into a human by touch alone. How easy would that make life, to substitute the consciousness of the human and control the body as it saw fit? When it grew bored, it could simply move on with another touch to a new body, and then another, and another.

Rose entered the brick Sogang gates and walked up the path towards the KLEC building. Carlos shook off his musings, quickly unshouldered his schoolbag to retrieve a notebook, and pretended to concentrate upon a scribbled page as she approached. When she was about to pass him, he said in English, "Excuse me, can you help me figure something out?"

Rose stood almost a meter shorter than him. She wore a modest pair of teal pants, a puffy purple jacket, and a knitted cap over her tightly twisted hair. She smiled warmly at him, and stepping up to him, placed a hand on his arm.

"What's wrong?" she asked, looking at him through her dark brown glasses.

"Do you have a list of conversation topics they're going to ask for the writing test?" He gave her a rueful grin. "I was rushing this morning and totally forgot my study notes."

She gave his arm a friendly squeeze. "You're in luck. I have them memorized," she replied, and rattled off eight general topics in Korean about school, friends, and family. Carlos, holding her gaze, listened intently, and when she finished, shook his head.

"So many," he said. "This is going to be wicked hard."

She peered closer at him. "Are you still in Level 4? I remember seeing you when I started the program last year. I would have thought you had graduated and gone home. Or gotten a job by now."

The angel froze. It hadn't considered the possibility that Rose would have seen this body when it still lived and attended the Korean Language Education Center last year. She gazed into his eyes waiting for a response. The angel cycled through a jumble of conjured excuses, but nothing seemed convincing enough. Carlos took a small step back from her, poised to flee but too hungry for power to run.

Then, she squeezed his arm again. "You don't have to be ashamed. Plenty of people fail these language classes a couple of times before completing the program. Korean's not easy to learn." She smiled at him. "As long as you pass the tests this time, that's all that matters, right?"

Carlos laughed with relief, his body relaxing at her assumption. "Yes, yes," he said in quick agreement. "I'm sure I'll pass this time." He paused. "You've been very kind. I'll let you know after exams how I did." He pointed to this spot. "I'll be right here waiting to tell you."

She took his pale hand in her dark ones. "I'll say a prayer for you, and will be right here waiting to hear. See you in a couple of hours."

§

All of the exams ended at 1:00, when the KLEC morning classes let out each day. Carlos waited outside by the same bench, a cigarette between his fingers. Throngs of chattering students poured out into the cold afternoon, their voices full of excitement or despair at potential test scores. The angel decided that Carlos would tell Rose that he passed this time around. All because of her good wishes. He mustered up the appropriate amount of youthful enthusiasm, and checked the time again.

1:10.

The flood of students dwindled to a trickle. Rose was late to exit the building, and with her death estimated between 1:00 and 2:15, the angel began to worry. Perhaps it'd happened inside the KLEC building. But how? A tumble down the stairs as she rushed to meet him? A sudden illness overtaking her in the classroom as she handed in her paper to the professor? He listened intently, but heard no voices in distress calling for assistance and saw no ambulances to indicate a person needing medical attention.

The angel swore. If she died outside its presence, it wouldn't be able to secure the soul before Rose started her journey into the plane above for judgment. Opportunities for individuals this pure came few and far between, and usually took months to triangulate. The next chance to barter with a soul singularly devoted to the Creator could be years in the future. Annoyance at the thought became a simmering rage at the opportunity lost.

And then through the glass lobby doors he spied Rose coming out of the elevator. Carlos flicked away the cigarette he'd just lit and waved to her as she exited the building.

"You're still here?" she asked in surprise as she walked down the steps towards him. "I'd have thought you'd left by now."

Carlos shook his head. "I was too excited. I'm sure I passed this time 'round, and it's all because of you."

Rose threw her head back and laughed. Her whole body shook with the force of it. Even the sunlight falling on her coal black skin seemed to glow with amusement. She peered at him through her glasses, and gasped out through the peals ringing forth from between her red lips, "I had nothing to do with it!" She clasped his arm. "Be prepared and have faith in the Lord, and there's no trial you can't pass."

A slight sneer curled Carlos' lips before he could twist them into a smile. Rose's gaze searched his face inquisitively, but her expression remained open and friendly.

"I'm sorry I'm late," she continued. "Me and my classmates got so busy taking pictures and exchanging information. Time just got away from us." She looked at her watch. "And looks like I'm going to have to get a taxi. There's another exam I have to take down towards my church that I'm just about to miss if I don't hurry."

"Your church tests you?" Carlos asked, surprised.

"Life is full of tests," Rose replied. Taking Carlos' pale hand in her dark ones, she said, "It's been nice to meet you. I hope you get everything you want this quarter."

She started to pull away, but Carlos held on. "Do you mind sharing a cab with me?" he asked. "I'm going towards Shin Chon anyway. Same direction. And I'll pay for the fare."

Rose inclined her head. "You knew my church was in Shin Chon?"

"I just figured it'd be nearby," Carlos quickly replied.

Rose nodded. "Okay, let's hurry, then."

Together, they walked down the path leading from the KLEC building back through the brick gates of Sogang University. They only had to wait a minute before flagging down a taxi that swerved out of the busy afternoon traffic to come to an abrupt stop meters ahead of them. Once inside, Rose told the driver their destination in Korean, and the taxi leapt back into the bustle of cars speeding down the street.

Carlos checked the time in the dashboard. 1:45. Less than half an hour was all that the girl sitting next to him had left to her. The angel had been in the last moments of life of humans often enough that he began to extrapolate exactly how it would happen. So when out of the corner of his eye, he saw a moped cut off a bus barreling towards the upcoming intersection, Carlos put his hand on the back of the seat and relaxed his body. The bus jerked away from the moped to avoid hitting it, then jerked again to miss a group of pedestrians waiting at the crosswalk. The huge speeding vehicle lurched toward the taxi and slammed into the car, flipping it over.

Glass rained in upon the three occupants. At the first tumble, the roof of the car caved in, and the angel picked up the sound of bones cracking. The second flip, which sent the taxi skidding into the wall of an adjacent building, crushed the side of the car where Rose sat and left her body mangled in steel.

Immediate silence dropped over them. *Finally,* the angel thought, and reached out to touch Rose's bleeding face. Her eyes fluttered open, and she tried to focus on him without her missing glasses. She must have recognized him regardless, because the first thing she asked was, "Are you okay?" Her voice gurgled up from her throat as a broken whisper. The angel nodded, even though its skin had ripped in places. It needed to get out of the wreckage fast and escape before too many humans pressed in around it. Even though they would not see its true form in the rips of its suit of flesh, they would still see *something*. An apparition that their minds would not be able to comprehend, and their attempts to process the appearance of the angel might attract attention from the Creator. That, the angel could not risk.

"I'm okay," Carlos replied. Rose nodded, relief flooding the dark features of her face. Her eyes gently closed, and without another sound, she passed away. The angel waited several breaths until a haze drifted up from the corpse in a series of concurrent waves. The angel reached out, and speaking in its divine language, said, "Come with me. I'll take you where you need to go."

The haze shifted as if on a breeze, paused, and simply hovered over the body for a brief moment before flowing towards the angel and saying, *"Come with me, and I'll take you where you need to go."*

The angel shrank away from Rose's soul speaking the divine language. What a source of inspiration this human may have become in the mortal realm had she lived. Truly had she been close to the Creator, communing with It in such intimate prayer that she had actually learned the language of the heavens.

Thinking quickly, the angel said, "There is nothing left here for you. Only I can take you where you need to be."

The haze drifted closer, and the angel pressed Carlos back against the twisted steel that tore further at its flesh.

"*There is nothing left here for you,*" the haze said. From some point behind it, a sudden pinpoint of bright light exploded into reality. The pinpoint grew, and brightened, a portal to the Creator's plane opening to engulf Rose's soul with a brilliant hue. "*Only I can take you where you need to be.*"

Through the portal, the angel saw the realm of the Creator. A transit hub of energy becoming form in reality, the center of which the Creator existed toiling endlessly in creation. The yearning to become part of Its cosmic plan again brought tears to the angel's three faces, and its six wings stretched in agitation against the suit of skin. To be welcomed back into the embrace of the Creator, to become a part of that light infused with the power to influence humans to acts of selflessness and love. The angel could once again be an agent of good, and it would feel so good to let go and have the warmth of the Creator shine over it as It had so long ago.

The angel reached out towards the portal, but then saw its bleeding fingers and ripped flesh. It remembered the human skins hanging in its closet. It remembered the experiences it'd had when it wore the body of men and women. And it remembered what it was like to be an angel in the mortal realm. To have no identity, to only be a bright light with no agency to forge a destiny of its own.

The angel's six eyes closed. "No," it said to the haze bathed in the bright light of the Creator. "I cannot go to that place with you."

"*No.*" Rose's soul repeated the word. The portal closed, and she was gone. But her last words lingered faintly in the air. *"I cannot go to that place with you."*

It was over. The merchandise had been lost, and the angel had to escape. Even as it climbed out of the car to see the concerned looks of the people who had crowded in around the accident, the angel studied their different faces, their hairstyles, their body shapes. It'd ruined one of its favorite suits, and the angel had no choice but to procure another.

About the Authors

D.H. Aire has walked the ramparts of the Old City of Jerusalem and through an escape tunnel of a Crusader fortress that Richard the Lionheart once called home. He's toured archeological sites that were hundreds, if not thousands of years old... experiences that have found expression in his epic fantasy series with a science fiction twist, *Highmage's Plight* and its companion *Hands of the Highmage Series. Hands of the Highmage,* Book 2, *Of Elves and Unicorns* is being published in October 2017. The seventh and concluding book of his *Highmage's Plight* Series, *Paradox Lost* was released in 2017.

Author of twelve fantasy and science fiction novels, Aire's short stories appear in a number of anthologies, most recently *Nowhere to Go But Mars* in Digital Science Fiction's *Alternate Facts* and *Grounding a Mockingbird* in Elder Signs Press' *Street Magick: Tales of Urban Fantasy.* A collection of his published short stories along with essays on his thoughts on a writer's journey, *Crossroads of Sin and Other Stories,* was published earlier this year.

A native of St. Louis, Missouri, Aire resides in the Washington D.C. metropolitan area. To learn more check out his website, www. dhr2believe.net.

Claire Davon has written on and off most of her life, starting with fan fiction when she was young. She writes across a wide range of genres, and does not like to limit herself to one. If a story calls to her, she will write it. Currently based in Los Angeles, she spends her free time writing and doing animal rescue. Learn more about Claire at her website, on Facebook and Twitter: www.clairedavon.com, https:// www.facebook.com/ClaireDavonindieauthor/, and @ClaireDavon

In all but one career aptitude test **Rebecca Gomez Farrell** has taken, writer has been the #1 result. But when she tastes the salty air and hears the sea lions bark, she wonders if maybe sea captain was the right choice after all. Currently marooned in Oakland, CA, Becca is a member of Broad Universe and an associate member of the Science Fiction and Fantasy Writers of America.

Her epic fantasy novel, *Wings Unseen*, debuted in August 2017 from Meerkat Press. Her short stories, which run the gamut of speculative fiction genres, have been published by *Beneath Ceaseless Skies, Pulp Literature,* and *The Future Fire,* among others. *Maya's Vacation*, her contemporary romance novella, is available from Clean Reads. Becca also co-leads the East Bay Science Fiction and Fantasy Writers Meetup group and runs the San Francisco chapter of the Women Who Submit Writing organization.

Becca's food, drink, and travel writing, which has appeared in local media in CA and NC, can primarily be found at her blog, theGourmez.com. For a list of all her published work, fiction and nonfiction, check out her author website at RebeccaGomezFarrell. com. Social Media Handle: @theGourmez.

Michael M. Jones lives in southwest Virginia with too many books, just enough cats, and a wife who helped dream up the Coyote Brothers, much to her dismay. His work has appeared in anthologies such as *Clockwork Phoenix 3, D is for Dinosaur, and Utter Fabrication.* He is the editor of Scheherazade's Facade, and the forthcoming Schoolbooks & Sorcery. For more, including a full list of stories set in Puxhill, visit him at www.michaelmjones.com.

Maxine Kollar is a wife and a mother of three. After receiving a degree in political science, she planned to save the world but then was all like, 'Nah'. Her works of poetry, creative non-fiction and fiction have appeared in various online and print publications such as *Mamalode, Funny in Five Hundred, Route 7 Review, Halfway Down the Stairs, Ironsoap, Wild Women's Medicine Circle, Edify Publications* and elsewhere. Most recently, her story was included in *MASHED*, a horror anthology from Grivante Press which is available in print, e-book and audio.

Jason J. McCuiston was born in the wilds of southeast Tennessee, where he was raised on a healthy diet of old horror movies, westerns, comic books, sci-fi and fantasy novels, and, yes, Dungeons & Dragons. He attended the finest state school that would have him where he studied art before coming to grips with the hard truth that his heart just wasn't in becoming a professional illustrator. Following his matriculation, he embarked on a whirlwind tour of underpaid and uninspired career paths until finally realizing that all his forays into role-playing games, comic books, and creative design were merely the manifestation of his innate desire to be a storyteller.

So, for the next twenty-odd years, he slogged his way through the jungles of terrible prose, waded the never-ending streams of form rejections, navigated through the cyclopean obelisks of scathing (yet often constructive) criticisms, and finally climbed the daunting peaks of Personal Growth, Craft, and Skill in search of his goal: the fabled Shangri La of becoming a published and prolific author.

He can be found on the internet at: jasonjmccuiston.wixsite.com/shadowcrusade and www.facebook.com/ShadowCrusade.

Adam Millard is the author of twenty-six novels, twelve novellas, and more than two hundred short stories, which can be found in various collections, magazines, and anthologies. Probably best known for his post-apocalyptic and comedy-horror fiction, Adam also writes fantasy/horror for children, as well as bizarro fiction for several publishers. His work has recently been translated for the German market.

Gregory L. Norris is a full-time professional writer, with work appearing in numerous short story anthologies, national magazines, novels, the occasional TV episode, and, so far, one produced feature film (*Brutal Colors*, which debuted on Amazon Prime January 2016). A former feature writer and columnist at *Sci Fi*, the official magazine of the Sci Fi Channel (before all those ridiculous Ys invaded), he once worked as a screenwriter on two episodes of Paramount's modern classic, *Star Trek: Voyager.* Two of his paranormal novels (written under his rom-de-plume, Jo Atkinson) were published by Home Shopping Network as part of their "Escape With Romance" line—the first time HSN has offered novels to their global customer base. He judged the 2012 Lambda Awards in the SF/F/H category. Three times now, his stories have notched Honorable Mentions in Ellen Datlow's Best-of books. In May 2016, he traveled to Hollywood to accept HM in the Roswell Awards in Short SF Writing. Follow his literary adventures at www.gregorylnorris.blogspot.com.

Evan J. Osborne is a writer from Temécula, California.

TJ Perkins is a gifted and multi-award winning author with thirteen books out in the mystery/suspense, New Age and fantasy genre for young readers. She has been published numerous times in a wide variety of magazines, anthologies and websites.

Jeffrey G. Roberts was born in New York City on February 24th, 1949. Yes, he's a Pisces. He was raised in New York, and South Florida, where he graduated North Miami Senior High. He attended Northern Arizona University, in Flagstaff, AZ, where he received degrees in writing and American history. Jeffery lives in Tucson, Arizona, land of mystical vistas of magnificent desolation, and brain-boiling summer temperatures. Also, a great mecca for UFO watchers, something he's very interested in.

He has two books available on Amazon: *The Healer* and *Cherries in Winter*. In May of 2018, his urban fantasy, *In the Shadow of the House of God*, will also be available.

Find Jeffery on twitter: @talejotter, Facebook: https://www.facebook.com/Atalespinner, his personal website: http://www.Atalespinner.weebly.com and the planet Mars: particularly the famous and eerie "Face on Mars," the subject of his novel *The Healer*. Jeffrey says, "I hope you enjoyed *One Day in the Hills of Milan!*"

Steven R. Southard's writing endeavors have soared to an impressive altitude. His uplifting tales have been published in over ten anthologies, including *In a Cat's Eye, Hides the Dark Tower, Dead Bait,* and *Avast, Ye Airships!* He penned the series, *What Man Hath Wrought,* a collection of fourteen alternate history stories. An engineer and former submariner, Steve has fluttered amid the cloudy genres of steampunk, clockpunk, science fiction, fantasy, and horror. A common theme of his stories is people striving to understand and adapt to new technology. Most often he glides like a lone eagle, far above the human plane, but he occasionally alights at www.stevenrsouthard.com, www.facebook.com/steven.southard.16, and www.twitter.com/StevenRSouthard.

Nancy Springer has passed the fifty-book milestone, having written that many novels for adults, young adults and children, in genres including mythic fantasy, contemporary fiction, magical realism, horror, and mystery—although she did not realize she wrote mystery until she won the Edgar Allan Poe Award from the Mystery Writers of America two years in succession. Her most popular books at this point are a series about Enola Holmes, Sherlock Holmes' younger sister, but she looks forward to the publication of another important novel, a heartfelt work of high fantasy, in June of 2018, just in time for her seventieth birthday. As of this writing, its title is yet to be finalized, but please follow Nancy Springer on Facebook or Twitter for more news of this special fantasy novel.

Todd Sullivan has a B.A. in English from Georgia State University, and a M.F.A. in Creative Writing from Queens College. He currently lives in South Korea, and has lived there for eight years. He's taught English as a Second Language, has studied the Korean language at Yonsei and Songang universities, and is a practitioner of kumdo, a Korean sword fighting martial arts. In 2019, he will take the teacher's test in kumdo, which will place him as a 4th degree black belt in the martial arts. He has published fiction in a variety of publications, including *Aurealis Science Fiction and Fantasy Magazine, Hellbound Books, Scarlet Leaf Review, Expanded Horizons Magazine, SciFan Magazine, Aurora Wolf Literary Journal, Eastlit Journal, Tokyo Yakuza Anthology*, and *Tincture Journal*. He is currently shopping around a speculative fiction/urban horror novel that takes place on Jeju, a small island at the southernmost tip of Korea. To learn more about Todd Sullivan, please visit his website at www.acrowsflying.com.

Brian Trent's speculative fiction appears regularly in *ANALOG, Fantasy & Science Fiction, Orson Scott Card's Intergalactic Medicine Show, Great Jones Street, Daily Science Fiction, Apex* (winning the Story of the Year Reader's Poll), *Escape Pod, COSMOS, Galaxy's Edge, Nature, Pseudopod,* and numerous year's best anthologies. The author of the historical fantasy series RAHOTEP, he is also a 2015 Baen Fantasy Adventure Award finalist and Writers of the Future winner. Trent lives in New England, where he works as a novelist, screenwriter, and poet. His website and blog are located at www.briantrent.com.

Nemma Wollenfang is an MSc Postgraduate and prize-winning short story writer who lives in Northern England. Generally, she adheres to Science Fiction—perhaps as a result of years in the laboratory cackling like a mad scientist—but she has been known to branch out, especially if there is a romantic twist to be had. Her work has appeared in several venues, including three of Flame Tree's bestselling Gothic Fantasy hardbacks: *Science Fiction Short Stories, Murder Mayhem and Pirates & Ghosts*. Her unpublished steampunk novel, *Clockwork Evangeline*, won the Retreat West First Chapter Competition in 2016, as well as gaining Honorable Mentions for two of the Speculative Literature Foundation's grants. She also has a Silver Honorable Mention from Writers of the Future, and won the Northwich LitFest Short Story Competition 2017. She can be found on Facebook, Goodreads and Twitter: @NemmaW.

Trisha J. Wooldridge writes grown-up horror short stories and weird poetry for anthologies and magazines—some even winning awards! Under her business, A Novel Friend (www.anovelfriend.com), she's edited over fifty novels for multiple small and mid-size presses, as well as indie authors; written over a hundred articles on food, drink, entertainment, horses, music, and writing for over a dozen different publications; designed and written three online college classes; copy edited the MMORPG *Dungeons & Dragons Stormreach*; edited two geeky anthologies; and has become the events coordinator and consignment manager for Annie's Book Stop of Worcester. Because she is masochistic when it comes to time management, she created the child-friendly persona of T.J. Wooldridge and had three scary children's novels published. She has two novellas through Pole to Pole Publishing, "Tea with Mr. Fuzzypants" and "Mirror of Hearts," and besides *Dark Luminous Wings*, you can find her most recent work in the 2017 anthologies *Gothic Fantasy Supernatural Horror, Now I Lay Me Down to Sleep*—a charity anthology for The Jimmy Fund, and New England Horror Writers' *Wicked Haunted*, and the collector's book of the Blackstone Valley Artists Association 2017 Art and Poetry Show.

About the Editors

Kelly A. Harmon is an award-winning journalist and author, and a member of the Science Fiction & Fantasy Writers of America. A Baltimore native, she writes the *Charm City Darkness* series, which includes the novels *Stoned in Charm City, A Favor for a Fiend, A Blue Collar Proposition* and *In the Eye of the Beholder*. Her stories can be found in many anthologies, including *Triangulation: Dark Glass; Hellebore and Rue; Deep Cuts: Mayhem, Menace and Misery;* and others.

Ms. Harmon is a former newspaper reporter and editor, and now edits for Pole to Pole Publishing, a small Baltimore publisher. She is co-editor of *Hides the Dark Tower, In a Cat's Eye and Dark Luminous Wings* along with Vonnie Winslow Crist. For more information, visit her blog at http://kellyaharmon.com, or, find her on Facebook and Twitter: http://facebook.com/Kelly-A-Harmon1, https://twitter.com/kellyaharmon.

Vonnie Winslow Crist, MS Professional Writing, has had a life-long interest in reading, writing, art, science fiction, fairy-tales, folklore, and legends. A cloverhand who has found so many four-leafed clovers that she keeps them in jars, she strives to celebrate the power of myth in her writing and art.

A Pushcart nominee, she is a member of Science Fiction & Fantasy Writers of America, Society of Children's Book Writers & Illustrators, and Pen Women. Her award-winning books include *The Enchanted Dagger, Murder on Marawa Prime, Owl Light, The Greener Forest, Leprechaun Cake & Other Tales, River of Stars* and *Essential Fables.* Her speculative stories can be found in *Chilling Ghost Short Stories, Cast of Wonders, Faerie Magazine, Dia de los Muertos, Les Cabinets des Polytheistes, The Great Tome of Fantastic and Wondrous Places* and elsewhere.

Editor of The Gunpowder Review, Ms. Crist co-edited Pole to Pole Publishing's *Hides the Dark Tower, In a Cat's Eye* and *Dark Luminous Wings* with Kelly A. Harmon. For more information, visit http://vonniewinslowcrist.com, http://vonniewinslowcrist.wordpress.com, http://facebook.com/WriterVonnieWinslowCrist, or http://twitter.com/VonnieWCrist.